R...

Roddy Doyle was born in Dublin in 1958. He is the author of twelve acclaimed novels including *The Commitments*, *The Snapper*, *The Van* and *Love*, two collections of short stories, and *Rory & Ita*, a memoir about his parents. He won the Booker Prize in 1993 for *Paddy Clarke Ha Ha Ha*.

ALSO BY RODDY DOYLE

Fiction

The Commitments
The Snapper
The Van
Paddy Clarke Ha Ha Ha
The Woman Who Walked Into Walls
A Star Called Henry
Oh, Play That Thing
Paula Spencer
The Deportees
The Dead Republic
Bullfighting
Two Pints
The Guts
Two More Pints
Smile
Charlie Savage
Two for the Road
Love

Non-Fiction

Rory & Ita
The Second Half (with Roy Keane)

Plays

The Snapper
Brownbread
War
Guess Who's Coming For Dinner
The Woman Who Walked Into Doors
The Government Inspector (translation)
Two Pints

For Children

The Giggler Treatment
Rover Saves Christmas
The Meanwhile Adventures
Wilderness
Her Mother's Face
A Greyhound of a Girl
Brilliant
Rover and the Big Fat Baby

RODDY DOYLE

The Complete
Two Pints

VINTAGE

1 3 5 7 9 10 8 6 4 2

Vintage
20 Vauxhall Bridge Road,
London SW1V 2SA

Vintage is part of the Penguin Random House group of companies
whose addresses can be found at global.penguinrandomhouse.com

 Penguin
Random House
UK

Copyright © Roddy Doyle 2012, 2014, 2017, 2019 & 2020

Roddy Doyle has asserted his right to be identified
as the author of this Work in accordance with the Copyright,
Designs and Patents Act 1988

'Bye Bye Love' Words and Music by Boudleaux Bryant and Felice Bryant
© Reproduced by permission of Sony/ATV Music Publishing Ltd.,
London W1F 9LD

Extract taken from 'Mid-Term Break' taken from
Death of a Naturalist © Estate of Seamus Heaney and
reprinted by permission of Faber and Faber Ltd

Two Pints first published by Jonathan Cape in hardback in 2012
Two More Pints first published by Jonathan Cape in hardback in 2014
Two for the Road first published by Vintage in hardback in 2019
The Complete Two Pints first published by Vintage in paperback in 2021

penguin.co.uk/vintage

A CIP catalogue record for this book is available from the British
Library

ISBN 9781529111279

Typeset in 10.5/13 pt Plantin MT Std
by Integra Software Services Pvt. Ltd, Pondicherry

Printed and bound in Great Britain by Clays Ltd, Elcograf S.p.A.

The authorised representative in the EEA is Penguin Random House
Ireland, Morrison Chambers, 32 Nassau Street, Dublin D02 YH68.

Penguin Random House is committed to a sustainable future for our
business, our readers and our planet. This book is made from Forest
Stewardship Council® certified paper.

Contents

Two Pints: 2011–2020   1

Two Pints: The Play   333

The Zoom Pints   407

TWO PINTS

2011–2020

24-5-11

— Tha' was a great few days.

— Brilliant.

— She's a great oul' one. For her age, like.

— Fuckin' amazin'. Great energy.

— An' B'rack. He must've kissed every fuckin' baby in Offaly.

— An' did yeh see the way he skulled tha' pint?

— No doubtin' his fuckin' roots, an' anyway.

— An' the speech.

— Brilliant.

— 'Yes, we can' – whatever it is in Irish. He made the effort.

— What is it again?

— Haven't a clue. But it's funny, isn't it? Such a simple thing – a few speeches and smilin' faces. A bit of hope. An' it feels like we're over the worst, we've turned a corner.

— Exactly. It's great.

— We're still fucked but, aren't we?

— Bollixed.

31-5-11

—You know your man Gaddafi?

— From the chipper?

— No. The Libyan nut.

—What about him?

— You know the way they're lookin' for a country to take him?

— I'm not in the mood for fuckin' politics.

— He should come here.

—Wha'?!

— A state visit, like. The hat-trick. It'd be great. The few words of Irish, green jacket at the airport, kiss a few babies.

— He'd strangle the fuckin' babies.

— Not if he's looked after properly. It'd keep the buzz goin'. And the Shinners wouldn't object this time. He could bring the Semtex himself – save on the post.

— Good point. Where's Libya, annyway?

— I don't know – the desert.

—Which one?

—Wha'?

— Which desert?

— The fuckin' sandy one. Ask fuckin' Peter O'Toole.

— D'yeh know who'd make a fuckin' great president?

— Who?

— Your one who does the weather.

— Which one?

— The glamorous one – looks like she used to hang around with the Human League.

— She's lovely. Yeh'd give *her* one.

— I would, yeah. If I worked in the meteorological service. No, but she'd be great for the state visits an' tha'. She'd be able to point to the clouds an' say, 'That's a cold front comin' in from the south-west, Your Majesty. But it'll have fucked off by this afternoon.' Impress them, yeh know – a scientist in the Áras. An' she's a woman as well. They're always better at visitin' the homeless an' lookin' like they give a shite. An' she's a gay icon.

— What's a gay fuckin' icon?

— Somethin' all the gays like.

— Wha'? Like chicken curry?

— No – I don't know. I think it's more people – singers – women. Madonna an' tha'.

— Can she sing as well?

— Who?

— The weather one.

— More than likely.

— She could sing 'It's Rainin' Men' at the whatsit – the fuckin' inauguration.

— Good idea. An' at the airport, when the IMF fuckers are gettin' off the plane.

12-6-11

— Did you hear your man, the Senator, on the radio there?

   — I fuckin' hate the radio. Which one?

   — The one that's running for President. He was goin' on abou' Plato.

   — The footballer?

— The ancient Greek – there's no footballer called Plato.

   — I bet there is.

   — Fuck up an' listen.

   — In Brazil, somewhere.

   — Shut up. He was sayin' abou' Plato. Young fellas came to him. Offerin' themselves, like. In return for sharing the wisdom of his fuckin' years. It was common enough – in ancient Greece.

   — Wha' kind o' wisdom?

   — I don't know – Remember to put the bins ou' the night before collection day. The bits of cop-on yeh pick up. In exchange for your moment of pleasure.

— Your moment of pleasure could go on all day, if you were talkin' abou' puttin' the fuckin' bins ou' while you were havin' it.

   — Tha' was what I was thinkin'.

   — The whole country would grind to a fuckin' standstill.

   — I was thinkin' that as well.

   — No wonder Greece is in fuckin' bits.

   — I'm with yeh.

   — Could they not have, like, just gone for a pint?

— See your man in America who twittered his dick.

— Wha'?

— The politician. Congressman or somethin'.

— Ah, not fuckin' politics again.

— No, listen. He sent his langer to some woman – by Twitter, yeh know?

— Cheaper than post, I suppose.

— A photograph, like.

— Wha' was he fuckin' up to?

— I'm not sure. I couldn't really figure it ou'.

— Well, I couldn't see any of our gang pullin' a stunt like tha', could you?

— They wouldn't have broadband, where most of them come from. The bog an' tha'.

— That's true.

— But I'll tell yeh one thing. They would, if they thought it would get them a few votes.

— That's true as well. Vote for me an' I'll come round to your house.

— Was it in the paper, was it?

— It was, yeah.

— Bet it didn't say langer or dick.

— No. Genitalia.

— It does nothin' for me, tha' word.

— I know what yeh mean. Are you on Twitter, yourself?

— Fuck off.

— We're after gettin' the Sky in.

— Anny good?

— Brilliant. The HD, yeh know. You can see fuckin' everythin'. On the news, like.

— Ah fuck off now. Yeh don't need HD to watch the fuckin' news.

— Will yeh just listen. Open your fuckin' head – for once.

— Go on.

— The riots.

— They're back.

— Big time. The Syrians. The Greeks.

— Fuckin' wasters.

— An' our own gang – above.

— An' the riots are better on HD, are they?

— It's not tha'. Some o' those black an' white riots – from the 60s. They're still brilliant. But it's the extra stuff.

— Wha' extra stuff?

— Well, like. I was watchin' the one in Belfast there. The first one. With the sound down. Mute, like. And I could still tell which side they were on. The young fellas throwin' the stones an' tha'. I knew they were fuckin' loyalists. Immediately.

— How?

— The tattoos. I could see every fuckin' one. Clear as if they were on me own arm here. UDA, No Surrender, The Pope's a Cunt – an' what have you.

— Sounds good. Does it make the fuckin' economy look better as well?

— Fuck off.

— How's the HD workin' out for yeh?

— Jesus, man, I'll tell yeh. It's fuckin' exhaustin'.

— How come?

— It's too real. Yeh can't relax. Every fuckin' spot an' ear hair. Your man, Richard Keys – they didn't sack him just cos he's a cunt. Tha' was just the excuse.

— He is a cunt, but.

— Ah yeah – no argument. But they got rid of him – the real reason – because he has hairy hands. A fuckin' werewolf interviewin' Beckham or wha'ever. They couldn't have it. That's why they're all gettin' Brazilians.

— On Sky Sports?!

— The gee hair, m'n – what's the official name for it? Pubic. It's Vietnam on HD.

— What fuckin' channels have yeh got?

— Yeh'd expect fuckin' Rambo to jump ou' – with his bandanna. Men as well – they're all gettin' it done. So I'm told an'anyway.

— Wha'?

— Gettin' the hair off. Arse hair as well. Drug dealers an' tha'.

— Wha?!

— In case they're caught on *Prime Time Investigates*. With the drugs hidden up there, like.

— They want to be lookin' their best.

— Exactly.

— It's not somethin' yeh'd want to do for a livin' but, is it?

— God, no – Jesus. If it can't go in the glove compartment, it isn't goin' annywhere.

— Would you be bothered hackin'?

  — Hackin'?

— Yeah. Could yeh be bothered readin' your man, the black prostitute fella – what's his name? Hugh Grant. Would yeh really want to read his fuckin' texts?

  — No.

  — Me neither. Borin'.

  — Unless it was somethin' unusual.

  — Like wha'?

— Well, say he was stickin' it into Colette from the Mint or your woman with the hair from Paddy Power's. That'd be worth knowin' abou'.

  — I'm with yeh.

  — Other than tha' but—

  — I've been hackin' me missis.

  — There's plenty of her to hack.

  — Fuck off now.

— Jesus, but. D'yeh have the technology an' tha' – to do it?

  — I do, yeah.

  — How d'yeh manage it?

  — I read her texts when she goes to the jacks.

  — Anny good ones?

— Not at all. The usual shite. Loads of fuckin' LOLs – an' the other one. PMSL. Don't know what it means.

  — P is for period.

  — An' M – that'll be the other one. Men's—

  — Men's wha'?

  — Menstruation.

  — Makes sense. What about the S an' the L?

  — Fuck knows.

  — One thing.

— Wha'?

— How come yeh didn't slag my missis after I slagged yours?

— Are yeh ready for another pint?

— After yeh answer my fuckin' question.

13-7-11

— Harper Seven.

— I'm not listenin'.

— It's wha' Beckham an' Posh are after callin' their latest.

— I know.

— But, like – who gives a shite?

— Fuckin' everyone. In our house annyway.

— It's not a bad oul' name, really.

— It's the Seven bit's the problem.

— I know. But they prob'ly have their reasons. Somethin' sentimental.

— Like the amount o' times he had to ride her.

— I'll tell yeh. You're never fuckin' predictable.

— Fuck off. My brother's young one's little fella. John. Know wha' his full name is?

— Go on.

— John Player Blue.

— Fuck off.

— Swear to God. It's like I said. Sentimental reasons. They met outside the boozer a few weeks after the smokin' ban kicked in. And John arrived soon after.

— That's kind o' nice.

— There now.

— They still together?

— No. Actually – he died. The husband.

— That's rough.

— Cancer. She was pregnant as well. A girl. Know wha' she called her?

— Wha'?

— Cancer.

— Fuck off now. I'm not listenin' to yeh.

— A tribute to his memory.

— Fuck off.
— D'yeh want to know the surname?
— No.
— Ward.
— Cancer Ward?
— A lovely kid. A breath of fresh air.
— Fuck off.

— How come the most borin' stuff is the most important?

— Wha' d'yeh mean?

— Well, look it. What's the best thing yeh saw on the news this week?

— Murdoch's missis slappin' the comedian.

— Me too. It was fuckin' brilliant. An' I bet you were sittin' there watchin', and wishin' your missis was Chinese. Amn't I righ'?

— Kind o'.

— Fuckin' sure I am. She threw her whole body into tha' slap. But – this is my point. It doesn't matter a fuck. It was only a laugh. But, now, all the EU leaders meetin' in Brussels tomorrow—

— Ah, fuck off. I'm not interested in those cunts.

— Exactly my point. The thought of it – it makes me want to lie down an' fuckin' die. But it's vital.

— Why?

— I don't fuckin' know. I just know it is. But the thought of tryin' to understand it – defaultin', an' Greece, an' all tha' shite.

— If they brought their wives an' husbands—

— That's it. Human interest. Sittin' behind them, like Murdoch's. An' Merkel says somethin' snotty abou' Ireland—

— Kenny's wife slaps her across the fuckin' head.

— Yeh'd watch.

— I might.

— Yeh fuckin' would.

— Okay.

— Did yeh like Amy?

  — I did, yeah.

  — A bit skinny.

  — Great fuckin' voice.

  — True.

  — Sad.

  — Desperate. The same age as my oldest.

  — A real singer. None o' the *X Factor* shite.

  — No.

  — Horrible week.

  — Fuckin' awful.

  — Norway.

  — Frightenin'.

  — Who'd shoot kids?

  — I haven't a clue.

  — Horrible.

  — Fuckin' horrible.

  — An' Somalia.

  — Stop.

  — Where is Somalia, exactly?

  — I don't even know where Norway is, exactly.

  — Well, at least we have the cunts in the Vatican to give us a laugh.

  — I'm not laughin'.

  — The fuckin' heads on them.

  — Thank Christ the football's back in a couple o' weeks.

  — What're yeh sayin'? Tha' none o' this would've happened if there'd been football on the telly?

  — Fuck off. It's not funny.

  — You're righ'. Sorry.

  — Okay.

— No massacres this week.

— Stop tha'.

— Were you across at Amy's funeral?

— I'll leave, I'm fuckin' tellin' yeh.

— Okay. Fair enough. Wha' abou' the ban on smokin' in cars? Can I mention tha'?

— It should be up to the kids.

— Wha'?

— The ban. It's when there are children in the vehicle, righ'?

— Righ'.

— So, the children should vote on it. In the back o' the car, like.

— They'd bribe the poor fucker tha' wants a smoke.

— Exactly. It'd teach them to be adults. Cash only. In little brown child-sized envelopes.

— You're not jokin'.

— No way am I. It's the problem with this fuckin' country. We're tryin' not to be corrupt. But we should be teachin' our kids to be even more corrupt. Like every other country in the world. Not just Greece an' the mad places – fuckin' everywhere. They're laughin' at us.

— I don't know. Yeh might have a point.

— I do have a fuckin' point.

— What if there's only one kid in the car?

— Then the dopey prick drivin' it should have no problem countin' the votes.

15-8-11

— How did Wexford go for yeh?

— I'll tell yeh. We were sittin' in the mobile, myself and herself. Watchin' the news. Cos it was fuckin' bucketin' outside. There's the riots in London. Then there's this stuff abou' how the euro is basically fucked. So she says, Fuck it, let's blow it. So, that's wha' we do. We get the Tesco bus into Gorey and we fuckin' spend it.

— Your jeans are new.

— Fuck off a minute. We're in this pub, Browne's, and we go out for a smoke. She takes ou' her BlackBerry an' she taps in some fuckin' thing. An' she puts up the hood of her pink hoodie. An' then – basically – she's gone. Like a fuckin' greyhound. Across to this shoe shop. Gaffney's. She takes a run at it an' kicks the fuckin' window.

— Did she break it?

— She missed it. But she has another go. An' then there are other women – middle-aged, like. An' they're all kickin' the window. They're only up from the fuckin' Garda station. An' sure enough, here's a Guard, an' they leg it. I haven't seen her since. Where were you, yourself?

— Magaluf.

— Where's tha'?

— I'm not sure – we went in a plane.

22-8-11

— I was ou' at the airport there.

— Doin' wha'?

— Lookin' at the boats – wha' d'yeh think I was fuckin' doin'?

— I don't know. Goin' somewhere, comin' back. Fuckin' lay off.

— We were ou' meeting her sister.

— Comin' back from somewhere.

— Yeah.

— Where?

— Can't remember – doesn't matter. We're at the arrivals place, yeh know, and I'm bored out of me fuckin' tree, cos her flight's late. So I start doin' imaginary passport control as all the people are comin' in off the planes – in me head, like. You can stay, you can stay, you can fuck off, you can stay. An' anyway, that's when I see him.

— Who?

— Gaddafi.

— From the chipper?

— No, the other one. From Libya.

— In Dublin Airport?

— Terminal 2.

— Fuck off.

— Swear to God. That's where he's hidin'.

— Fuckin' hell. An' he'd just arrived, had he?

— No, this is the genius bit. He was moppin' the floor.

— Gaddafi was?

— Fuckin' brilliant, isn't it?

— Colonel Gaddafi?

— They'll never find him there.

— You're sure it was him?

— Course I am. I winked at him.
— Wha' did he do?
— He winked back.

30-8-11

— That's a fuckin' jumper.

— Birthday present.

— Purple's your colour.

— Fuck off.

— I'm serious. Man o' your age. It's brave.

— Fuck off.

— D'yeh get annythin' else?

— This.

— Wha'?

— This – hang on. I've to get it – it's around me neck.

— What's tha'?

— Kind of a dog tag.

— What's it say there? I am neutered and chipped. It *is* a fuckin' dog tag.

— Yeah.

— Who fuckin' gave yeh tha'?

— She did.

— Why, but?

— She got it off the dog. She died, like.

— Your missis?

— No, the fuckin' dog. A few months ago there. D'yeh remember?

— I do now, yeah. What was it again?

— Mongrel – bits of fuckin' everythin'.

— No, wha' killed it, I meant.

— Ah, just fuckin' fat – yeh know yourself. Great oul' dog, but. An' anyway, she held on to the collar.

— That's nice. Considerate.

— I thought so. An' that's not all. The chain.

— What about it?

— Gold.

— No.

20

— Yeah. Her idea. Somethin' she heard on the radio. It'll hold its value long after the euro goes down the fuckin' jacks.

— So, it's not just romantic.

— It's me fuckin' pension. An' it's goin' back under me new purple jumper.

21

4-9-11

— I need this pint.

— I know.

— No. I really need it.

— Yeh look a bit flaked alrigh'. Wha' were yeh up to?

— Writin' my response to the Vatican.

— Wha'?!

— Well, like, I responded to the Vatican's response yesterday to Enda fuckin' Kenny's response to the child abuse inquiry in – it'll come back to me in a minute – Cloyne.

— Say tha' again. No – don't. But. Am I righ'? You wrote to the fuckin' Vatican.

— I did, yeah.

— To the fuckin' Pope.

— Yeah.

— Fuckin' hell – fair play. Wha' did yeh say?

— Fuck off.

— I was only askin'.

— No. That's wha' I said. Tha' was my response. And I think I spoke on behalf of the vast majority of the Irish people. The Dubs an'anyway.

— You told the Pope to fuck off?

— I did, yeah.

— How?

— The usual way.

— Yeh shouted? He wouldn't have heard yeh from here.

— No, email.

— You emailed the Pope?

— I did, yeah.

— Fuckin' hell. Did he answer?

— Not yet. Come here, but. Yeh know the way you're angry sometimes but yeh cop on an' calm down. But other times you're angry an' yeh know you're righ' to be.

— Yeah.

— Yeah, well, this was one o' those times.

— Did the Pope get back to yeh yet?

   — He did, yeah – this mornin'.

   — Did he? Jesus. Wha' did he say?

   — Well – like, it was in Latin.

   — D'you know any Latin?

   — We wouldn't speak it much at home, no. But listen. I found this English–Latin dictionary yoke. Google, like. An' there's a box for the Latin. So, I typed in his – the fuckin' Pope's email – it's only short. An' the English came up.

   — Wha' did it say?

   — Tell your sister I was asking for her.

   — Fuckin' hell. The Pope wrote tha'?

   — In fuckin' Latin.

   — So, wha' did yeh do?

   — I told me sister – I phoned her. I knew which one he meant.

   — And wha' did she say?

   — Tell him he was a terrible ride an' he can fuck off back to Poland.

   — Tha' was the last one.

   — Tha' was the one she meant, I think. So, annyway, I translated it into Latin an' sent it to the fuckin' Vatican. An' I said I expected a reasoned response by the end o' the week.

   — He'll deny he's Polish.

   — I cheated there. I changed it to German.

   — He can't deny he's German.

   — No, but he mightn't admit it, either. They're slippy fuckers.

— Have yeh recovered yet?

— Ah fuck, man. What a day. I'm still a bit – I don't fuckin' know – overwhelmed.

— Know wha' yeh mean. I had to lie down on the bed for a bit.

— I cried.

— Me too.

— Fuckin' hell.

— I never thought I'd see it happen again.

— No – same here. It's been so long – I'd given up hopin'.

— But the way he took tha' ball.

— Incredible.

— Fuckin' incredible. Here, look it. Give us a hug.

— Hang on, hang on. You're not upstairs in the fuckin' lounge.

— Sorry.

— No, you're grand. Have a suck o' your pint.

— Yeah – thanks.

— You're grand.

— Somethin' to tell the grandkids, wha'.

— Exactly, yeah.

— We saw it.

— That's it. The day Fernando Torres scored a fuckin' goal.

Man Utd 3–1 Chelsea

— Who'll yeh be votin' for?

   — Fuck tha' – not interested.

   — Come on. Be a citizen. There's the Senator.

— Which one's he?

   — The James Joyce wanker.

   — Got yeh. He did somethin', didn't he?

   — He wrote a letter defendin' an Israeli paedophile.

   — Could he not've defended one of our own paedophiles?

   — His patriotic duty. I never saw it tha' way before.

— Who else is runnin'?

   — Dana.

   — Ah, for fuck sake. Louis Walsh in a fuckin' dress. Who else?

   — McGuinness.

   — Has he given up managin' U2?

   — Different McGuinness.

— The Provo?

   — He says he left them in 1974.

   — He's lying through his arse, so. No change there. Who else?

— Your man from *Dragons' Den*.

— Tha' cunt?

   — He says he won't be havin' anny posters.

   — Not surprised, the fuckin' head on him. Who else?

   — Gay Mitchell.

   — For fuck—. Who else?

   — Michael D. Higgins.

— Which one's he?

   — Squeaky voice, poetry, Nicaragua.

   — Is he still alive?

   — At the moment, yeah – far as I know.

— Who else?

— Mary Davis.

— Who?

— Special Olympics.

— Did she win a medal?

— She ran the thing – organised it. Yeh feel guilty now, don't yeh?

— No.

— Yeh feel horrible.

— I don't – fuck off.

— Yeh do – go on.

— Okay, I do – fuck off.

— Have yeh made your mind up yet?

— A pint – same as always. I haven't had to make me mind up since—

— I meant the election.

— Ah, shove it.

— Well, it's either tha' or the Greek default.

— Alrigh' – fuck it. Who's goin' to win?

— Hard to say. They're all shite.

— I seen Mary Davis's *Sex an' the City* posters.

— There yeh go. An' Mitchell. He said you can see the house he grew up in – in Inchicore, like – from the window of the Áras. An' he's goin' to look out at it every mornin'.

— An' shout, Fuck you, Inchicore.

— He could get the Queen to do it with him the next time she's over.

— A bondin' exercise.

— Exactly. She probably never gets the chance to say Fuck at home.

—Talkin' abou' fuck an' the Queen. What's McGuinness up to?

— Says he'll only pay himself the average industrial wage.

— The fuckin' eejit.

— I'm with yeh. He says he'll employ six young people with the money left over.

— Cuttin' the grass an' washin' diesel. What about the Senator?

—Ah Jaysis. It looks like Greece is goin' to miss its deficit target an' has fuck-all chance of avertin' bankruptcy.

— Wha' d'yeh think of the poll?

  — He's alrigh'. He pulls a reasonable pint.

  — I meant, the election poll.

  — Ah, fuck the—. Go on.

  — Michael D.'s leadin'.

  — Followed by Mitchell.

  — No. The *Dragons' Den* fella.

  — Fuckin' hell. How did tha' happen?

— Well, he's scutterin' on abou' community an' disability an' tha'. But, really, he's an ol' Fianna Fáil hack. Up to his entrepreneurial bollix in it. Annyway, my theory.

  — Go on.

  — People still love Fianna Fáil.

  — But they'd hammer them if they had a candidate.

  — Exactly. But they can vote for this prick without havin' to admit it.

  — Brilliant.

  — But I think Michael D. will get there.

  — How come?

  — He was goin' on abou' the President not bein' a handmaiden to the government.

  — What's a handmaiden?

  — I'm not sure. But if I was lookin' for one in the Golden Pages, I wouldn't be stoppin' at the Michaels. Annyway, he suddenly stops, an' says he broke his kneecap when he fell durin' a fact-findin' mission in Colombia. Wha' does tha' tell yeh?

  — He was ou' of his head.

  — Exactly. Fact-findin' mission me hole. He's lettin' us know – he's one o' the lads.

  — Well, that's me decided.

  — Me too.

— Tha' must've been some party.

— Wha' party?

— The one in Tallaght. Five stabbin's.

— Is tha' your idea of a good party?

— Not necessarily, no. An' I didn't say it was 'good', so fuck off.

— Well, I'm sorry. And?

— An' wha'?

— Wha's your fuckin' point?

— Well, for a start. I thought you'd be happy tha' I'm not talkin' about the fuckin' election.

— Oh, I am.

— Grand. So, annyway. It said on the news tha' they were taken – the ones tha' got stabbed, like – to different hospitals, to make sure there wouldn't be a continuation of the hostilities.

— Well, tha' makes sense.

— Exactly. That's what I thought. The thinkin' tha' went into it. The infrastructional plannin'.

— The wha'?

— When they were buildin' Tallaght hospital, they must've thought, we'd better leave James' Street open as well, just in case.

— In case there's a scrap?

— You're with me. An', well – I think that's worth celebratin'. Cos we don't hear enough good news these days – fuckin' success stories.

— So. You're sayin' we should celebrate five stabbin's in Tallaght?

— It's only a fuckin' suggestion.

14-10-11

— D'yeh ever read poetry?

— Wha'?!

— D'you ever—

— I heard yeh. I just can't fuckin' believe I heard yeh.

— Well, look it—

— G'wan upstairs to the lounge if yeh want to talk abou' poetry.

— Just let me—

— Unless yeh can talk abou' the football in rhyme. 'There was a young player called Blunt'.

— There's no player called Blunt – far as I know.

— You're missin' me point.

— I'm not. I heard yeh. Yeh didn't hear me.

— I did.

— You feel threatened by it.

— No, I don't.

— Yeh do. Yeh even moved your stool there.

— I didn't.

— Yeh fuckin' did. To get away from anny mention of poetry. It's mad.

— Well, it's a load o' shite.

— I agree with yeh. That's wha' I'm tryin' to say.

— Yeh've lost me now.

— So listen. My young's one's youngest lad, Damien.

— The kid with the cheeks.

— That's him. He's good in school – the great white hope. Annyway, he has to read a fuckin' poem an' write a bit about it. The homework, like.

— Okay.

— So, he's in our place, cos his ma's visitin' the da. An' he asks me to, yeh know, look at the poem. So I get the oven gloves on an' I give it a dekko. 'The Road Not

31

Taken' – some bollix called Robert Frost. Have yeh read it, yourself?

— I won't even say no.

— Two roads diverged in a yellow wood. Stay where yeh are; I'm just givin' yeh a flavour o' the thing.

— And – wha'?

— Well, this cunt – Robert Frost, like – he's makin' his mind up abou' which road to take an' he knows he'll regret not takin' one o' them. An' that's basically it.

— He doesn't need a fuckin' poem for tha'. That's life. It's common fuckin' sense.

— Exactly. I go for the cod, I regret the burger.

— I married the woman but I wish I could be married to her sister.

— Is tha' true?

— Not really – no.

— Annyway. Yeh sure?

— Go on.

— So annyway, the poor little bollix – Damien, like – the grandson. He has to answer questions about it. An' the last one – it's really stupid now. What road do you think you should never take? An', like, I tell him, The road to Limerick.

— Did he write tha'?

— He fuckin' did. An' guess where the fuckin' teacher comes from? An' guess who's been called up to the fuckin' school, to explain himself to the fuckin' headmaster?

— Brilliant.

— Tomorrow mornin'.

— Serves yeh righ' for readin' poetry.

— I agree. A hundred fuckin' per cent. Two roads diverged in a yellow wood me hole.

15-10-11

— Wha' d'yeh think o' Dana's sister sayin' that her –

    — No! No – please—

    — Okay.

    — Thanks.

    — Can I just say one thing abou' Miriam O'Callaghan's outrageous bullyin' of poor Martin McGuinness in the *Prime Time* debate? An' then we'll move on.

    — Okay. One thing.

    — Only one – thanks. She can bully me anny time she fuckin' wants.

    — That it?

    — That's it.

    — The first sensible thing yeh've said in weeks.

    — Months.

    — Ever.

— So Gaddafi's gone.

— From the chipper?

— Ah, listen – look it. You're goin' to have to broaden your fuckin' horizons.

— Oh, the other one.

—Yeah, the other one.

—Yeah, I seen tha'. The man with the golden gun.

— Didn't do him much fuckin' good, did it? See they found him in a drainage pipe?

—Yeah.

— I'll tell yeh. The last couple o' months must've been rough. Cos he wouldn't've fitted into tha' pipe a few months back.

—We'll kind o' miss him.

— We will in our holes. An' d'yeh see ETA's declared a ceasefire?

— Thank fuck. That's great news.

— Oh, you're interested in tha' one, are yeh?

— Fuckin' sure – the noise she was makin'.

— Hang on – wha'?

— A woman of her age, buyin' a fuckin' drum kit with her redundancy – her fuckin' lump sum. Thinks she's Keith fuckin' Moon at three in the fuckin' mornin'.

— Hang on—

— It's a disgrace.

— Hang on. Not Eithne.

— Oh.

— ETA.

— The Spanish cunts who aren't Spanish.

— Exactly.

— Shite.

1-11-11

— Wha' does 'thinkin' outside the box' mean?

— You were watchin' *The Apprentice* last night, weren't yeh?

— I was, yeah.

— Me too.

— Wouldn't've thought it was your cup o' tea.

— It isn't. But we had to give the dog half a Valium, cos of all the fuckin' bangers and fireworks. An' he conked ou' on top o' me. So I was stuck – couldn't reach the remote.

— Yeh saw it, so.

— Load o' shite.

— I'm with yeh. But they're all runnin' around – the contestants, like – an' they're all, I'm thinkin' outside the box, Bill. What's it fuckin' mean?

— Comin' up with somethin' new. Thinkin' a bit different.

— That all?

— Think so.

— For fuck sake.

— Last time I thought outside the box I tried to get off with me mother-in-law.

— Fuck off.

— Before she died, mind.

— Ah, fuck off. I'll give yeh an example. My young one's lad. Damien. The grandson. He goes into the chipper, with his chipmunk.

— His—?

— Chipmunk. An' he tells Gaddafi he'll fuck it into the fryer unless Gaddafi pays him a tenner.

— I'm impressed. And?

— Gaddafi tells him to fuck off.

35

— And?
— D'yeh ever taste deep-fried chipmunk?
— That's thinkin' outside the snack box.
— It fuckin' is.

9-11-11

— So annyway, I was listenin' to the news there.

— Oh fuck.

— No, fuck off a minute. This is important. *Morning Ireland*, it was. The posh news.

— Go on.

— An' the headline – this was one o' the headlines. Italian parliament under pressure to take out Berlusconi. Take out was wha' he said, the news cunt. An' he didn't mean bringin' him ou' for a nosebag an' a few drinks in the lounge.

— He meant kill him.

— Assassinate him, yeah.

— Why would the Italian parliament be under pressure to assassinate Michael Jackson's doctor?

— Wha'?

— Berlusconi is Wacko's—

— You're gettin' your stories mixed up.

— Got yeh there, bud.

— Ah, fuck off. So, annyway. There's that. The *inappropriate* language. An' then there's the story itself.

— How d'yeh mean?

— Well, the bondholders aren't happy with Berlusconi, so he has to go. But then I'm thinkin', just who do these fuckin' cuntin' poxy bondholders think they fuckin' are? Berlusconi's a prick but he's an elected prick. Who elected the bondholders? Fuckin' no one.

— Were yeh a Frazier or an Ali man?

— Frazier. An' the Stones.

— I was Ali. An' the Beatles.

— Go upstairs to the lounge, where yeh fuckin' belong.

— Are yeh goin' to Poland?

— I'm only after gettin' back from the jacks. Give us a fuckin' chance.

— I meant the football, yeh gobshite.

— I know yeh did, yeh cunt.

— Well, are yeh?

— Don't think so. It's cold there, isn't it?

— Not in fuckin' June – I don't think.

— Summer there then, is it?

— I'd say so, yeah.

— I'll tell yeh wha' it is. The football's shite. The way we play.

— It's always been shite. We play ugly.

— We are fuckin' ugly.

— That's it – spot on. We're the ugliest cunts on the planet and we still sing. Especially when there's a recession.

— The Mexicans are way uglier than us.

— That's fuckin' debatable.

— No way is it. They're un-fuckin'-believable. And the Welsh.

— The fuckin' Welsh?

— Yeah. You know your man, the Snag? He's over there, beside the picture of the Dubs. Don't look – don't fuckin' look!

— Is he Welsh?

— No, but he was conceived in Holyhead when his ma an' da missed the ferry.

— Ah, fuck off. It's great but, isn't it? Qualifyin' for the football.

— It is, yeah.

— Gives the place a lift.
— It's not as good as the Queen's visit, but.
— Fuck, no. Tha' was the best.

Estonia 0–4 Republic of Ireland

— Will the euro last?

  — I've enough left for a couple o' pints, an'anyway.

  — I mean the currency. Is it fucked?

  — I don't care.

  — Ah, fuck tha'. Yeh have to have an opinion.

  — Why should I? Fuck it.

  — But—

— We were able to enjoy the occasional pint before the euro. Yeah?

  — Yeah.

— We'll still be able to do tha' if the euro goes. Life'll go on.

  — You're righ'.

  — Wha'?

  — You're probably righ'.

  — I am.

— We'll still be able to buy Cornettos for the grandkids when they come over on Sundays.

  — No fuckin' way.

  — Ah now, would yeh begrudge—

  — It's Magnums in our house.

  — Yeh posh cunts.

— It's Magnums or nothin'. I told her. If we can't afford Magnums for the grandkids, we might as well turn on the gas.

— Yeh don't want to be too hasty. There mightn't be anny in the shop.

  — Yeh know what I mean.

  — I do, yeah.

— Every Sunday. Magnums for everyone. Even the youngest. She's lactose-intolerant, God love her. Yeh should see the state of her by the time she's finished. Try takin' it off it her, but – she'll bite your ankle through to the bone.

— She has respect for family tradition.

— She fuckin' does.

— Did yeh get tha' flu yet?

— You've been its victim, yeah?

— Did yeh not notice I wasn't here?

— I thought yeh'd gone quiet alrigh'.

— Fuck off now. It was fuckin' desperate. I had a temperature of 123.

— Is tha' fuckin' possible?

— So she said, an'annyway. An' she gave the yoke a good shake before she put it under me arm.

— Yeh can't argue with science.

— That's another thing.

— Wha'?

— I'm in the bed, feelin' woegious. An' there's this smell. Un-fuckin'-believable. First of all, I think it's me. But it's comin' from downstairs. So I go down. I have to cling to the banister, the sweat's drippin' off me. An' young Damien's in the kitchen – the grandson, like. An' there's a mouse in the fuckin' toaster.

— Ah Jaysis.

— So I say it must have fallin' in – to comfort him, like. But he says, No, Granda, I thrun it in.

— Is this the same lad tha' threw the chipmunk into the deep-fat fryer?

— That's him.

— Do yeh detect a fuckin' pattern here?

— He's goin' to be a scientist – a biologist.

— D'yeh reckon?

— Fuckin' sure. We can all love animals, yeah?

— I suppose.

—Well, Damien takes it further. He's curious abou' them.

42

— Isn't it great tha' we can hate the Brits again?

— Brilliant, yeah. It's a load off me mind.

— Good oul' Cameron.

— The baby-faced prick. Wha' is it he's after vetoin', exactly?

— I haven't a fuckin' clue. It doesn't matter.

— Fuckin' gas, isn't it?

— Brilliant. All tha' matters is tha' the news will make sense from now on. The Brits will be to blame for everythin'.

— It's fuckin' great. After three years of not understandin' wha' was happenin'. Now but. The bondholders.

— Brits.

— Every fuckin' one o' them.

— The Brits are to blame for where we are now.

— Yep.

— And for blockin' all attempts to get us ou' of our fuckin' predicament.

— Bastards.

— I love them.

— All the Queen's hard work – up in smoke.

— Thank fuck. It was too complicated. But do we have to start hatin' her again as well?

— There's always a downside, unfortunately.

— The fuckin' wagon.

— Good man. You're adaptin' to the new reality.

— I fuckin' am.

— You're a good European.

— Come here, but. It's a pity Cameron isn't Thatcher, isn't it?

— Ah, Jaysis. I've died an' gone to heaven.

— My pint's not the best. How's yours?

43

— Only so-so.
— The fuckin' Brits.
— Cunts.

— See the Queen's goin' to mention Ireland in her Christmas speech.

— Ah, great. I might mention her in mine.

— It's a big deal.

— Not really. I just say a few words to the family.

— The Queen's one, I meant.

— Fuck 'er – she has it easy.

— She's goin' to say Ireland's great or somethin'.

— She can hardly say we're a bunch o' cunts.

— They'd sit up an' listen.

— That's my point. They won't sit up when she says we're grand. It's borin'. I suppose yeh have all your presents bought, do yeh?

— The ones I didn't rob.

— Yeh girl.

— Fuck off.

— Wha' did yeh get young Damien? A wolf?

— God, no. Nothin' like tha'.

— Wha' then?

— A hyena.

— Where the fuck did yeh get a hyena?

— Wicklow. There's a fella rears them – in a caravan, like.

— Where is it now?

— In the attic.

— Does Damien know?

— Not yet. But he stayed with us there a few weeks ago. An' he tells me tha' the hyena's reputation for bein' a scavenger isn't deserved. Tha' they kill 95 per cent of wha' they eat. Yeh should've heard him. Like fuckin' Attenborough.

— An' it's in your attic?

— Yeah.
— Gift-wrapped?
— Not yet, no. That's her department.

23-12-11

— Are yeh all set for the Christmas?

— Fuck the Christmas.

— Ah now—

— There was no way he was the son of God.

— Who?

— Jesus.

— Which one?

— Wha'?

— Which Jesus, like? You man over there or the Israeli fella?

— The Israeli, o' course. Your man over there – that's only his nickname. His ma was called Mary an' the post-man's name was Joe. His real name's Larry. Annyway, Christmas is a load o' bollix.

— Is your eldest comin' home this year?

— No.

— Too far?

— Yeah. So he says.

— Where is it he's gone again?

— Drogheda.

— That's only up—

— I'm messin'. Melbourne.

— New Zealand.

— Exactly. Nearly all his pals have gone. All over the place. An' there now. Jesus. Jesus over there, like. His lad – Danny. D'yeh know wha' he's up to?

— Wha'?

— He's a Somali pirate.

— Fuck off.

— True as God. He saw it on the news an' liked the sound of it. So off he went.

— Did he do a course or somethin'?

47

— Not before he left – far as I know. I don't think there's a piracy course here. Yet.

— He'll hardly be home for the Christmas.

— No, this is their busy time.

— So. The high points an' the low points of last year.

— No fuckin' way.

— Ah, go on.

— Listen, bud. I already have me low point for this fuckin' year.

— Christ – sorry. Wha' happened?

— Young Damien's hyena.

— Go on.

— I had to put him out of his misery this mornin'. The hyena, like. Not Damien.

— Was it sick?

— Not really.

— Wha' happened?

— Well, the hyena was Damien's Crimbo present, like. Yeh remember tha'?

— I do, yeah.

— So, all's grand – on the day itself. The fuckin' thing never stopped laughin'. It was fuckin' gas, actually. Burstin' its shite laughin'. Even durin' *Downton Abbey*. An' tha' takes some doin'. Laughin' through tha' shite. Annyway but, the trouble starts the day after. When Damien lets it ou' the back for a dump.

— Oh God.

— Rita next door. Her chickens, yeah?

— Gone.

— You betcha. An' Larry Hennessey's English bulldog.

— Fuckin' hell.

— I'm not finished.

— Go on.

— One o' Stella Caprani's twins.

— It didn't eat a fuckin' twin.

— Not all of it – in fairness. A fair bit, though. So annyway. Tha' was tha'.

— How did yeh do it?

— Shovel – the usual.

— Sad.

— Desperate.

— Poor Damien.

— Ah, he'll be grand. He has his eye on a gorilla.

—You're like me, I'd say, are yeh?

— I fuckin' hope not. How?

—Yeh hate havin' your dinner interrupted.

—Well, yeah. I'm with yeh there. Definitely.

— It drives me spare.

— Me too. The bell, the phone – they can fuck off till I'm done.

— Same here.

— Sometimes, like, she even expects me to talk to her. While I'm eatin', yeh know.

— It's fuckin' unbelievable. Annyway. You're just startin' the dinner when the cruiser hits the rocks. Do yeh finish it or leg it to the lifeboats?

— Depends. Wha' is it?

— Risotto.

—What's tha'?

— Rice.

— On its own?

— No. It's nice. Like Chinese, except it's Italian.

— I'll finish it, so. Anny idea what else was on the menu?

— No. It just said risotto in the paper.

— Grand. An' I wouldn't rush it either. We don't want heartburn.

—We'd eat first, then climb over the women an' children to get to the lifeboats. Like the lads – the crew, like.

— My fuckin' heroes.

— Especially the captain.

— Francesco Schettino.

—They should put him in charge o' the euro.

— He'd know when to quit.

— He fuckin' would.

24-1-12

— Wha' d'yeh think of cancer?

　— I'm all for it.

　— I'm serious.

　— Well, like – what's there to think?

　— Which one would yeh prefer? If yeh had to choose, like?

　— Well, definitely not the balls.

　— We're too old for tha' one.

　— Really?

　— Yeah.

　— Fuckin' great. How d'yeh know, but?

　— Me cousin. He had to have a medical an' they told him, an' he's the same age as us.

　— That's great. What's left?

　— Bowels.

　— God, no.

　— It's not usually fatal.

　— Don't care. I'd prefer the lungs.

　— That's one o' the worst.

　— I don't give a shite. It has more style.

　— Wha'?!

　— Okay. Listen. Say you're chattin' to a bird. Your missis has died or somethin'. Whatever – and you're chattin' to this woman. You tell her you have lung cancer, you're home an' dry. She'll think you're Humphrey Bogart. But tell her you've bowel cancer?

　— She's gone.

　— Exactly.

　— What about prostate?

　— I'm not even sure what it is. What's it do?

　— Don't know. Me cousin said it's the one we should be worried about. At our age, like.

52

— What's the test?
— Finger up the hole.
— Doctor's finger?
—Yeah, has to be a doctor. It's fifty quid extra for two fingers. The cousin said.

— Would you ever let yourself be digitally enhanced?

— Wha'?

— Would you ever—

— I heard yeh, but wha' the fuck are yeh talkin' abou'?

— You're chosen to be the face of L'Oréal.

— Me?

— Yeah. So—

— L'Oréal. That's the butter tha' spreads straight from the fridge.

— No—

— Wha' would they want my fuckin' face for?

— It's not – You know fuckin' well what it is.

— Go on. They've called to the house an' asked me to be their face. An' I've said, Yeah. Have I?

— Yeah.

— Grand. Go on.

— So they do the shoot – the filmin', like.

— 'Because you're worth it.' How was tha'?

— Very good.

— Did it give yeh the horn?

— Not really.

— Okay. I'll put the pint closer to me lips. Because you're well fuckin' worth it. Better?

— I felt a bit of a tingle tha' time, alrigh'. But annyway, they decide to digitally enhance yeh. Like they did with Rachel Weisz.

— Rachel – ?

— Stay with me. They decide to make yeh look younger.

— Wha'? Fifty-four, like?

— Forty.

— Fuckin' great.

— Is it not unethical, but?

— What age is Rachel?
— Forty-two.
— Does she go for younger men?
— She might.
— Well then. Unethical, me hole.

— Poor oul' Whitney, wha'.

— Sad.

— Desperate.

— She was a great young one.

— She was forty-eight.

— But she was always a young one. D'yeh know what I mean?

— An' forty-eight's young these days annyway.

— True. She's at home, fuckin' devastated.

— Whitney?

— Stop bein' thick. The wife. She felt a special – I don't know – a link, I suppose. Our youngest, Kevin, yeh know – he was conceived after we saw *The Bodyguard*.

— In the fuckin' cinema?

— No, we made it home. Well – the front garden.

— Nice one.

— We stopped at the boozer – here actually, upstairs. An' the chipper.

— Romantic.

— Fuck off. The chips were her idea.

— The ride was yours, but, was it?

— No, no. She took the initiative there as well. Thing was, she thought the fillum was the best thing she'd ever seen an' I thought it was a load o' shite.

— Bet you didn't tell her that.

— I forgot. So anyway, Kevin arrived the nine months later.

— Hang on. Kevin Costner.

— Exactly; yeah.

— An' if he'd been a girl, it would've been—

— Whitney; yeah.

— Ah God. I'm sorry for your troubles, bud.

— Thanks.

24-2-12

— D'yeh know the way they're thinkin' o' frackin' Leitrim?

— I can't believe I understood tha' question. But, yeah.

— An' you know what frackin' involves, do yeh?

— Kind o' – yeah.

— Well, young Damien reckons we'd find gas in our back if we fracked it.

— Does he?

— So he says. All the animals we've buried ou' there. The hyena an' tha'. Remember?

— I do, yeah.

— Well, he says there should be enough gas to supply our road. So, like – I left him to it.

— Hang on. Young Damien is frackin' your back garden?

— Yeah.

— What's he usin'.

— Her Magimix.

— Is she happy with tha'?

— She doesn't know. She's still over at Whitney's funeral.

— So she went?

— She did, yeah. Cleaned ou' the fuckin' credit union. But I'm worried. About the frackin', like.

— Why?

— Well, it's – like – controversial, isn' it? An' dangerous. I don't want to, yeh know, impede young Damien's natural curiosity, but we could've gas comin' out the fuckin' taps. There was a fella, a geologist like, on *Prime Time* last nigh'. An' he said we aren't even spellin' it right. He said there's no 'K'.

— Don't mind him. He can just fuc off.

— See the Monkee's dead.

   — Young Damien's monkey?

   — Young Damien doesn't have a monkey.

   — Does he not? I thought he did.

   — No, he doesn't. Not yet an'anyway.

   — It's on his list.

   — Yeah, but fair play to him. He wants to see if the wallabies survive first. No, your man from the Monkees.

   — Davy Jones.

   — The English one – yeah.

   — The singer.

   — Except – there now. What was their one really good song?

   — Jaysis. Hey hey we're the—

   — No.

   — Cheer up sleepy—

   — No.

   — Then I saw her face.

   — Exactly. 'I'm a Believer'. But he didn't sing it.

   — Did he not?

   — No. Micky Dolenz, the drummer – he sang it.

   — So you're saying – wha'? We shouldn't give much of a shite tha' poor oul' Davy's after dyin'?

   — No.

   — Just because he didn't sing 'I'm a Believer' an' he happens to be English?

   — No, I'm not—

   — You're fuckin' heartless. My sisters used to love Davy Jones. He did more for Anglo-Irish relations in our gaff than anny of the fuckin' politicians. Him an' Tommy Cooper.

   — I only said he didn't sing 'I'm a Believer'.

— An' I didn't sing '24 Hours from Tulsa'. Will you be as fuckin' blasé when I die?

- - - -

— Well?

— Yeh know the way there are no snakes in Ireland?

— Yeah.

— Well, it's not true.

— No?

— Young Damien was tellin' me. People who bought snakes but can't afford them any more. They're releasin' them back into the wild. So—

— Yis went searchin' for snakes.

— A boa constrictor.

— Where?

— Up the mountains. Pine Forest.

— Anny luck?

— Hang on. We brought one o' the wallabies. As bait, like. An' tied him to one o' the trees. It was all very scientific. An' we're sittin' there. An' your man slides right up – an' he coils himself aroun' the wallaby. No complaints from the wallaby.

— Probably thought it was a woman.

— I was thinkin' tha', meself. She has her arms around you, an' by the time yeh know she's stranglin' yeh, you don't really care. So, anyway. The mouth – there's no jaw. It just keeps openin'. Swallows the fuckin' wallaby. An' sits there, digestin' it.

— That's probably why the gangland guys bring the bodies up the mountains.

— Might be. But I was thinkin'. We're sitting there, in this scenery. With the rain an' the sandwiches. An' the boa eatin' the wallaby. Well, there's no other country in the world where yeh'd get tha'.

— You know this Norwegian cunt?

   — The guy in court?

   — Him – yeah.

   — Breivik – or somethin'.

— Yeah.

— What about him?

   — Yeh know the way he starts the day with the Nazi salute – his version of it, like?

— Yeah.

— Would you do tha'?

— No.

— Grand.

   — Why would I start me day doin' the fuckin' Norwegian Nazi salute?

   — So you'll stick with the fartin', yeah?

   — Fuck off now.

   — It's hard to get your head around it, isn't it?

— Wha'?

   — Norwegian Nazis.

   — We gave those cunts a hidin' in 1014, an'annyway – in the Battle of Clontarf.

   — Tha' was the fuckin' Danes.

   — Same thing.

   — Is it?

   — Not now. Back then, but.

   — Really?

   — Yeah. Back then, 'Danes' referred to all the Nordies – annyone north of the airport.

   — The fuckin' airport?

   — Where it is now, yeah.

   — So – say – all the fuckers in Dundalk were Danes.

   — Yeah. Except worse.

— How come?

— Well, yeh know the way the Danes – the genuine ones, like – left Denmark in their fuckin' canoes, so they could pillage an' rape everythin'?

— Yeah.

—Yeah, well, the Dundalk Danes didn't bother leavin'. They just pillaged stuff they already owned and raped their cousins an' their fuckin' cattle an' tha'.

— It hasn't changed, so.

— Not much, no.

16-5-12

— See tha', over there?

— Yeah.

— It's the Opera House, yeah?

— Think so.

— The roof, like. Is it an accident or is it meant to be like tha'?

— How could it be a fuckin' accident?

— Well, it's opera. That's wha' goes on in there. Opera. Singin', like. So you'd have Pavarotti, singin' the World Cup song an' tha' – full blast. And other opera cunts as well. Belting it out. All fuckin' day. So I thought maybe it'd do structural damage. The vibrations, like – eventually.

— No.

— Yeh don't think?

— No. I know what yeh mean, but I'd say they wanted it like tha'. Deliberately fucked up an' stupid-lookin'.

— D'yeh reckon?

— I'd say so.

— An' there's another thing.

— Wha'?

— It's the Sydney Opera House. That's its full name, like.

— Yeah.

— So, like – we're in Sydney.

— Yeah.

— Well. How did we get here?

— Haven't a fuckin' clue.

— Somethin' in the pints, maybe.

— That'd be my fuckin' guess.

The author looks out his hotel window

— See Donna Summer died?

    — Did she?

— Yeah.

    — That's bad. Wha' was it?

— Cancer.

    — Ah well. Cancer of the disco. It gets us all in the end.

— I met the wife durin' 'Love To Love You Baby'.

    — You asked her up.

— No.

    — No?

— I asked another young one an' she said, Fuck off an' ask me friend.

    — An' tha' was the wife.

— Her sister. An' she told me to fuck off as well. So. Annyway. Here we are.

    — Grand. She'd a few good songs, but – Donna.

— 'MacArthur Park'. That was me favourite.

    — A classic. Until Richard fuckin' Harris took it an' wrecked it.

— It's all it takes, isn't it? Some cunt from Limerick takes a certified disco classic an' turns it into some sort o' bogger lament.

    — Someone left the cake out in the rain.

— They wouldn't know wha' cake was in Limerick. They'd be puttin' it in their fuckin' hair.

    — An'anyway, they'd've robbed the fuckin' cake long before it started rainin'.

— Is she upset about Donna – the wife?

    — Stop. Jesus, man, we were just gettin' over Whitney. An' now this.

— Will she go over for the funeral?

    — She's headin' down to the fuckin' credit union.

— See the second-last of the Bee Gees is after dyin'.

— I used to have one o' them suits.

— Wha'?

— One o' the white ones. Like John Travolta's.

— They weren't a bad oul' band.

— Wha' fuckin' eejit ever decided tha' white suits were a good idea?

— Well, you had one.

— Fuck off. I had to – I'd no choice. The weddin'.

— D'yeh still have it?

— Not at all. The state of it – after the weddin', like. It was never goin' to be white again. Or even grey.

— They'd some good songs.

— They'd some big teeth as well.

— D'yeh know wha'? You're a heartless cunt.

— How am I?

— The man dies an' all you can say—

— Fuck up a minute now. Hear me out.

— Go on.

— The songs are great. No question. 'I've Gotta Get a Message To You', 'Night Fever', 'How Can Yeh Mend a Broken Heart'—

— Did they write tha' one?

— There now. I know more about them than you fuckin' do. They'll live a long time – the songs. An' so will the teeth. Long after the rest of him is gone. That's all I'm sayin'.

— So?

— Well, it's depressin', isn't it? The teeth might last longer than the songs.

— Did yeh buy any Facebook shares?

— For fuck sake, m'n. I had to grope behind the fuckin' couch to find the money to pay for this round. Annyway, they're way overpriced.

— I'm not even sure wha' Facebook is.

— A social network.

— What's a fuckin' social network?

— There was a fillum about it.

— *Legally Blonde*.

— That's the one. Anyway, it has millions o' customers – users.

— How's the money made?

— That's the point. Ads. Little ads. But they'll never make their money back. It's like this place. It's a social network as well, really.

— This kip?

— People meet here an' chat – LOL.

— Wha'?

— Never mind.

— There's no little ads here, but.

— That's no problem. We'd just all agree to put in an ad after everythin' we say. Like, Will yeh look at the tits on your one – Fly Emirates.

— Gotcha. Go on.

— So this place might've been worth – wha'? – a million. Before everythin' went mad.

— Okay.

— So then they sell it for ten million. It'll never make sense. We'd never be able to drink the new owners into profit. An' all the bankers an' bondholders who bought Facebook shares at tha' price are a dozy bunch o' cunts – Vorsprung durch Technik.

— Are yeh votin' Yes or No tomorrow?

— No.

— You're votin' No?

— No. I'm not talkin' about it.

— But—

— I'm goin'.

— Hang on – okay. I won't mention it.

— Austerity, me hole. The Yes crowd, righ' – they want us to do wha' the Germans want us to do but the Germans won't fuckin' do wha' they expect us to do. Are yeh with me?

— Yeah—

— So, anyway – historically – doin' what the Germans want yeh to do isn't always a good idea. Fuckin' hell, man, they could make us invade fuckin' Poland the next time we need a dig-out.

— That's a bit far-fetched.

— Exactly wha' the Poles said in 1939. Annyway. There's the No crowd. The anti-austerity brigade.

— Yeah.

— Have yeh ever seen a more miserable-lookin' bunch o' fuckers? They're supposed to be against misery. Half o' them don't even have jackets – an' they never fuckin' smile.

— Mary Lou smiles.

— Only cos she has to.

— Wha'?

— The young Shinners have been trained to smile. So yeh won't think they're goin' to kneecap yeh when you open the door an' they're on the step.

— That's ridiculous.

— I fuckin' agree. But it's true. They've been trained to smile – by the Libyans.

13-6-12

— Wha' d'you make of the football?

    — We won't mention Ireland.

    — Fair enough.

    — Boys in green, me hole.

    — We'll move on. I thought Ukraine were a breath o' fresh air.

    — Brilliant, yeah.

    — Shevchenko, wha'.

    — Amazin'. At his age.

    — An' he was fuckin' brutal when he was at Chelsea.

    — Ah but, when you're playin' for your country.

    — Fuckin' McGeady was playin' for his country.

    — We won't go there.

    — Tha' cunt should be playin' for fuckin' Narnia.

    — Shevchenko, but.

    — Yeah.

    — He— Don't get me wrong now. An' listen. This is between ourselves.

    — Go on.

    — Well, like. I've never fancied a man in me life.

    — Go on.

    — But. If I ever did fancy a man – if I could. It'd be Shevchenko.

    — I'm the same with Torres.

    — You fancy Torres?

    — I do, yeah.

    — But he's shite. You're always sayin' it.

    — He is. It's fuckin' tragic. But it's more of a paternal thing, I think. I just want to cuddle him. Tell him it'll be grand, he's not half as shite as he looks. Is it the same with you an' Shevchenko?

    — Not really – no.

— Grand.

— Wha' about the Irish lads? Could yeh see yourself cuddlin' anny o' them?

— It's your round.

— You must've given Torres a fair oul' cuddle before our match against Spain, did yeh?

— Fuck off, you.

— You must've well an' truly—

— One more fuckin' word an' I'll be lettin' your missis know you're thinkin' of Andriy Shevchenko every night when you're slidin' into the fuckin' bed.

— Keep your voice down, for fuck—

— Fuck off.

— It's not true.

— Just fuck off.

— It's not.

— Grand.

— Wha' d'yeh think of Theo Walcott?

— As a footballer?

— Ah, for fuck sake! Yes! As a fuckin' footballer!

— Yeh know what's happened?

— Keep your fuckin' voice down.

— You've ruined it.

— Wha' – how?

— With your Shevchenko revelations. We'll never be able to talk about the football again. There's the quarter-finals, the semis, the final, the new season comin' up – the rest of our fuckin' lives. It's *Brokeback* fuckin' *Mountain*.

— Not at all – calm down. Listen. Wha' d'yeh think of Ronaldo?

— Selfish little step-over cunt. There's no disputin' his talent but he doesn't give a shite about his team. He plays for Ronaldo an' he disappears on the big occasions.

— Brilliant. Great analysis. Wasn't so hard, was it?

— No.

— So. Movin' on. Wha' d'yeh make of Oxlade-Chamberlain?

— He's—

— Yeah – go on.

— He's lovely.

27-6-12

— See the Queen is back.
  — Wha' queen?
  — The Queen of fuckin' England. What other queen is there?
  — Where is she?
  — Here.
  — Where?
  — The North.
  — That's not here.
  — Yes, it is.
  — No, it isn't. It's England.
  — Northern Ireland is England?
  — Yeah.
  — That's fuckin' mad.
  — It belongs to England.
  — No, it—
  — Do you want it?
  — No.
  — Shut up then. What's she doin' up there, an'anyway?
  — Shakin' hands with McGuinness.
  — God love her. At least his hands'll be nice an' soft.
  — Wha'?
  — The gun oil.
  — Ah, for fuck sake—
  — They all use it up there. It's great for the hands. All the massage parlours – they use it.
  — I'm not listenin'.
  — They butter their fuckin' bread with it.
  — Not listenin'.
  — Will he tell her a joke?
  — Wha'?
  — McGuinness.

— I doubt it.

— Get her to laugh, like he did with Paisley. Here, Your Majesty, did yeh hear the one abou' the priest an' the donkey?

— He says he won't be callin' her Your Majesty.

— That's a pity. Cos it's a great joke. An' she loves donkeys.

— Horses.

— Same thing.

— See the weather in England?

— Fuck the weather in England. We've loads of our own.

— It's unbelievable.

— Desperate.

— Fuckin' relentless.

— But I'll tell yeh. It's handy enough for the polar bear.

— The polar bear?

— Young Damien's.

— You gave in.

— Ah, yeah.

— You're a gobshite.

— Ah now. He's grand. He's only a pup.

— Young Damien?

— The bear.

— It's a cub.

— Wha'?

— Not a pup. Seals have pups.

— Don't remind me.

— Is the bear in the house with yis?

— God, no. He's ou' the back. An' happy enough, in all the rain an' tha'.

— Wha' d'yis feed him?

— You can smell it, can yeh?

— Wha'?

— I rubbed half a lemon all over meself. Stung like fuck as well.

— Why did yeh do tha'?

— To get rid o' the smell.

— Wha' smell?

— Whale.

— Jesus, m'n. Did yeh buy him a fuckin' whale as well?

— No way – no. We heard it on the news. A dead whale on the beach.

— Where?

— Sligo.

— Yeh went to fuckin' Sligo?

— That's where the fuckin' whale was. They don't sell them in SuperValu.

— Yeh spent the day cuttin' up a whale?

— Most of it was gone by the time we got there. But we got a good vanful.

16-7-12

— See your man from Deep Purple died.

   — Cancer again. Did yeh like them?

   — No. Well, yeah. They were brilliant.

   — 'Smoke on the Water'.

   — Tha' one takes me back.

   — Go on.

   — I was seventeen.

   — Like Janis Ian.

   — Fuck off. I was in this place called Club 74.

   — I remember it.

   — 'Smoke on the Water' was playin' an' I was with this young one, an' she had a few rum an' blacks in her. Annyway, her tongue was all over me face. But she eventually finds me mouth. So – grand. The national anthem comes on and I say, We'll give it a miss, will we? An' we're out o' there an' straight into St Anne's.

   — Now we're talkin'.

   — Listen. She leans back against a tree. Her own idea, now. One thing leads to another – I couldn't fuckin' believe it. An' I'll tell yeh, when I—

   — Came.

   — Exactly. I thought I'd never stop. Premier Dairies couldn't've kept up with the demand.

   — An' what about her?

   — She'd gone.

   — Wha'?

   — She wasn't there.

   — So, hang on – wha'? You're tellin' me yeh rode the arse off a tree?

   — Basically.

   — Jaysis. Wha' sort of tree was it?

   — Don't know. I don't know much abou' trees.

— It's was Magnums all round in our place tonigh'.

— How come?

— My young one's fella – young Damien's dad, like. I told yeh about him.

— Yeah.

— He got ou' today.

— Great.

— An' he already has a job.

— Go 'way. Doin' wha'?

— Security.

— Great. Where?

— The Olympics. In London, like.

— Fuckin' hell. How did tha' happen?

— Well, the security company tha' got the contract—

— G4S.

— They've been makin' a balls of it. Their own staff aren't turnin' up an' the army lads over there don't want the gig either cos they signed up to shoot Iraqis an' tha'.

— Grand. So what'll he be guardin'?

— Sand.

— Fuckin' sand?

— The beach volleyball sand. It's special. They don't use the stuff off the beach. The Yanks would object to broken glass an' condoms an' tha'. The stadium isn't ready but the sand is.

— So he'll be guardin' sand.

— No.

— Hang on, you – no?

— He sold it.

— Wha'?

— He's buddies with a chap who knows a fella who's got the job fixin' some o' them houses with the pyrite, yeh know. So they're headin' over to London with a lurry.

— What'll the poor beach volleyball young ones do?

— They'll have to go to the fuckin' beach.

30-7-12

— Were yeh watchin' the women's archery?

  — Missed it.

  — Big girls with bows an' arrows.

  — Grand.

  — The bows – fuckin' hell. They're like out of a video game. The type o' thing yeh'd bring with yeh into a room full o' Batman fans.

  — Fuckin' stop tha'.

— Wha'?

  — Stop.

  — How's the polar bear?

  — It's interestin'.

— Yeah?

  — Well, the weather's picked up, so he's strugglin' a bit. She gives him the ice out of her fuckin' mojitos an' I was thinkin' o' bringin' him in to watch the synchronised divin'. Thought it might remind him o' home. The water an' tha'.

  — Makes sense.

  — No.

  — No?

  — Not accordin' to young Damien. He doesn't know he's a polar bear, Granda, he says. An' he explains it me – his experiment, like.

  — Go on.

  — We're – the humans, like – we're the only ones tha' know wha' we are. The animals haven't a clue. So why should a polar bear struggle in the heat if he doesn't even know he's supposed to be cold?

  — Hang on—

  — So we're pretendin' he's a dog. See how it goes. Took him ou' for a walk an' all.

— An'?
— He killed a couple o' dogs.
— That's encouragin'.
— Young Damien was pleased enough.

— See Maeve Binchy died.

— Sad tha'.

— It is, isn't it? D'yeh ever read any of her bukes?

— No.

— Me neither.

— I read the covers. In the bed, like. Whenever she had her hands on a new Maeve Binchy buke, yeh knew it was goin' to be a quiet fuckin' night.

— Same in our place.

— Still, but. No hard feelin's.

— No.

— I liked her on the radio.

— Yeah. I was thinkin' tha' meself earlier, when the news was on, like. I was lookin' ou' the kitchen window. An' young Damien was ou' there, sittin' in the deckchair, yeh know – takin' notes. Watchin' the polar bear peelin' the skin off o' Larry Hennessey's new English bulldog. An' I said to meself, Maeve would've seen the funny side o' tha'.

— I know wha' yeh mean.

—Wha' for us would be just a normal everyday domestic scene. She would've made it look funny.

— Exactly.

8-8-12

— You're in early.

— So are you.

— I need a fuckin' pint.

— You were watchin' Katie Taylor, yeah?

— Brilliant.

— Fuckin' brilliant.

— Did yeh ever think watchin' a girl boxin' the head off another girl would make yeh feel so proud?

— Gas, isn't it?

— Will she win the gold but?

— Foregone conclusion.

— No doubts at all?

— None.

— How come?

— She's from Bray.

— Wha'?

— Did yeh ever walk through Bray on a Saturday nigh', did yeh?

— No.

— It's either boxin' or sprintin'.

— Makes sense. See the Brits were claimin' her, but. The *Daily Telegraph* or somethin'.

— Never mind the Brits. We'll start worryin' if the Germans start claimin' her.

— Or the IMF – we'll eliminate the debt in exchange for Katie Taylor.

— No deal, lads. We'll take the debt.

— She's ours.

— She is.

— An' see your man, the showjumper – the one with the horse tha' cheated – he's doin' well too.

— Fuck'm.

— Yeah.

9-8-12

— Jesus, man – me heart.

— It was close.

— Jesus –

— But she won.

— She's brilliant.

— Just brilliant.

— I love her.

— Me too. Your man on the telly's right. She's a fuckin' legend.

— She's a born-again Christian as well. Did yeh know tha'?

— God is my shield – yeah. That's what's made her a gold medallist.

— Wha'?

— The religion.

— Wha'?

— No, listen. If she was a Catholic, righ', she'd've been happy with the bronze.

— Wha'?!

— It's always the same. We qualify for somethin' or we get to a final or a semi-final and that's grand – we're there for the fuckin' party. But the born-agains – Jesus.

— You're serious.

— It was the same with the War of Independence. We won three-quarters o' the country and then we said, That'll do us. An' we went home for our fuckin' tea.

— But if we'd been born-again Christians, we'd've kept goin'?

— The fourth green field, yeah – no bother. And on into Scotland – an' Iceland – an' fuckin' Zimbabwe.

— Yeh might be righ'.

— Think about it.

—When was the last time we won a gold without cheatin'?
— Twenty years – Michael Carruth.
— So maybe honesty is the best policy.
— Ah now – calm down.

— Pussy Riot.

   — That's just middle age. It'll sort itself ou'.

   — No. The Russian young ones. The group, like.

   — What abou' them?

   — I can't get me head around it. Hooliganism motivated by religious hatred. What the fuck is tha'?

   — It's just the excuse.

   — Wha'?

   — It's nothin' to do with religion. They're in jail cos Putin doesn't like them.

   — Is that all?

   — Listen. Remember punk – back in the day, like?

   — The Sex Pistols. 'God Save the Queen' an' tha'.

   — Exactly.

   — Brilliant.

   — I wasn't mad about it meself. But annyway. It blew the other music away.

   — Glam rock.

   — Putin loves it.

   — Wha'?

   — Glam rock.

   — Fuck off.

   — Serious. He's mad into Gary Glitter.

   — Tha' makes sense. They prob'ly like the same videos.

   — Ah now. Annyway. Fuckin' Putin an' the other cunts in the Politburo all have platforms an' silver suits, an' he mimes along to 'I'm the Leader of the Gang' an' 'Do Yeh Wanna Touch Me?'.

   — Ah, fuck off.

   — I'm tellin' yeh. He's been doin' it for years. He fuckin' hates punk.

— An' that's why those young ones are in jail?

— The Pistols made Gary Glitter look ridiculous an' those three young ones make Putin look even more ridiculous.

21-8-12

— See the *Top Gun* fella died.

— Tom Cruise?

— No, the director. Tony Scott. Killed himself.

— I seen that alrigh'. It's sad.

— It is, yeah. D'yeh ever see *Top Gun*?

— God, no. No fuckin' way. I put the foot down after *Flashdance*.

— Good man.

— Had to be done. Hand on me heart now – I've never seen a fillum with Tom Cruise in it.

— None o' them?

— Not fuckin' one.

— Not even the *Mission: Impossibles*?

— Is he in them?

— Yeah – 'course.

— Well, I've seen them alrigh'. But I never noticed him.

— He's there alrigh'.

— For fuck sake. He was chargin' around so much an' bashin' into glass, I never saw his fuckin' face. Are yeh sure about this?

— Yeah, yeah. He's in all o' them. He's the star, like.

— Fuck – I feel a bit violated now.

— Still but. Those action fillums – it doesn't really matter who's in them, sure it doesn't?

— Unless it's one o' the *Die Hards*.

— Ah, but they're different.

— Cos o' Bruce.

— He's one o' the lads.

— Yippee-ki-yay, motherfucker.

— He was in here takin' notes before he went to Hollywood.

— He fuckin' was.

3-9-12

— How's young Damien gettin' on?

— Well –

— Yeah?

— He was a bit low in himself.

— After yis buried the polar bear?

— Maybe a life o' science isn't for me, Granda, he says. Broke me fuckin' heart.

— I can imagine.

— So – yeah. But then. He starts cuttin' up stuff – bits o' cloth, like. An' he asks for the lend of his granny's sewin' machine.

— Oh Jesus.

— Yeah –

— You're worried.

— I *was*. I'm ashamed to admit it. I think the world of him – he's a great little lad. But annyway, he's lookin' at magazines and chattin' to the granny an' tellin' her all his fashion ideas.

— God—

— Now, I'd never want to interfere with his – like, his natural leanin's. You with me?

— Yeah.

— But I did.

— How?

— I bought him a tiger. A cub, like.

— To turn him away from the sewin' machine?

— I hated meself. When I realised what I was up to. But I needn't've worried.

— How come?

— He went to school this mornin' wearin' a little tiger-skin waistcoat.

— He made it himself?

— He smelt like the back o' the chipper after a long weekend. But I'll tell yeh—

— Naomi Campbell will be wearin' his stuff.

— She'll be fuckin' lucky.

— Did yeh see your man winnin' his medal last nigh'?

— Brilliant.

— What's his name again?

— McKillop.

— Wasn't he brilliant?

— Fuckin' amazin'.

— But I'll tell yeh – the bit tha' got me. When his ma – like, when his ma presented him with the medal. I was nearly cryin'.

— It was a fuckin' disgrace.

— Wha'?!

— Did yeh not hear?

— Hear wha'?

— The story.

— Wha' fuckin' story? If you're—

— Just listen, will yeh.

— Go on.

— Righ'. They had Kylie Minogue lined up to give the poor lad his medal.

— Fuck off.

— Serious.

— Jesus. Why Kylie, but?

— Ah, for fuck –. Listen. Say you've just won a medal. There's an Oul' Lads Olympics an' you've won gold for – say – the synchronised arse scratchin'. Okay?

— Okay.

— Can yeh think of annyone you'd prefer to see comin' at yeh with your medal than Kylie?

— No.

— Well, that's wha' they had set up for poor McKillop.

— You're fuckin' messin'.

— It's on YouTube. His ma pushed Kylie out o' the way – split her head open against one o' the pillars. And she walked ou' with the fuckin' medal.

— Fuck off.

— Poor Kylie needed stitches.

— I'm not listenin'.

— Made me ashamed to be Irish.

— Fuck off.

19-9-12

— Wha' d'yeh make of the photographs?
  — Wha' photographs?
  — Kate Middleton.
  — Who's she?
  — You're jokin'.
  — I'm not.
  — You have to be.
  — I'm not. I lose track o' them all.
  — She's – look it, she's married to Prince William.
  — Which one's he?
  — For fuck sake—
  — I know who yeh mean. Topless pictures.
  — Exactly.
  — An' riots in all the Arab places because o' them.
  — No, listen—
  — Egypt an' Australia an' tha'.
  — No – that's a fillum abou' Muhammad.
  — Topless?
  — No – that's the French cartoons.
  — Wha'?
  — Let's just concentrate on the Middleton pictures.
  — Your man, Muhammad – he's dead, isn't he?
  — You're gettin' distracted. Listen.
  — Wha'?
  — You're out on your balcony.
  — I don't have a balcony.
  — You're out the back. An' it's a lovely day.
  — Okay.
  — You take your top off—
  — So I'm topless.
  — You are.
  — An' me tits are bigger than your woman's.

— They are.

— Serious – they are.

— So are mine.

— Desperate, isn't it?

— We'll get back to tha'. Annyway. You don't know it, but someone's takin' photos of yeh.

— The cunt. Who?

— A paparazzi. Me, say. An' I sell the pictures to the *Star*.

— Okay.

— For a fortune.

— Fair enough.

— I brought me camera.

— Give us a hand with this zip.

— *Top o' the Pops.*

— Wha'?

— D'you remember watchin' *Top o' the Pops* when you were a kid?

— Yeah – 'course.

— Pan's People.

— Fuckin' hell. The first women.

— Wha'?

— For me, like. That was wha' it felt like. I remember them dancin' durin' a Status Quo song.

— 'Down Down'.

— You remember it as well.

— I do, yeah.

— They were un-fuckin'-believable.

— They fuckin' were.

— An' I remember thinkin' – it sounds fuckin' ridiculous – but I remember thinkin', They're women!

— A eureka moment.

— Something like tha', yeah.

— An' it made you very happy.

— It fuckin' did.

— An' it still does.

— A bit, yeah.

— An' Jimmy Savile. When yeh saw him on *Top o' the Pops*. Wha' did yeh think?

— Fuckin' eejit.

— Yeah – me too. A gobshite. But never annythin' else.

— No.

— Yeh never thought you were lookin' at a fuckin' paedophile.

—Well, look it, I went to the Christian Brothers. I didn't have to look at *Top o' the Pops* to know what a paedophile looked like.

— It's horrible but, isn't it?

— Fuckin' horrible.

— Makes yeh wonder how many more television celebs an' tha' were paedophiles back then.

— Nearly all o' them, I'd say.

— The lot.

— Except Morecambe an' Wise.

— They were sound.

7-10-12

— See Enda Kenny's on the cover of *Time*.

— Give me a shout when he's on the cover of *Playboy*.

— It's a big deal, but. He's the first Irishman to make the cover since, well – probably Obama.

— He's not Irish.

— Obama?

— Kenny – he's not fuckin' Irish.

— Wha'?

— He's from Mayo, yeah?

— Think so – somewhere over there.

— Then he's Moroccan.

— Wha'?

— I seen it on a thing – on the telly. The Moroccans came up from wherever the Moroccans come from—

— Morocco.

— Yeah. An' they settled in Mayo an' Galway an' tha'. Took it over, basically. An' the locals never noticed.

— Says nothin' abou' Morocco on the cover. The Celtic Comeback, it says.

— Me hole.

— Annyway, listen. They interviewed him—

— Did they interview Reilly as well, did they? Doctor fuckin' James.

— I don't think so—

— The Celtic Cunt. He'd try to sell them a second-hand ol' folks' home.

— Annyway—

— An' relocate New York to fuckin' Swords.

— Just fuckin' listen. Kenny wants to bring us back to the late '90s.

— Wha'?

— So he says.

— What's he on?

— Somethin' Moroccan, I'd say. But I'll tell yeh, if we are goin' back to the '90s, it's just as well yeh held on to tha' shirt.

— Fuck off.

— D'yeh read much?

— Wha'? Books an' tha'?

— Yeah.

— A bit. History – I like. The Nazis an' tha'. Why?

— I wouldn't mind readin' your man Mitt Romney's new one.

— He has a book?

— *Binders Full o' Women.*

— Great fuckin' title.

— It's kind of a man's version o' *Fifty Shades o' Grey.* Far as I can make ou'.

— What's it abou'?

— The Governor of Massachew—. The one the Bee Gees used to sing about. Annyway, the women—

— The binders o' them.

— Yeah – exactly. They're attracted to him and they want to ride the arse off him.

— Grand.

— Cos he's a bollix.

— Sounds realistic. A bit strange, but, isn't it? A presidential candidate havin' a book like that ou' a few weeks before the election.

— He's after the men's book club vote, I'd say.

— Could be his downfall, but.

— How?

— The word – binders. Remember our own presidential fella who mentioned the brown envelope in the debate an' tha' was the end of him?

— Yeah.

— Well, binders might be Mitt's brown envelope.

— He's fucked.

— An' not like the fella in his book.

— *Brown Envelopes Full o' Women*. Would yeh buy tha' one?

— Jesus, m'n, you're makin' me weak.

— Which way are yeh votin'?

— I can't vote, bud.

— How come?

— I'm not American.

— Not tha' one. Our own one – the referendum, like.

— Another one? It's not fuckin' Europe again, is it?

— No—

— Fuckin' Hitler had the right idea there—

— Relax, for fuck sake. Take a fuckin' chill pill. This one is abou' protectin' children's rights.

— What's the point o' tha'? Jimmy's Savile's dead.

— It's not about Jimmy Savile.

— I know. There's Gary Glitter ou' there as well, an' the rest of them.

— No, listen—

— No, you listen. They – children, like – they already have their Xboxes an' their – fuckin' – tha' place where the young fellas nearly show off their tackle.

— Abercrombie an' Fitch.

— That's the one – in town. They have tha'. Wha' do they want rights for as well?

— You're just bein' thick.

— Ah, I know. Kids are grand. Take them away from their mothers. It's for the best.

— I'm not listenin'.

— An'annyway, it looks like the American election mightn't be goin' ahead now.

— How come?

— It's rainin'.

7-11-12

— Wha' did yeh make of the result last night?

— Glad to see the back of them.

— Who?

— Man City, the fuckin'—

— No, no. I mean in America.

— The presidential yoke?

— Yeah.

— Our man got in.

— Good oul' B'rack.

— I love the way he talks.

— Wha'?

— The way he talks – the speeches, like.

— Is this one o' your Andriy Shevchenko moments?

— Fuck off – no. I'm just sayin'. Him an' Morgan Freeman. An' your man, the dead one. Martin Luther King. They're great fuckin' talkers.

— They're all black.

— That's part of it, yeah. It's the style o' the thing.

— Wha' the fuck are you on?

— No, listen. 'We have picked ourselves up.' He stops an' they cheer. 'We have fought our way back.' Same again. 'An' we *KNOW* in our hearts.' They're goin' fuckin' mad. 'Tha' for the United States of America.' He makes them wait, then, 'The-best-is-yet-to-come.' It's fuckin' brilliant, tha'. 'The-best-is-yet-to-come.'

— It *is* a Shevchenko moment.

— It fuckin' isn't. Not with Michelle beside him.

— Now you're makin' sense.

— Gorgeous.

— Fuckin' gorgeous.

— The election, but. What's a swing state?

— I'm not sure, but you should probably think o' fuckin' movin' to one.

101

— Are yeh votin' Yes or No tomorrow?

— Well. I had one small doubt, but I think I'm covered.

— Wha'?

— Well, every Stephen's Day I dangle the grandkids by their feet over the side o' the pedestrian bridge in Fairview. It's a family tradition. Hot chocolate after.

— Nice.

— So. My worry was tha' if the thing is passed an' children get their rights, then they'd have the righ' to dangle me.

— It'd take a fair few six-year-olds to hold on to you.

— Tha' was the worry. But I was assured, by a chap handin' out the leaflets, that tha' possibility is covered under existin' weights and measures legislation. The holder of the legs must be four times heavier than the holdee. So I'm grand. An' then as well—

— Wha'?

— I seen tha' prick on the telly.

— Which one?

— The bald fella with the long hair. Yeh know him?

— The oul' 'if-Jesus-had-lived-a-bit-longer' look.

— That's him. He came last in the Eurovision.

— It's some fuckin' achievement.

— Anyway, he made a remark abou' foster-parents. Suggested tha' they're in it for the money. An' I says to myself, tha' cynical cunt would say annythin' for a No vote. So fuck him – I'm votin' Yes.

21-11-12

- - - -
  - - -
  - - - - - -
— So, look it.
— Wha'?
— We're goin' to have to get past this.
- - Okay.
— I'll say it – I don't mind.
— Okay.
— Just the once.
— Okay.
— An' then we can move on.
— Grand. Go on.
— Righ' – okay. Yeh ready?
— Yeah – go on.
- - - Abortion.
- - -
— Tha' wasn't too bad.
— No.
— We're over the hump.
— Yeah.
— Grand.
- - -
- - - -
- - Is—?
— Yeah?
— Is it okay if we have another pint now?
— Fire away, yeah.
— Thanks.

— See the Pope says there were no donkeys in the stable.

— Rafa Benitez.

— Was he in the fuckin' stable?

— Rafa fuckin' Benitez.

— Good man.

— Rafa fuckin' cuntin' Benitez.

— Get it out o' your system.

— I mean – how can he get away with it?

— Who?

— Tha' Russian—. What's the word for a rich Russian fella – begins with 'o'?

— Cunt.

— How can he just play with my fuckin' heart?

— D'yeh want a hug?

— Fuck off. Look it. I've been followin' Chelsea twenty years longer than I've known my missis.

— That's two fuckin' disasters, so.

— Fuck off. Look. In all the years – all the managers an' tha'. Goin' way back. To the '60s, like. Tommy Docherty, Dave Sexton. I've never liked it when the manager was sacked. Never. But I never felt any hostility towards the new man comin' in. Even tha' fuckin' eejit, Hoddle. But Rafa fuckin' Benitez – ah, fuck. I'll be watchin' them tomorrow—

— Don't watch it.

— I fuckin' have to. An' I'll be shoutin' at the telly – 'Fuck off back to Spain, yeh scouse cunt.' An' yeh know what'll happen?

— Wha'?

— Torres will score two an' the next time I'm down here I'll be callin' him Rafa.

4-12-12

— See Kate Middleton's pregnant.

— Who's the da?

— Ah, stop it now. She's a nice young one.

— Serious. Who is it? I always forget.

— It's – fuck. I forget now, meself. His name, like.

— Just to be clear. She's not the one on *I'm A Fuckin' Celebrity Get Me Ant And Dec Are A Pair O' Twats Out O' Here*?

— No.

— Or the one with the cookery book.

— I don't think so – no.

— Grand. Tha' narrows it down.

— William.

— Wha'?

— That's who's she's married to.

— William who?

— Prince William.

— Okay. An' he's the da, is he?

— Yeah.

— Yeh sure?

— Ah, fuck off now.

— Did yeh never watch *The* fuckin' *Tudors*, did yeh not?

— That's just telly.

— They'd get up on annythin', them royals.

— Annyway. She's pregnant.

— So wha'?

— Ah, lay off.

— I'm serious. So wha'?

— Well, it's just a bit o' good news—

— It isn't news at all. It's only fuckin' gossip.

— Well, d'yeh want to talk abou' tomorrow's Budget instead?

— It might be twins, apparently.

— Cos o' the strength o' the mornin' sickness.
— Spot on, yeah.
— How were yeh feelin', yourself, this mornin'?
— Ah Jesus, man – fuckin' triplets. Definitely. All boys.

5-12-12

— Take a look at tha'.

— What is it?

— A property tax voucher.

— A wha'?

— I was listenin' to the news there. The Budget, like. An' they're goin' on abou' the property tax. An' I just thought – Bingo. Last year I bought a goat – online, like.

— For young Damien.

— Exactly, yeah. A stockin' filler. But annyway. I'd actually bought the goat for some family in fuckin' Somalia or somewhere. An' all I got was a voucher an' a picture of a fuckin' goat. You with me?

— Eh—

— So annyway, the oul' brainwave. I get young Damien to give me a hand. I do up a PDF—

— A wha'?

— Stay with me. I bring the memory stick up to the late-night chemist, to the chap at the back who does the photographs. He's got a state-o'-the-art photocopier in there with him. So he does me five thousand copies.

— It's a lovely job. How's it work but?

— This one here, look. For fifty euro. Yeah?

— Yeah.

— Yeh give – whoever – the voucher an' a photograph of the thing you were goin' to give them before they announced the fuckin' property tax.

— Brilliant.

— Two euro a pop, includin' the envelope.

9-12-12

— See the spacer died.

— Wha' spacer?

— The *Sky at Night* fella.

— Bobby Moore.

— Patrick Moore.

— That's him, yeah. Did he die?

— Yeah.

— That's a bit sad. He was good, wasn't he?

— Brilliant. Very English as well.

— How d'yeh mean?

— Well, like – he'd look into his telescope an' his eyebrows would go mad cos he was so excited abou' all the fuckin' stars an' the planets an' tha'. An' the words—

— They fuckin' poured out of him.

— Exactly. It was brilliant. But if he'd been Irish, he'd just've said, So wha'? They're only fuckin' stars. There's no way it would've been the longest-runnin' programme in the history o' television if it'd been Irish.

— You might be righ'.

— Think about it. Our attitude is just shite.

— I remember once, but. He was goin' on abou' how the light from stars took millions o' years to reach here and how the light we saw might be comin' from stars tha' were long dead – cos it took so long, like. An' well—

— Wha'?

— Maybe he died years ago an' we're only findin' out about it now.

16-12-12

— Did yeh go past my place on your way?

  — I did, yeah.

  — Notice annythin'?

  — It's still there.

  — You'll need to be a bit more fuckin' specific.

  — Lovely tree.

  — No.

  — Big Santy in the garden.

  — Union Jack.

  — Wha'?

  — The flag. Hangin' off the chimney.

  — Well, it's fuckin' night-time. So, no, I didn't—. Are yeh serious?

  — I am, yeah.

  — You've the flag o' Britain on top o' your house?

  — Yeah.

  - - - Why?

  — The Shinners in Belfast voted to get rid of it, off the top o' City Hall – yeah?

  — The riots an' tha'.

  — Yeah. Except for fifteen days o' the year. So I bought one.

  — A Union Jack?

  — Off eBay, yeah.

  — Okay, grand. Fuckin' why, but?

  — Show the cunts it works both ways. I'm hangin' me flag for fifteen days o' the year. Paddy's Day, Easter Monday. All the biggies.

  — Why today?

  — Excitement. When I opened the package, like. I was straight out to the ladder.

  — Jaysis.

— Sure, it's Christmas.

— What abou' Continuity Carl across the way? You're not worried he'll lob a petrol bomb at yis?

— With his one remainin' hand.

— Yeah.

— No. Tha' fucker wouldn't take tha' hand ou' of his tracksuit bottoms for an Ireland free.

22-12-12

— Anny idea wha' you're gettin' for Christmas?

— Bottle o' the Brad Pitt stuff.

— Wha'?

— Inevitable.

— Wha'?

— If it works for Brad, it'll work for me. Slap a bit on after I shave an' I'll be beatin' the women off me.

— Hang on—

— Poor oul' Brad. Angelina's too busy with all them orphans she bought in Somalia.

— Was tha' not Madonna?

— There was a sale. So, annyway, Brad has a shave an' slaps on the Inevitable an' he says, 'I'm just goin' ou' for some milk an' nappies, love,' an' he—

— Yeh missed somethin'.

— Wha'?

— He has a beard.

— So?

— He didn't shave.

— It's only one o' them little Three Musketeers ones—

— It's not aftershave.

— I know – they don't call it aftershave—

— It's not called Inevitable.

— Wha'?

— It's Chanel No. 5.

— I don't give a fuck what it is—. Hang on. The fuckin' perfume?

— Yep.

— Women's perfume?

— Well spotted.

— I never fuckin' noticed. What's tha' dopey cunt doin' on an ad for women's perfume?

111

— Makin' a few quid.

— For fuck sake. She asked me what I wanted an' I told her a bottle of Inevitable, an' she just smiled an' said Grand.

— Wha' did you get her?

— *FIFA Manager 13.*

31-12-12

— Fiscal cliff.

— He's shite.

— Wha'?!

— He's just copyin' the other fella.

— Wha' the fuck are yeh talkin' about?

— The rapper.

— Wha' rapper?

— Fiscal Cliff.

— There's no fuckin' rapper called—. You're messin', yeh cunt.

— I am, yeah.

— It's serious, but. Isn't it? The fiscal cliff.

— Seems to be.

— How?

— Don't know. Spendin' cuts, deficits – the usual shite.

— America goes into recession.

— An' so do we.

— Wha' the fuck are we in at the moment?

— Exactly. We're already fucked.

— Still though. A crap end to a crap year.

— They're all crap.

— Wha'?

— Every fuckin' year I've lived has been crap.

— Ah now.

— It's all shite.

— Hang on – calm down. The birth of your oldest.

— A great day in the middle of a fuckin' shite year.

— Your youngest.

— My ma died the same day. Fuckin' dreadful.

— Your weddin'.

— I remember half an hour an' the rest o' the year I was hung-over an' out o' work.

113

— Your first ride.

— Five minutes. The rest o' the '70s were fuckin' unbearable. An' the fuckin' '80s.

— I'm not listenin'.

— A waste o' time – I'm tellin' yeh. As for the '90s—

— Ah, fuck off.

— Happy New Year.

— Fuck off.

— God, you're fuckin' miserable.

14-1-13

— See the new boss o' the Bank of Ireland is a lighthouse keeper.

— He can't be anny worse than the dozy cunts that've been runnin' it up to now.

— True. Although – did yeh see the ad, did yeh?

— I did, yeah.

— So. You've your man arrivin' at the lighthouse.

— In the pissin' rain, yeah.

— To change the light bulb.

— An' he manages it all righ'.

— It's comfortin' tha', isn't it? Tha' the new boss o' the bank can change a bulb.

— An' he turns on the light as well, don't forget.

— Fair enough – it's a busy day.

— An' the voice is goin', 'We recognise tha' for the last few years the waters have been particularly stormy.'

— Un-fuckin'-believable.

— An' this bit. 'That's why we want – an' need – to renew our commitment to look ou' for you.'

— You know it off by heart.

— I fuckin' do.

— But did you notice his bike?

— Wha'?

— When he's inside in the lighthouse lookin' ou' for us, his bike's outside. Parked against the wall, like.

— Yeah – okay. And?

— The fuckin' eejit forgot to lock it.

— Did he?

— Annyone could fuckin' rob it.

— So it's business as usual at the Bank of Ireland.

— Exactly.

115

15-1-13

— When was the last time yeh ate a burger?

— Jaysis – I don't know. A good while back. This mornin', I think. Maybe last nigh' – not sure. Why?

— Did yeh not see the fuckin' news before yeh came ou'?

— I did, yeah.

— How they found traces of horse an' pig DNA in beefburgers, in Tesco's an' Dunne's an'—

— So?

— So? Fuckin' so?

— It's still meat.

— But it's not fuckin' beef.

— The beef isn't beef either. I couldn't give a shite. Long as it's not slugs or maggots or eyeballs an' tha'.

— You're fuckin' serious.

— Long as they taste alrigh' – what's the fuckin' fuss?

— Wha' abou' standards?

— This is fuckin' Ireland, bud – cop on.

— So – say—

— Go on. You're goin' to say somethin' stupid.

— Fuck off now, an' listen. Say it was human DNA?

— Grand. It's meat.

— Yeh wouldn't mind eatin' human?

— No. But it depends.

— On wha'?

— Wha' sort o' human it was.

— Wha' d'yeh mean? Not race—

— God, no. No – fuck tha'. No, I could never eat a Man United supporter. It'd make me fuckin' sick.

— I'm with yeh. Or a City fan.

— No meat on those fuckers.

— Or a child.

— Not one o' me own, no.

18-1-13

— You look a bit lost.

  — Ah fuck it—

  — Wha'?

  — She caught me smokin'.

  — At home?

  — Ou' the back, yeah.

  — How long have yeh been off them?

  — Ten years – officially.

  — Jesus. Wha' did she say?

  — I've to go on *Oprah Winfrey*.

  — Wha'?!

  — She's comin' to the house.

  — Hang on – *the* Oprah Winfrey?

  — Yeah.

  — She's comin' to your fuckin' house?

  — To interview me, yeah. To hear me confession.

  — Fuck off.

  — Don't believe me – I don't give a fuck. She's fuckin' furious.

  — Oprah?

  — The wife. She's makin' me do the hooverin' before your woman arrives. With her 112 fuckin' questions.

  — Will you admit it?

  — I will, yeah – no problem. But listen. She – the wife – says it was the most sophisticated, organised and professionalised sneaky smoke in the history of sneaky smokin'.

  — She's a way with the fuckin' words.

  — Well – between ourselves now – she can fuck off. I'll be tellin' Oprah that all people my age – tha' generation – we all fuckin' smoked. There were East Germans smoked a lot more than me. I was quite conservative. But yeah,

I'll admit it. Then I'll be back on the bike – with a bit o' luck.

— Will yeh say you're sorry?

— I will in me fuckin' hole.

26-1-13

— See Heffo died.

— Sad.

— Heffo's Army, wha'.

— Good days.

— Were yeh one of the lads yourself back then?

— No, I wasn't big into the Gaelic at all. But it wasn't tha'. It wasn't the football.

— Wha' d'yeh mean?

— It was the whole Dubs thing. The pride, yeh know. When they started winnin'.

— We were Dubs.

— Exactly. We were Dubs. Against the rest of the country.

— The culchies.

— The kids call them boggers.

— Well, they'll always be culchies in my heart. Especially the Kerrymen.

— No argument. They're the best culchies of the lot.

— I worked with a chap from Kerry. Nice enough fella but I couldn't understand a fuckin' word he said. I'm pretty certain it wasn't English.

— Irish, maybe.

— Maybe, yeah. His sandwiches, righ'? They were so big – he'd lift it to his mouth an' his whole fuckin' head would disappear behind it. Only his fringe, like – hangin' over the edge.

— See they're thinkin' of allowin' drink-drivin' in Kerry?

— Great idea.

— D'yeh think?

— No question. Think of it. Tourism. Telly. You'd come in after a few pints an' there's a programme on called *Drunk Kerry Drivers – Live*. You'd watch it.

— I'd get locked just to watch it.

— See the last o' the Andrews Sisters died.

  — Whose sisters?

  — The Andrews Sisters. They were singers.

  — Oh.

  — Durin' the war.

  — A bit weird, tha'.

  — Wha'?

  — They stopped singin' when the war ended. Were they Nazis or somethin'?

  — Ah, fuck off. My da loved them.

  — Did he?

  — He did, yeah – loved them. He was in the RAF.

  — Was he?

  — He was, yeah. Did I never tell yeh?

  — Hang on – your da was fuckin' Biggles?

  — Well, there now. There was once – I was a kid, like – an' I ask him what he was in the RAF. An' he looks at me an' he says, 'Well, son, I was a fuckin' air hostess.'

  — Brilliant.

  — He was great, me da. He was a mechanic.

  — Fixed the planes.

  — Exactly. But he never mentioned it much. In case some fuckin' eejit called him a Brit an' took a swing at him. But he loved the Andrews Sisters. Had the record.

  — Give us one o' their songs.

  — There was one abou' sittin' under the apple tree.

  — Give us a few bars.

  — No – fuck off. Not here.

  — Ah, go on. Did he play it a lot?

  — He did, yeah. Specially after me ma died.

  — Ah shite – sorry.

  — No, you're grand – you're grand. It's your round by the way. The barman wants yeh.

4-2-13

— See Richard the Third was found dead in a car park.

— Who?

— Richard the Third.

— Who was he?

— The King of England.

— Wha' happened the fuckin' Queen?

— Before her.

— He was her da?

— I think so, yeah. Grandda maybe. Annyway, they found him.

— They took their fuckin' time.

— Yeah – yeah. I'd like to think that if I got lost my gang'd try a bit fuckin' harder.

— He was probably a bit of a cunt.

— Safe bet. They're all cunts.

— Wha' happened him annyway?

— He couldn't find his car.

— So he just lay down an' fuckin' died?

— Well, like. If you're used to people doin' everythin' for yeh—

— Ah, fuck off.

— I'm only messin'. He was in a fight. Swords an' all.

— The car park was in fuckin' Swords?

— No – the fight. There were swords. He was brutally hacked – accordin' to the English guards.

— How do they know it was him? He must've been there for ages.

— His DNA.

— What about it?

— It was 45 per cent horse.

— Ah well, then he was definitely one o' the British royal family.

— Science is incredible, isn't it?

— Brilliant.

121

— See the Trogg died.

— I saw tha', yeah. Reg Presley.

— With a name like tha' he was never goin' to be a plumber, was he?

— It wasn't his real name.

— Was it not?

— No. His real one was Reg Ball.

— You were a bit of a fan, were yeh?

— I was, yeah. I was only a kid when 'Wild Thing' came ou'—

— It made your heart sing.

— That's the one. One of me brothers had the record an' he left it behind when he got married, so it was always in the house.

— Great song.

— Brilliant song. Still.

— Could you get away with it now?

— Wha'?

— Callin' a woman a wild thing.

— I don't see why not. I called my missis exactly tha' this morning after the news.

— An' she was grand with it?

— Fuckin' delighted. I put me arms around her – I was a bit emotional, like. An' I sang it to her.

— Nice.

— In the kitchen.

— An' tell us – without invadin' your privacy. Did it develop into a bit of a Jack Nicholson, Jessica Lange moment? On the table.

— Not exactly, no. But she put an extra dollop o' jam into me porridge.

— For fuck sake.

— Blackcurrant.

— Nice.

7-2-13

— So. Anglo's gone.

— Liquidated.

— Great fuckin' word.

— But—

— Wha'?

— Is it good news or bad news?

— That's the fuckin' problem, isn't it? We don't really know.

— An' no one else does either. Not one o' those cunts on the telly or the radio has a fuckin' clue.

— 'Cept your man, the economist fella. Constantin.

— Constantin Gurdgiev.

— Him – yeah. He looks like he knows wha' he's on abou'.

— Only because he's the only one tha' doesn't look like he's tryin' to sell yeh his wife or a second-hand Hiace. His face, like.

— Buster Keaton.

— Exactly.

— So, does he think we're any better off?

— I couldn't really understand him. But he said none o' those Anglo season ticket holders—

— Bondholders.

— Yeah. None o' them should've got their money back. They could fuck off with their promissory notes.

— Did he say tha'?

— More or less.

— He's one o' the lads, so. One thing, but.

— Wha'?

— Yeh know the way no one really gives a shite abou' the horse DNA in the burgers?

— Yeah.

123

—Well, it's the same with this Anglo shite, isn't it? They can't scare us annymore.

— 'Cept Buster.

— Fair enough. He's a bit fuckin' scary.

10-2-13

— What's wrong?

   — I stuck twenty euro on a horse.

   — An' it lost.

   — No, it won.

   — Wha'?

   — Listen. Me cousin texts me – yesterday. Stick a few quid on Paddy's Boyband, in the four o'clock at Leopardstown. So I do. An' he wins.

   — The horse.

   — Yes, the fuckin' horse. So. I go into Paddy Power's – just now. An' the young one at the hatch tells me he's disqualified. He failed a fuckin' test.

   — Dopin'.

   — No. DNA. They found traces of horse DNA.

   — In the horse?

   — 73 per cent.

   — Hang on – fuck off. The horse was only 73 per cent horse?

   — Yeah.

   — But—. Wha'? 27 per cent of the horse wasn't fuckin' horse?

   — Yeah.

   — Wha' was it?

   — Beef.

   — Fuckin' beef?

   — Here's me theory, righ'. They've been puttin' horse DNA into the beefburgers, yeah?

   — Okay.

   — So there's the problem. They need to get rid of the beef they took ou' of the burgers to make room for the horse.

   — Hang on—

— So they shove it into the horses.

— Shove?

— Inject – I'd say.

— Fuckin' hell. How can a horse that's more than a quarter cow win a fuckin' race?

— We've been underestimatin' cows for years.

— Are you fuckin' havin' me on? - - - Are yeh?

13-2-13

— Pope's gone.

— Fuckin' tragic.

— There's a thing.

— Wha'?

— Wha' was his name?

— Jesus—. I can't remember. I never really got the hang of it.

— Gas but, isn't it? Can you imagine – back in school, say? Not rememberin' the Pope's name. We'd've been murdered.

— Shows yeh how times've changed.

— Gas.

— An' he resigned. I didn't know they could do tha'.

— He's frail. I heard a lad on the radio. Why he resigned, like. Wha' d'yeh think tha' means?

— He's gay.

— Ah stop it. You're not usin' your imagination.

— That's wha' she says, at home.

— Why?

— We won't go there. He's frail.

— Yeah. But what's it mean?

— Go on.

— Say – tonigh'. We have a few pints more than the normal. How will yeh feel tomorrow?

— Shite.

— Grand. An' as well as tha' you'll feel a bit—?

- - - Frail.

— Good man.

— So, you're sayin' he drinks.

— It's a theory.

— He's one o' the lads.

— Far-fetched. But is it impossible?

— No.
— After work, like. He puts on jeans an' a jumper.
— An' has a few cans.
— But he can't cope annymore.
— Mass in the mornin's.
— Meetin' African nuns.
— Fuck it, he says.
— In German.
— I'm out o' here.

— See they found traces o' greyhound DNA in the horse meat they've been puttin' in the burgers.

— Borin'.

— Borin'?

— I've moved on.

—Well, before yeh do—

— Go on.

— There was a chap on the radio – a food scientist. An' he says, if yeh handle a piece o' meat you leave traces of your DNA on it.

— So?

— So? For fuck sake – listen. I had a bit o' steak earlier. I handled it an' the missis handled it.

— Why both o' yis?

— We're makin' the dinner together these days. Some shite she read at the dentist's. Adds excitement to the fuckin' marriage.

— How?

— Movin' on. The butcher handled it.

—Wearing the plastic gloves.

— I've no proof o' tha'. He gave the wife a hug before he left the house. You're sittin' up now, yeh cunt.

— I fuckin' am. It's the name of a book, I think.

— Wha'?

— *The Butcher's Wife.*

— I bet it's a good one. Annyway. I had me steak, so I ate the cow, meself, the wife, the butcher, the butcher's wife an' maybe her sister, if the rumours are true. An' that's borin', is it?

— Which sister?

— Does it matter?

— It kind o' does, yeah.

— See the French bird says there's good news on the horizon.

— Wha' French bird?

— Your woman with the scarf. The IMF boss – what's her fuckin' name.

— Madame Lagarde.

— That's the one. She's very happy with us. We've been very good, apparently.

— It's International Women's Day.

— Yeah. So?

— Yeh just called the head of the IMF the French bird.

— She is fuckin' French. Unless she's just messin'. Wha' d'yeh think the good news is? She didn't say.

— Yeh can't call the head of the IM fuckin' F a bird.

— Why not? Hang on – I've sussed it. You've done it again, haven't yeh?

— Wha'? No – fuck off.

— Go on, yeh cunt. You've fallen in love with her.

— Fuck off.

— Jesus, every time. A woman in any sort of authority – an' you're fuckin' smitten.

— You're talkin' shite.

— Your woman, Bhutto.

— She was gorgeous.

— Okay.

— An' tragic.

— Yeah, yeah. But Condoleezza?

— She was lonely.

— For fuck sake. An' Hillary?

— She could've done better than Bill.

— Wha' – you?

— No – fuck off. Not necessarily.

— Does your missis know you're in love with half the world's politicians?

— She's gone.

— Fuck – where?

— Chavez's funeral.

— For fuck sake.

— Well, she let me go to Benazir's.

— Fair enough.

— Would you take penalty points for your missis?

— Not 'would', bud. Did.

— Did yeh?

— A few years back. When we went from miles to the other yokes.

— Kilometres.

— Yeah.

— Wha' happened?

— She took the van down to the chipper.

— Why didn't she just walk?

— Big order, an' her back was at her. So anyway, a couple o' Gardas seen her burnin' the rubber on the way back. An' they order her to stop. But she panics – so she said. The priority was to get the chips home.

— The maternal instinct.

— Yeah, yeah. So the fuckin' Guards ring the bell—

— Oh fuck.

— An' she said I'd been the one drivin'.

— Did they believe her?

— No.

— Where were you?

— Out the back. So, annyway. The day we're up in the district court, she drags me down to the fuckin' hairdresser. Gay Larry – d'yeh know him?

— I do, yeah.

— A fuckin' genius. By the time he's finished with us we're fuckin' twins. An' we stand side by side in the court, same hair, an' in our leisure gear, yeh know. An' the judge – he just gives up.

— Brilliant.

— But—

— Wha'?

— He fuckin' winked at me.
— The cunt.
— Fuckin' ugly as well.

— He isn't black.

  — Who? Stevie Wonder?

  — The Pope.

  — The fuckin' Pope?

  — He isn't black.

  — Is he – like – is he supposed to be?

  — Yeah.

  — Well, he's only new. Give him a chance. What's the problem?

  — Cheltenham.

  — Wha'?

  — I was in Paddy Power's earlier – stuck a tenner on Back In Focus in the openin' race.

  — Hang on – he won.

  — Yeah, but—

  — Wha'?

  — It was a double. Back In Focus to win the National Hunt Chase an' a black pope by the end of the day. Hundred to one.

  — Fuckin' hell. An' Black Pope wasn't a horse?

  — No. Black Pope was a black fuckin' pope. So, like – I'm watchin' it on telly. White smoke. Fuckin' great – he's elected today. Then they're sayin' – the fuckin' experts – they're saying he'll be Italian cos the election was so fast. An' I'm thinkin' unless they've elected Mario Balotelli I'm fucked. But then they announce he's from Argentina. An' I get a bit giddy. I kind o' mix up Argentina an' Brazil. There's loads o' black Brazilian footballers, so I'm still in with a chance. But then this white prick walks out onto the balcony.

  — Pope Frankie.

  — The bastard.

25-3-13

— My young one is in trouble. An' her fella.

— Ah, no.

— The mortgage, yeh know.

— They can't handle it?

— They're fucked, God love them. They've been into the bank an' tha', to try an' sort somethin'. But—

— No joy?

— It's fuckin' madness. Her fella was in the chipper last nigh'. He gives his order, then sees the onion rings an' he tells Gaddafi he'll have one. Then someone taps him on the shoulder an' he turns, and this cunt in the queue says, 'You can't have the onion ring.'

— Fuck off.

— That's exactly wha' my young one's fella says. An' your man, the other fella, takes out his ID an' flashes it. Bank of Ireland.

— No!

— An' he proceeds to tell him he can have the chips – but only once a month. An' he can't have the onion ring. Ever. Or until the mortgage is fully paid.

— Wha' did your lad say?

— He said the onion ring was one of his daily five an' the prick from the bank could fuck off with himself.

— Wha' then?

— The bank prick follows him home. Shouts in the letterbox, 'Hope that's not Sky Sports you're watchin'!'

— It's fuckin' harassment.

— It's the future.

— Jesus. It's like New Year's in here.

— An' it's only a fuckin' Monday. He wouldn't take money for the pints.

— Who wouldn't?

— The miserable cunt tha' owns this dump. The pints are for nothin' till closin'. So he says.

— Fuckin' hell. It's a pity Thatcher couldn't die every fuckin' day.

— We'll make the most of this one, so.

— I never called a woman a cunt in me life.

— Except Thatcher.

— You're the same?

— I am. Yeh know what I hated most about her?

— I won't bother guessin'.

— She made me think like a Provo.

— Wha'?

— Every time she opened her mouth about Ireland. With her 'Out, out, out'. Remember?

— I fuckin' do.

— An' durin' the hunger strikes. Every time she spoke. She hated us.

— I always thought – she couldn't figure out tha' we weren't British. She was a bit thick.

— You're probably righ'. Anyway—

— She's gone.

— Cheers.

— Cheers. Come here, but. Who d'yeh think she's sittin' beside in hell?

— Some fucker with an accordion.

— Playin' 'Kevin Barry'.

— Out of tune.

— For all fuckin' eternity.

— Longer.

14-4-13

— Anny news?

— It's war.

— Oh, fuck. Korea?

— Fuck Korea. At home – in the house, like. Herself.

— Hate tha'. What's the story?

— She's goin' across to Thatcher's funeral.

— Wha'?!

— I know – I fuckin' know. I can't fuckin' believe it. She says – listen to this. She says she's always modelled herself on Thatcher.

— Fuckin' hell. Did you ever notice?

— Fuck, no – Jaysis, no. No, no. She's lovely, sure. Isn't she?

— Go on.

— Sure, she collected for the miners back in the day, an' she named the fuckin' dog Las Malvinas. But there's no remindin' her. She's on the Holyhead boat tomorrow.

— Jesus—

— It's un-fuckin'-believable. So I went on the counter-attack, o' course.

— Thatcher-style.

— Fuck off. I was a bit mean, like. I told her I'd never seen a picture o' Thatcher sittin' up in the bed in a pink onesie, playin' Texas holdem on her grandson's tablet.

— An' wha' did she say?

— The usual. An' fair enough. But then – I'm not proud o' this – I called her a scanger. I just whispered it, like.

— Oh, boy. What did she say then?

— The scanger's not for turnin'.

— Did yeh ever bite anyone?

— God, yeah.

— Wha'?

— Loads o' times.

— Not when you were a baby, like.

— I know, yeah. I know exactly wha' you're at. Yeh want me to join the witch-hunt against poor Luis Suárez.

— But—

— Just cos he bit a Serb in the penalty area.

— Fuck off a minute. I'm serious.

— So am I. So sit back there, yeh cunt, an' I'll tell yeh the problem. The root of it, like. An' not just scapegoatin' fuckin' Suárez.

— Okay. Go on.

— Christianity.

— Wha'?

— Fuckin' Christianity. I'm tellin' yeh. All these fuckin' players – you've seen them. They bless themselves goin' on the pitch, or look up to the sky – talkin' to God, like. An' the first thing they do is rake their studs down some poor fucker's shins. Or they dive – they hit the deck like they're bein' ridden by a bear. But it's grand, because they're Christians an' they talk to God an' he's obviously told them they can kick an' cheat an' pull jerseys as much as they like. They're fuckin' crusaders. An' Suárez was just showin' God how much he loved him.

— By bitin' Ivanovic?

— Exactly. It was fuckin' heroic.

1-5-13

— See they're talkin' about legislatin' for the right to an abortion in the event of your team bein' relegated.

— Fuck off – you're sick.

— Serious. I heard it on the radio – I think I did, annyway.

— Fuck off.

— But it has to be actual relegation, not just fear o' relegation – or the *ideation* o' relegation.

— I'm not listenin'.

— An' it'll have to go before a panel of three people. Two doctors – an obstetrician, like, an' a psychiatrist. An' one o' the lads from *Match of the Day*.

— Fuck off.

— So I heard. If there's a genuine prospect of the team bein' relegated an' the woman wants an abortion, the HSE will call in Alan Shearer—

— Fuckin' Shearer?!

— Or Dion Dublin.

— Ah, for fuck sake. It's fuckin' typical. What's wrong with one of our own punters?

— So. If I'm right—. You think it's okay for a woman to have an abortion if she gets the all-clear from Brian Kerr or Kenny Cunningham.

— Yeah – no. Fuck off.

— Or Lawrenson.

— Fuck off.

— Or Roy Keane.

— She'd listen to Roy.

— See he's gone.

   — Jimmy Tarbuck?

   — Fuck off – Sir Alex.

   — An' for the same reason.

   — Don't start now.

   — Why d'yeh think he held on to Giggs and fuckin' Scholes for so long?

   — You're fuckin' sick.

   — Buyin' their silence. They were only little lads when they were forced to join tha' fuckin' club. Fuckin' kidnapped they were.

   — I'm not listenin'.

   — On their way to Chelsea.

   — Wake me up when you're done.

   — An' poor little Beckham as well. But Posh rescued him, thank God.

   — Are yeh finished?

   — Go on.

   — It's the end of an era.

   — Is tha' the best yeh can do?

   — Well, it fuckin' is.

   — Okay – grand. What is a fuckin' era, annyway?

   — I don't know. A long time – ages – fuck off.

   — Why's he leavin'?

   — His hip.

   — His fuckin' hip?

   — He's havin' it replaced.

   — Why can't he fuckin' limp like the rest of us? An' who's replacin' him?

   — Mourinho.

   — Wha'?! José? Fuck off. He's comin' back to us.

— Not accordin' to the bookies.

— Fuck the bookies. Tell yeh wha' – Sir Alex can have my hip. If it'll make him change his mind. D'yeh have a saw on yeh?

18-5-13

— So. Beckham retired.

— Tha' cunt retired years ago.

— Ah, for fuck sake – relax. Just accept it. He was a great player.

— He wasn't great. He was okay for a couple o' years. Before he met Spice Rack or wha'ever her fuckin' name is.

— God, you're a fuckin' eejit.

— An' I'll tell yeh exactly why he retired.

— G'wan. Why?

— To upstage Angelina.

— Wha'?!

— They couldn't cope – him an' Posh – with all the attention she was gettin' an' all the praise. An' Posh didn't have an illness or a condition of her own to announce, cancer or depression or a second hole in her arse or annythin'. So he says, 'Fuck it, love, I'll announce me retirement.'

— Actually. You're probably righ'.

— I'm definitely righ'.

— Would you tattoo your kids' names on the back of your neck?

— They wouldn't fit.

— I suppose it wouldn't be too bad if the name was Romeo or Brooklyn. But your man over there – Badger.

— What abou' him?

— The tattoo.

— Where?

— On the back of his fuckin' neck

— That's not a tattoo. That's just dirt.

— But look – it says 'John Paul'.

— Coincidence.

— Fuck off.

— An' annyway, it's spelt wrong – look. 'John Pal'.

25-5-13

—Were yeh ever breathalysed?

— Yeah.

— Did yeh pass it?

— No – failed. Fuckin' miserably. But I wasn't drivin'.

— Wha'?

— I wasn't even in a fuckin' car.

— Wha'?!

— I was walkin' home – from here. An' I swerved into the wrong garden an' up to the wrong fuckin' door. An', like, the key wouldn't turn for me. I was so locked, it never occurred to me that I was tryin' to get into the wrong house.

— Whose gaff was it?

— Widow McCarthy's.

— She's not a widow.

— Married to tha' cunt, she might as well be. Annyway, she phoned the Guards. An' that's how they found me – with me key in your woman's lock.

— But yeh weren't in a car.

— No. But the Guard says if I'd been drivin' and I'd taken a wrong turn like tha', I'd've killed meself. An' he breathalysed me, to prove his point.

— Fuckin' eejit.

— Ah, he was grand.

— But – come here. Alan Shatter.

— An' his fuckin' asthma.

— I had asthma – when I was younger, like. An' if I couldn't've done a breathalyser, I'd've either been on me way to A&E or fuckin' dead.

— So, he's lyin' through his arse.

— He can manage tha'. His arse doesn't have asthma.

— What's wrong?

    — Nothin'.

    — Is someone after dyin'?

    — No.

    — Well, there's something wrong with yeh. I can tell. Come on, ou' with it.

    — Well—

    — Yeah?

    — Mourinho's back.

    — I know. I expected you to be dancin' on the fuckin' counter.

    — Well, I'm not.

    — But you like Mourinho.

    — I fuckin' love Mourinho.

    — So, what's the problem?

    — Well. I made a pact.

    — With the fuckin' devil?

    — No. God.

    — Mourinho?

    — No, the other one. The hairy one, like – the real one, I suppose you'd call him.

    — Just – hang on. Just so I'm clear here. You made a pact with God.

    — Yeah.

    — Do you even believe in God?

    — Not really. But – I don't know. I kind o' do.

    — Wha' was the pact?

    — I'd give up the drink if Mourinho went back to Chelsea.

    — For fuck sake. When?

— At me cousin's funeral there, a month ago. In the church. On me knees, like. I said, I might as well give it a go while I'm down here.

— But, look it, Mourinho was on his way long before tha'.

— Ah, I know.

— An' did God actually answer yeh?

— Not really.

— Annythin' in writin'?

— No.

— Fuck'm, so. You'll have a pint.

— Okay. Grand. Yeah. Thanks.

— Poor oul' Mandela.

— Yeah.

— He's on the way ou'.

— D'yeh know wha', but? He should never've left the Four Tops.

— Fuck off now – just fuck off.

— Okay – sorry. Sorry.

— Okay. D'yeh remember the time he was in town? He was gettin' the freedom o' the city or somethin'.

— Same day the Irish team came home from the World Cup. Italia '90.

— That's righ'. You were with me, yeah?

— Yeah, 'course. We'd most o' the kids with us.

— The ones tha' were born.

— Some fuckin' day.

— I had two o' mine on me shoulders. All fuckin' day. I don't think I ever recovered.

— Great day, but.

— Brilliant. Seein' him. My kids still remember it.

— Good to have done it, so. Gone in, like.

— 'Ooh aah, Paul McGrath's da'. D'yeh remember?

— Brilliant.

— An' him walkin' out o' jail. D'yeh remember tha'?

— Amazin'.

— The dignity, like.

— My cousin. Danno. A mad cunt. He was up in court. Did I ever tell yeh this?

— When was this?

— 'Bout the same time – back then. Anyway, the judge says to him, 'Why did yeh rob the bookie's?' An' Danno says back, 'So I can walk out o' jail like Nelson Mandela.'

20-6-13

— See Tony Soprano died.

— Sad, tha'.

— Only a young fella really.

— Fifty-one.

— Frightenin' – a bit. Isn't it?

— Yeah. He was fuckin' brilliant but, wasn't he?

— Amazin'. *The Sopranos* was the first television series I watched. As an adult, like.

— I know wha' yeh mean.

— The other shite was on but I never really watched any of it. *Dallas* an' all tha'. Fuckin' J.R. an' Bobby an' John Boy.

— Tha' was *The Waltons*.

— Doesn't matter – same fuckin' shite. An' the soaps were no better.

— Then Tony arrived.

— There were times I'd be lookin' at his face an' I'd know wha' he was thinkin'.

— Cos he was a man.

— Real, yeah.

— One o' the lads.

— Wouldn't go tha' far. Great actor, but.

— Brilliant. It's been a shite week, hasn't it?

— They're all shite. What else happened?

— Well, Michelle Obama. Goin' for a pint with fuckin' Bono. Wha' the fuck was she at?

— She could've come here.

— Exactly. Instead she had to listen to tha' prick scutterin' on abou' global poverty an' himself.

— Her loss.

— Big time. Yeh know what's tragic about it?

— Wha'?

— She went back to America without ever havin' tasted Tayto.

— Tony would've liked Tayto.

— He would.

— The Anglo tapes, wha'.

   — Don't get me fuckin' started.

   — I keep remindin' meself tha' it happened five years ago.

   — But it doesn't help, sure it doesn't?

   — No.

   — 'Get the money in, get the fuckin' money in.'

   — Our money.

   — Yeah.

   — Laughin' at us, they were.

   — Bastards.

   — If it'd been us – people like us. Lyin' through our arses, commitin' fraud an' tha' – we'd be in the Joy now.

   — We went to the wrong school.

   — But we paid the fuckin' bill. It's sickenin'. Jesus, man, my young one was cryin' last nigh' – she was askin' us for the money to buy shoes for little Caitlin – the gran'daughter, like. For fuck sake.

   — Your man who reported it – Paul Williams.

   — He's good, yeah.

   — He usually does the gangland guys, doesn't he?

   — Yeah.

   — An' he always uses their names – The General an' The Monk an' tha'.

   — Why doesn't he do the same now?

   — Yeah, exactly.

   — Which one is the laugher?

   — Bowe – I think.

   — John 'The Hyena' Bowe.

   — Not bad – a bit gentle.

   — The Fuckin' Hyena.

   — Better. What abou' Fitzpatrick?

— Peter 'The Thick-Lookin' Dopey Fuck' Fitzpatrick.
— Tha' captures the man alrigh'. An' Drumm?
— David 'The Cunt' Drumm.
— Put it on his fuckin' birth cert.

— The fuckin' weather.

   — What about it?

   — The heat.

   — It's not tha' bad.

— This is fuckin' Ireland. It's unnatural. It's – your man said it on the radio. It's an absolute drought.

   — It hasn't rained for two weeks. So wha'?

   — Well, it must be affectin' you. You've taken your hoodie off.

   — That's nothin' to do with the weather. It's a security measure.

   — Wha'?!

   — I took it off in case some prick decides to shoot me when I'm walkin' past his house. D'yeh remember 1976, do yeh?

   — I do, yeah.

   — Tha' was weather.

   — Un-fuckin'-believable.

   — Our dog died o' the heat tha' summer.

   — Ah.

   — An' we didn't notice till October.

   — What abou' the stink?

   — We thought it was me da.

   — Fuck off – you're messin' again. One thing, but.

   — Wha'?

— The colour of the grass. With the heat an' tha'. And Ireland is famous for bein' green. We even have the four green fields – the provinces, like. An' all those republicans fightin' an' dyin' for the four green fields.

   — Go on.

— Well, would they have got as worked up if the fields had been brown?

— What're yeh sayin'? We'd still be part o' the British Empire if the weather had been better?

— It's just a thought.

23-7-13

— See she had the baby.

— Who – the big girl from Paddy Power's?

— No. Kate Middleton.

— Who?

— Ah, don't fuckin' start again – pretendin' yeh don't know.

— She's the Queen's cousin or somethin', is she? I get mixed up – I don't give much of a shite.

— She's the Queen's granddaughter-in-law.

— For fuck sake – draw me a fuckin' diagram.

— I don't give much of a shite either, to be honest with yeh.

— Boy or girl?

— Stop fuckin' pretendin'.

— What'll they call him?

— It'll be announced in due course.

— Wha' they should do – if they'd anny imagination or guts . . .

— Wha'?

— Did yeh see the YouTube tha' was doin' the rounds a few weeks back? The missis showed it to me. The fuckin' eejit talkin' to the other pair o' fuckin' eejits abou' how she judges kids by their names.

— Seen it, yeah.

— The fuckin' head on her. Annyway, she objected to Chantelle an' – was it Tyler?

— Think so.

— That's wha' they should call him, so. Tyler. Show solidarity with their people. For once.

— Prince Tyler?

— Why not? The first royal rapper.

— King Tyler.

— The First.

— Or Jamal.

— Jamal the First? Sounds too like a pope. The fuckin' Orangemen would be riotin' again.

31-7-13

— See Pat Kenny's gone.

  — To Celtic?

  — Wha'?

  — Has he gone to Celtic?

  — Fuckin' who?

  — Kenny. The young lad tha' plays for Home Farm. Celtic and Colchester were lookin' at him an'—

  — Pat Kenny. From RTE.

  — What about him?

  — He's gone.

  — 'Course he's gone. It's the summer. They all fuck off for the summer in tha' place.

  — No—

  — Replaced by even bigger fuckin' eejits than themselves.

  — No—

  — Even the news. Kids from Transition Year do the reportin' an' tha'. Little fellas an' girls standin' on boxes so their faces can reach the camera.

  — Will yeh fuckin' listen—

  — While the other red-faced fuckin' wasters get the same holidays as the teachers they're all married to an' fuck off to France an' Donegal.

  — He's fuckin' gone, I'm tellin' yeh!

  — Who?

  — Kenny! He's gone. For good.

  — For ever, like?

  — Yeah.

  — Did he bring Joe Duffy with him, did he?

  — Not as far as I know.

  — So. Just to be clear. Pat Kenny doesn't work for RTE annymore.

— No.

— Well, my God. Where's he gone?

— Newstalk.

— An' come here. Seriously. Are we supposed to give a fuck?

— Yeah.

— But do we?

— No.

— No, we don't.

14-8-13

— Thirty-five grand.

— What about it?

— It'd buy yeh a lot of gargle.

— It fuckin' would.

— Thirty-five thousand cans of Dutch Gold. Just for example.

— Fuck – I'm not sure that's an attractive thought annymore.

— I'm just givin' yeh a simple picture. An idea of the scale o' the thing.

— You're talkin' about the amount o' booze tha' got delivered to the Garda station in Belmullet.

— In 2007 – yeah.

— Who gave it to them again?

— Shell – or some gang o' cunts workin' for Shell.

— The Garda inquiry said there was no evidence.

— 'Course not. They fuckin' drank it, didn't they?

— Wha' did they do with the empties?

— Threw them in the fuckin' sea on their way to hammerin' the heads off the protesters.

— Tha' makes sense.

— It's efficient. But yeh know the really mad thing about it?

— Wha'?

— There was only ten Guards in the station.

— That's, like, three an' a half thousands' worth of drink per pig.

— Yep.

— Does tha' include mixers?

— Good question.

— Or crisps an' nuts.

— I know wha' yeh mean. Accessories, like.

157

— Were yeh ever in Belmullet?

— No – thank fuck.

— Yeh'd need a lot o' free jar to survive a year in tha' fuckin' kip.

20-8-13

— See Elmore Leonard died.

    — The singer?

    — The writer.

    — Which one was he?

    — American, brilliant – *Get Shorty*.

    — Was tha' him?

    — Yeah. Look at me.

    — Wha'?

    — He wrote loads o' them. Look at me.

    — Wha'?

    — *Out o' Sight, Jackie Brown, Rum Punch, Killshot*. Look at me.

    — I am lookin' at you. Why d'yeh keep fuckin' sayin' tha'?

    — It's a quote.

    — Wha'?

    — It's a line. John Travolta says it.

    — In *Get Shorty*.

    — Yeah – good. Yeh know it.

    — I do, yeah. 'Course. An' I'm goin' to make an educated guess here. Look at me.

    — Wha'?

    — I bet it's the only line yeh remember from the fuckin' fillum.

    — No, it isn't.

    — Go on, so. Give us one.

    — Fuck off.

    — There. I knew it – yeh cunt.

    — Wha'?

    — Yeh couldn't think of another line.

    — I just did.

    — Wha'?

— Fuck off.

— Tha' doesn't count. Tha' line is in nearly every fillum worth watchin' tha' was ever made. *Taxi Driver, The Godfather, Adam an' Paul, Bambi*—

— Fuckin' *Bambi*?!

— The rabbit says it, if you're listenin' carefully – when the young prince's birth is announced.

— Fuck off.

— He's a bit of a Shinner, tha' rabbit.

— Look at me.

— Wha'?

— It's your round.

24-8-13

— D'yeh remember 'Kitty Ricketts'?

 — I fuckin' married her.

 — The song.

 — The song, the attitude, the whole fuckin' shebang.

 — The song – stop messin'. Yeh know what I fuckin' mean.

 — I do, yeah.

 — You remember it.

 — Yeah.

 — It was brilliant, wasn't it?

 — Yeah – brilliant. There were great songs back then.

 — Great gigs as well.

 — Yeah, yeah. The Blades, The Atrix.

 — The Radiators from Space.

 — Songs about Dublin.

 — Made us proud, didn't it?

 — Still does.

 — The fella tha' wrote tha' one, 'Kitty Ricketts'.

 — Philip Chevron – yeah.

 — There's a testimonial for him tonigh'.

 — Football?

 — In the Olympia.

 — Football in the Olympia? Fuckin' brilliant. The Radiators from Space versus A Republic of Ireland Eleven – from space.

 — Niall Quinn up in the gods.

 — His natural fuckin' habitat.

 — Eamon Dunphy on drums.

 — Tha' makes sense.

 — Philip Chevron on the left wing.

 — With his mazy runs an' silky skills. Slashin' at his opponents' shins with his guitar.

161

— He isn't well.

— Yeah.

— Yeh know wha' tha' means – 'isn't well'? For men our age, like.

— I do – yeah.

— Okay.

— Chevron, but. What sort of a name is tha'?

— It's Irish. He dropped the O.

— O'Chevron?

— Exactly. It means son of the unfortunate fucker who couldn't get the odds together to emigrate.

— Here, look it. We don't normally do this. But we'll lift the glass for Philip, will we?

— No – we won't.

— Why not?

— Cos punks don't do tha' shite.

— Could you ever see the Irish Army usin' chemical weapons?

— Well, I could see them goin' into Limerick with a bottle o' Harpic.

— Seriously.

— Why?

— Well – like. The Syrians gassin' their own people.

— Ah, fuck off. Is this one o' those 'we're nicer than the Arabs' conversations?

— No—.

— Cos we're not.

— I know. Although our music's better.

— Not by much.

— Okay. But the gassin' an' tha'. An' the Yanks an' the Brits plannin' on—

— The French as well.

— Never mind the French. They're all mouth, those fuckers. But do none of them have kids or mas or – just, families?

— People they love.

— Exactly. Have they no fuckin' imaginations?

— I nearly gassed the kids once.

— I'm serious.

— I know. They'll tell us they're doin' it for the good of the world but wha' they'll actually be doin' is destroyin' families.

— That's it – it's desperate. If they – Obama an' Cameron an' the headbangers – if they'd think of a great family moment, yeh know, everyone laughin' or something, before they do—. D'yeh know what it is? I'm scared.

— I know wha' yeh mean.

— Do yeh?

— I think so.

30-8-13

— See Seamus Heaney died.

— Saw tha'. Sad.

— Did yeh ever meet him?

— Don't be fuckin' thick. Where would I have met Seamus Heaney?

— That's the thing, but. He looked like someone yeh'd know.

— I know wha' yeh mean – the eyebrows an' tha'.

— He always looked like he liked laughin'.

— One o' the lads.

— Except for the fuckin' poetry.

— Wha' would possess a man like tha' to throw his life away on poetry?

— Exactly.

— Although, fair enough – he won the Nobel Prize for it.

— He'd probably have won it annyway.

— For wha' – for fuck sake?

— I don't know. Football, plumbin' – annythin'. Tha' was wha' was special about him. He was brilliant but he looked like he came from around the corner. The poetry, but.

— I feel a confession comin' on.

— I was givin' one o' the grandkids a hand with the homework.

— Go on.

— She had to write about one of his poems. 'Mid-Term Break', it's called.

— Yeah, go on.

— Well, it was fuckin' unbelievable. Just shatterin' – brilliant. About a child's funeral.

— 'A four foot box, a foot for every year.'

— You read it as well.

— You're not the only man in the shop with grandkids.

164

— See fruit's bad for yeh.

— I always said it.

— All tha' one-in-five bolloxology.

— Fuckin' scientists – they're fuckin' eejits. How could fuckin' kiwis be good for yeh?

— She's fuckin' furious – at home. She's thinkin' o' suin'.

— Suin' who?

— Fuckin' everyone – far as I can make ou'. Says she's suffered permanent spinal damage carryin' all them bananas home from SuperValu.

— So – she's suin' Africa? The country of origin, like?

— Africa's not a country – strictly speakin'.

— Okay—

— An' in fairness to the Africans, I don't think they came up with this one-in-five shite. They'd have different priorities, I'd say. I think what's really got her goat is the fact tha' she can't claim tha' the blackcurrant in her rum an' black is one of her daily five. She'll have to replace it with celery or broccoli or somethin'.

— Vegetables are still officially healthy, are they?

— For the time bein'.

— I hate them.

— Yeah. Little green cunts.

— Useless.

— It's gas but, isn't it? How we get suckered in. Some prick in a white coat says if you eat all o' your peas Gina Lollobrigida will sit on your face.

— An' we fall for it.

— Every fuckin' time.

— So Trap's gone.

   — He was never here.

   — Ah now, that's a bit fuckin' harsh.

   — I'm only statin' a fact. His interpreter—

   — Manuela Spinelli.

   — Exactly. Yeh know the way she stood beside him, noddin' at everythin' he said—

   — It was kind o' sexy.

   — It fuckin' was. Exactly wha' yeh want in a woman. Anyway. The very first press conference, when he got the job, like. He says somethin' in Italian. An' she's noddin' away but you can see it in her eyes.

   — Wha'?

   — Panic.

   — Okay. Why?

   — Cos he thinks he's in Iceland.

   — Wha'?!

   — He thinks he's the new manager of Iceland. Tha' he's in Copenhagen.

   — Reykjavik.

   — Exactly.

   — Fuck off.

   — I'm serious – you fuck off. Look at it on YouTube. She decides – yeh can see it clearly, in her eyes, like – she decides not to give the game away, and she starts goin' on about how he's lookin' forward to workin' with the Irish lads, when he's actually sayin' he's a big fan o' Björk an' he can't wait to see the fuckin' volcanoes.

   — Fuckin' hell.

   — An' she's been at it ever since. Basically.

   — She's – Jesus. Did she choose the teams as well?

   — Someone had to.

— D'yeh think there'll ever be a mad fella with a gun in Ireland like they have them in America?

— Did yeh miss the fuckin' Troubles?

— Yeh know what I mean, but.

— The country's full o' mad cunts with guns. They're always shootin' one another.

— Yeah – one another. The drug fellas an' tha'. But that's just business, isn't it?

— S'pose.

— They're only a bit mad. Wha' they are is cold-blooded businessmen an' the madness is actually an asset. It's wha' you'd be lookin' for in the job interview, like. 'Would yeh work well as part of a team?' 'I'd shoot the fuckin' team.' 'You're in.'

— Okay.

— But the Americans. Like the latest one – a Buddhist with a history o' violence. Yeh couldn't make it up.

— Stop there now. Your man over there – don't fuckin' look!

— Tonto?

— Yeah – Tonto. He's a fuckin' Buddhist.

— Is he?

— Kind of a Catholic Buddhist, but yeah. An' he has a history of violence. An' here's the point. He's still violent. He'd kill us all now, except – why?

— He doesn't want to be barred.

— And?

— He doesn't have a gun.

— Exactly. There's mad fellas everywhere but in America they give them guns.

4-10-13

— See Stephen Ireland's granny died.

— About fuckin' time.

— Jesus, man. That's fuckin' harsh.

— Yeah – okay. I'm sorry for her troubles.

— She's dead.

— Grand. An' it's sad. But it can't've been easy bein' that prick's granny. Sure, he announced she died – how long ago?

— Six years.

— Is it six?

— Yeah.

— Where did they fuckin' go?

— Incredible, isn't it? I can't even remember now why exactly he said she'd died.

— Did he not say tha' more than one granny died?

— A selection of them, yeah. They all denied it.

— Some fuckin' tulip. Imagine not playin' for your country.

— I've never played for me country, so I find it easy to imagine.

— Yeh know what I mean. You get the call—

— At my age?

— No, listen—

— I was always shite at football.

— Just listen. Yeh get the call. No. One of your grandkids – a few years down the line – gets called up to play for Ireland.

— Okay.

— You'd be chuffed.

— Oh yeah.

— But he says he can't play cos his grandda's after dyin'.

168

— Tha' would be me, would it?
— Yeah.
— An' I wouldn't be dead.
— No.
— I think I'd see the funny side.
— Would yeh, but?
— No.

— See Dublin is the twentieth most reputable city in the world.

— Tha' right? What's above us? Baghdad, Limerick, the other African one – what's it? – Kajagoogoo. An' Damascus. Am I righ'?

— No, you're way off. It's based on reputation.

— Yeah.

— Good reputation.

— Good?

— Yeah.

— I think that's the first time I've ever heard 'good' go beside 'reputation'. I remember, this cunt of a Christian Brother – this was me first day in secondary school – he grabbed me by the hair beside me ear an' he said he'd heard I had a reputation an', I'll tell yeh, it wasn't a fuckin' compliment. There was nothin' good about it. Stamped me for life, it did.

— Well—

—The wife even hesitated when the fuckin' priest asked her if she wanted me to be her lawfully wedded husband.

— Did she?

— She looked at the best man – my fuckin' best man – an' he nodded, an' then she said, 'I do.' It was touch an' go, but.

— Who was the best man?

— That's a different story. But these fuckin' polls. They're all me hole, aren't they?

— Hang on.

— Wha'?

— I was your best man.

— No, yeh weren't. Were yeh?

— Think so.

— Fuck. Wha' weddin' am I rememberin' then?

— Wha' colour are your kids' eyes?

— Ah Jesus. Is this me local or *University Challenge*?

— Okay. An easier one. How many kids have yeh? Is it the four?

— Think so, yeah. I get them confused with the grandkids.

— Same here. But you've four, yeah?

— Yeah.

— Grand. Movin' on, so. Eye colour?

— Okay. Righ'. There's three blues, like herself, an' a brown.

— One brown?

— One kid, two fuckin' eyes – both brown.

— Okay. Say the Guards came into your house an' took him away cos one o' your neighbours said he looked nothin' like the other kids.

— Wha' neighbour?

— Don't worry about the fuckin' neighbour. Stay with me. You'd have to show proof tha' he was yours – a DNA test an' tha'. An' you'd be the first item on the mornin' news an' the RTE crime correspondent would be there, even though no crime was committed. It'd be fuckin' appallin'.

— Yeah, but the blue-eyed kid in Greece—

— That's the thing, but. Here, like. In fuckin' Ireland. A blue-eyed kid in among the dark eyes. A little angel in with the gyppos. Must be stolen. But a dark-eyed kid in among all the fair hair? Where's the fuckin' crime correspondent then?

— At home.

27-10-13

— See Lou Reed died.

— Wha'?

— Lou Reed.

— He's after dyin'?

— Yeah.

— He can't've.

— I know wha' yeh mean. But he has.

— But – he – ah, fuck it.

— Sorry.

— There are – listen. There are the ones tha' die young—

— Like Hendrix.

—Yeah. Amy Winehouse an' tha'. An' there are the ones tha' don't die. Ever.

— Keith Richards.

— Exactly. An' Iggy Pop.

— An' Lou.

— You're positive about this now?

— Yeah. He's definitely dead. It was in the news.

— Fuck.

— He was good.

— He was fuckin' brilliant. Remember tha' one, 'Vicious'?

— I do, yeah.

— I smashed me ankle cos o' tha' song.

— How come?

— Dancin'. Fell off me fuckin' platforms.

—Yeh wore platforms?

— Once. Bought the fuckin' things tha' day. Executin' one o' me dance moves on the kitchen floor – an' gone. Jesus, m'n, the fuckin' pain. It still gives me grief when the weather's damp.

— Great song, but.

— No argument. Tha' whole album, *Transformer* – one o' the best.

— 'Walk on the Wild Side' – he shaved his legs an' became a she.'

— When yeh hear words like tha', when you're a teenager. In the early 70s, like.

— Did yeh ever shave your legs?

— No. Decided against.

— Same here. How's the ankle?

— Fuckin' killin' me.

— See the chap with no arms was convicted for arms possession.

— Wha' the fuck are you on about now?

— It was in the news. The body parts they found in Meath. An arm found in the woods an' the torso in the river an' tha'.

— What exactly is a fuckin' torso, an'annyway?

— I know what yeh mean – where does it start an' end. Annyway, they named the fella that owned the various bits – the Guards did. They knew him, an' he had a prior conviction for arms possession. It'd make yeh laugh.

— No.

— No. You're probably righ'. It's ironic, but.

— Everythin's fuckin' ironic. Isn't it? These days. Do we even know what it fuckin' means?

— Only kind of.

— I forgot me keys – oooooh, that's fuckin' ironic.

— Calm down, for fuck sake. Yeh goin' home early to watch *Love/Hate*?

— Fuckin' sure. Have to watch it live.

— Best thing ever on Irish telly.

— No argument. Come here, they'll probably find an arm that used to be owned by a fella tha' did time for arms possession.

— That'd be a bit far-fetched.

— True. But the lads diggin' up your man's dead ma last week was brilliant, wasn't it?

— Class.

6-11-13

— See Yasser Arafat was poisoned.

   — Was he? Hang on but – is he not dead?

   — I just told yeh. He was poisoned.

   — A good while – did he not die ages ago?

   — 2004.

   — So, why – just to be clear. He was the Palestinian fella, yeah?

   — Yeah.

   — With the scarf.

   — That's Yasser.

   — So, why did it take so long to find this ou'? Was it the HSE did the tests?

   — They had to dig him up – exhume him, like – to prove it.

   — Wha' was it – Chinese?

   — Why would the fuckin' Chinese poison Yasser Arafat? No, the smart money's on the Israelis.

   — No – the food, I meant.

   — Chinese food?

   — Yeah.

   — For fuck sake.

   — Are yeh seriously tellin' me there isn't a Chinese takeaway in Bethlehem?

   — Listen—

   — Kung Po Camel.

   — It was radioactive polonium.

   — Then it was the Russians. That's their department. Or—

   — Wha'?

   — The Shinners.

   — Sinn Féin killed Yasser Arafat?

   — Maybe.

— Come on – fuckin' how?

— Shergar.

— The horse?

— They sold him to the Chinese.

— The Palestinian Chinese?

— An' the Russians injected the stuff into Shergar. The Kung Po camel was really Kung Po poisoned racehorse.

— What abou' the Israelis?

— They hadn't a clue.

7-11-13

— Was Gerry Adams in the IRA?

    — Is he dead?

    — No. Was he in the RA?

    — 'Course he was.

    — He keeps sayin' he wasn't.

    — He's lyin'.

    — How d'yeh know?

    — It's obvious.

    — But how can yeh know? For certain, like. Were you in the IRA?

    — Don't be fuckin' thick. Yeh might as well ask me did I play for Tranmere Rovers.

    — Now you're the one bein' fuckin' thick. Tranmere Rovers never shot an' 'disappeared' innocent people. Did they?

    — Not as far as we know. But, look it, John Aldridge managed them for a while an' Aldo would never do annythin' like tha'. Or anny of the Italia 90 squad.

    — What about Roy?

    — Roy wasn't in Italy.

    — But Adams.

    — He's lyin'.

    — Yeah. Why, but?

    — He's been sayin' it for fuckin' years. It's part of the story – the fuckin' narrative.

    — So he can't back down?

    — He can. But he won't. But I'll tell yeh wha' he can do.

    — Wha'?

    — He can fuck off to his cottage in Donegal an' live with his memories.

    — Retire?

—Yep. Get off the stage an' let Mary Lou an' the other young fella take over. It must kill all those relatives every time tha' lyin' prick opens his mouth.

5-12-13

— See Ireland is the best country in the world for business.

— Fuck that drivel.

— It's official – it was in a magazine.

— *Shoot?*

— *Forbes.*

—Yeh know wha' that fuckin' means then? Just change 'best country' to 'country where you can do what yeh want and no one'll give much of a fuck', then you'll know why we're top o' the list.

— Ah now, that's a bit cynical.

— 'Young, educated workforce' means 'no tax'.

— Okay, okay – sit down. Where are we on Nigella?

— We're not on Nigella. That's the problem. She's a great young one.

— She's fifty-three.

— Exactly.

— She took cocaine.

— Even better. I love her. Anyway, she only took the cocaine when her first husband was dyin'.

— So she says.

—Yeh doubt her? Yeh cunt. When my first wife died—

— Hang on, hang on – fuck. Wha' first wife? Were you married before?

— No.

— Then what the fuck are yeh on abou'?

— Empathy.

—Wha'?!

— I imagined I had a first wife, dyin', like – just to see if I'd snort cocaine as well.

— And did yeh?

— Ah, yeah.

— Wha' was she like?

— The first wife?

— Yeah.

— Lovely.

— A bit like Nigella – was she?

— A bit, yeah.

— Just like mine, so.

6-12-13

— See Mandela's after pushin' Nigella off the front pages.

— Anyone else, I'd've been furious.

— Great man.

— That's puttin' it fuckin' mildly. Just walkin' out of tha' jail – d'yeh remember?

— I never thought somethin' as ordinary as watchin' someone goin' for a walk could be so incredible.

— D'you remember the Dunne Stores women?

— The strikers? I do, yeah. The wife's cousin was one o' them.

— Amazin', really. There we were, eatin' South African oranges an' tha'—

— Outspan.

— That's right – Jesus. And your woman on the checkout—

— Was it Mary Manning?

— Think so. She refuses to handle them. An' she's suspended an' there's the strike an' we all stop buyin' the oranges an' then the government bans them.

— Tha' would've been before Mandela got out o' jail.

— Yeah. Great fuckin' women.

— Nigella would've joined them.

— Probably, yeah. And d'you remember the day he came to Dublin?

— Same day the Irish team came home from Italy.

— That's righ' – Italia 90.

— Best tribute to him really, isn't it? The best Irish footballer ever an' the best politician in the world, side by side in the one chant.

— OOH AHH PAUL McGRATH'S DA – SAY OOH AAH PAUL McGRATH'S DA.

181

—We're out of the Bailout an'anyway. A nation once again, wha'.

— Fuck the fuckin' Bailout.

— What's wrong with yeh? Are yeh not happy tha' you can have your pint without worryin' tha' Merkel will whip it away from yeh?

— I'll tell yeh what's wrong with me.

— Go on.

— Fuckin' *Lawrence of Arabia*.

— Wha'?

— I go home a few nights ago an' she's cryin' – in the kitchen.

— Merkel?

— Fuck off. The wife.

— Why?

— I told yeh – *Lawrence of Arabia*.

— Was he in the kitchen as well?

— Fuck off. She's not cryin' like when Whitney died. She's really bawlin'. Fuckin' inconsolable.

— Cos o' Lawrence?

— Peter O'Toole, yeah. Turns out, all these years, she's fuckin' loved him – adored him. From fuckin' afar.

— Ah, that's just—

— He was tall, yeah?

— Yeah.

— Am I?

— Yeh would be, if you were up on a camel.

— He had beautiful blue eyes.

— Fuckin' beautiful?

— Wha' colour are mine?

— Kind o' grey an' red.

— Not blue.

— Not really. Maybe she just thought he was a good actor. Hang on but—. Is this a Fernando Torres thing? Did you fancy him too?

- - -

— An' now you have to share him with the missis? Is that it?

- - -

28-12-13

— How was the Christmas?

— Code fuckin' Red.

— Wha' happened?

— The mother-in-law.

— I thought she died.

— The new one.

— Oh fuck.

— Annyway. They all come to the house – the whole gang, like. An' she reacts badly to the stuffin'. A Nigella recipe, as it happens. Sausage meat an' Red Bull.

— Sounds lovely.

— Yeah, but she started expandin'.

— Well, it was the Christmas dinner. We all fuckin' expand.

— Really quickly. Like a thing in a fillum.

— Fuck.

— Exactly wha' I said. Anyway, then there's the lotto – who'll bring her to A an' E. An' they're all lookin' at me. Cos, like – A. I'm the fuckin' host, an' B. I have the van an' your woman's gettin' even bigger, so we'll be just about able to get her in the side door. But—

— Wha'?

— Well, it's Christmas. I want to stay at home with me family.

— But—

— Anyway. I say – listen to this. I say – as a matter of principle, like – I'm not willin' to bring anyone to hospital until I'm assured tha' the car-parkin' charge isn't goin' to top up some chief executive's salary.

— Jesus.

— Well, it seemed clever when I was sayin' it.

184

31-12-13

— How was your year?

— Ah, fuck off.

— Same here.

— Same shite.

— Death an' fuckin' disaster.

— I was shavin' this mornin', righ', an' there was this huge fuckin' hair growin' out of me ear. Two inches long, it was.

— An' tha' was your year's work, was it?

— Overnight. It wasn't there when I was brushin' the teeth last nigh'.

— Jesus, are your teeth in your ear as well?

— Fuck off. It's growin' old. Every fuckin' day – a bit less. I can hardly remember the names of me kids. The grandkids are fuckin' impostors.

— But yeh know, the worst thing about this year is findin' out the Yanks are watchin' us.

— Not me an' you, like.

— Yeah.

— Why the fuck would they be watchin' us? Now, like – here?

— Maybe.

— I thought it was only emails an' twitters an' tha'. So, if we change the order from two pints, say, to two pink gins, they'll tell Obama?

— They might.

— We'd better stick to the pints, so. To be on the safe side.

— Yeah. Fuckin' worryin', though, isn't it? Happy New Year, by the way.

— Fuck sake – I'm not fuckin' deaf!

— I wasn't talkin' to you. I was talkin' to Obama.

— See the Everly Brother died.

   — Saw tha'. Sad.

   — The lungs.

   — Fuckin' cruel, isn't it? He gave so much pleasure to people usin' them lungs, for decades, like – more than fifty years. An' then they go an' fuckin' kill him.

   — That's life.

   — You said it, bud.

   — 'Cathy's Clown'.

   — Great song.

   — Before our time, but, weren't they – a bit?

   — No. No, I know what yeh mean. I don't remember seein' them on *Tops o' the Pops* or annythin'. But when you heard them on the radio—

   — You always knew it was the Everlys.

   — Exactly.

   — An' it was always brilliant.

   — Exactly – yeah.

   —'Bye Bye Love'.

   — There now – here's somethin'. My mother sang that every mornin' when me da was goin' to work. Goin' out the back door, like.

   — Ah, that's nice. Isn't it?

   — Yeah.

   — That's a great memory to have. Cos o' Phil Everly.

   — She sang it at the funeral as well.

   — In the church?

   — At the grave.

   — God. Tha' must've been somethin'.

   — It was. We all joined in at the end. *'Bye bye, my love, goodbye.'*

— They loved each other.
— They did.
— So, how come you're such a miserable cunt?
— Well, I can't blame Phil.

—Yeh know the way we're goin' to be payin' for the water?

— Well, fair enough. It hasn't rained since this mornin'.

— And yeh know the way this new company, Irish Water—

— Good name.

— At least it's in English.

— They prob'ly paid a gang o' fuckin' consultants to find the best way to get across the point that they're Irish an' they'll be sellin' the water.

— That's the thing, but. They've paid fifty million to consultants. But, like, what is a consultant?

— A cunt.

— That all?

— With a jockey's bollix.

— A cunt with a jockey's bollix?

— Basically. A fuckin' chancer who's happy enough to take money from a useless bunch o' pricks who haven't the guts or the brains to make their own decisions, an' call it expertise.

— But, say—

— An' they all went to the same schools. The pricks an' the cunts. It's business as usual in Ireland fuckin' Inc.

— But—

— An' it's our money.

— Will we have another pint?

— I've the money for the round but I don't have the consultancy fee.

— Wha' fuckin' consultancy fee?

— D'yeh expect me to answer tha' question on me own? 'Will we have another pint?' It could take fuckin' years.

31-1-14

— See all the Uggs tha' got stolen?

   — Wha' – the whole family? The kids as well?

— What are you on abou'?

— The Uggs, tha' live over the bookie's.

— That's only their nickname.

— Fuck – is it?

— I meant the boots. That all the young ones wear.

— And one or two o' the oul' ones.

— Anyway, there was a million quids' worth stolen.

— Where?

— Cork.

— Ah well.

— The lads were caught but, like, some o' the Uggs got away – you with me?

— Grand.

— An', Cork bein' Cork, they've ended up in Dublin.

— That's not a pair yeh have on yeh there, is it?

— No – fuck off. These are desert boots.

— They're nice.

— I've had them a few years. Anyway. I know a chap might be able to find some – Uggs, like. Especially suitable for girls with different-sized feet.

— Ah, for fuck—

— No – it's a scientifically proven fact. We all have different-sized feet but it's usually not tha' big of a difference. But anyway, these Uggs would be a fuckin' godsend for a young one with, say, one size-four foot an' the other one size seven.

— Which is which?

— Left, four. Right, seven.

— I'll get workin' on it.

— See Shirley Temple died.

— There's a thing.

— Wha'?

— Shirley Temple. There was a fella in my class – in primary school. He'd curly hair – loads of it, like. An' a baby face. Mind you, we all had baby faces. We were only fuckin' six or somethin'. But the teacher – a righ' fuckin' monster – I can't remember her name. But anyway, she called him Shirley Temple. An' it stuck.

— The poor cunt.

— All his life.

— Did he die?

— Today.

— No. Same as Shirley?

— Same day, not sure abou' the time. Yeah, he was always called Shirley. An' he went bald in his thirties.

— Hang on. Tha' Shirley? Is she a man?

— Different one – you're barkin' up the wrong Shirley. Tha' Shirley just shaves her head – it's a lifestyle choice, like. You wouldn't've known this lad. He moved to England, somewhere.

— To get away from bein' called Shirley.

— Tha' an' a job, yeah.

— Come here, but. Shirley Temple. The real one, like – the original one. You know – all those fillums. The little dresses an' 'On the Good Ship Lollipop' an' tha'.

— Wha'?

— It was fuckin' weird. Wasn't it?

— Very fuckin' weird.

— See the city's full o' Nazis.

— Wha'?

— Nazis.

— In Dublin?

— So I heard. Bono was talkin' to them.

— Well, tha' would turn anyone into a Nazi, havin' to listen to tha' cunt. Wha' was Bono doin' talkin' to fuckin' Nazis?

— There's a conference of them. In the Convention Centre. The Nazis an' Fine Gael.

— Hold on. Fine Gael aren't fuckin' Nazis.

— Merkel's there as well.

— She's not a fuckin' Nazi. She's only a German. Yeh can't be callin' the Germans Nazis. They're grand, the Germans. I like Merkel.

— I kind o' do as well. There's somethin' about her – she doesn't give a shite.

— That's it. She's one o' the lads. Annyway, look it. It's the European People's Party that's in the Convention Centre. They're not Nazis. They just look a bit odd.

— No uniforms, no?

— No.

— Shite. I was goin' to bring the grandkids down to have a look at them.

— No, they're just right of centre. A bunch of heartless cunts, but not Nazis – in fairness. Borin' as fuck, I'd say. Imagine goin' for a pint with a gang of Fine Gaelers an' Christian Democrats from Belgium.

— An' Bono.

— Fuck sake. Give me the Nazis, anny day.

— See Christine Buckley died.

— Saw tha'. Sad.

— Very sad. Great woman.

— Great fuckin' woman.

— Wha' was the name o' tha' place, where she exposed the abuse?

— Goldenbridge.

— That's it. Hard to imagine a place with a name like tha' could be so fuckin' evil, isn't it?

— I know wha' yeh mean. You'd kind of expect hobbits in a place called Goldenbridge.

— Well, tha' was the problem, wasn't it? If the place had been run by hobbits, they'd have looked after those poor kids properly. A bit of love an' tha'. Not like the fuckin' nuns, batterin' them.

— It's nearly twenty years.

— Wha'?

— Since tha' programme Christine Buckley was in.

— Yeh serious?

— Yeah. 1996. Said it on the radio. Is the country any better, d'yeh think?

— Well, if it is, it's because o' Christine Buckley, an' them.

— I met her once.

— Did yeh?

— Corner o' Mary Street an' Jervis Street. She was standin' there, like she was waitin' for someone. An' I knew I knew her, but I didn't know her – d'yeh know wha' I mean? I knew her face. An' I said, 'Are you—?' An' she goes, 'That's right – Diana Ross.' An' she bursts ou' laughin'.

8-4-14

— Peaches Geldof.

— Jesus, man, it's sad.

— So fuckin' – just—. Sad.

— I know nothin' about her. Except she's Geldof's daughter an' she was in the magazines.

— She was only twenty-five.

— Terrifyin'. It'd have yeh wanderin' around the house, checkin' the windows.

— Textin' the kids an' grandkids, makin' sure they're alrigh'.

— Exactly. I drove past my young one's flat, just to make sure. I didn't go in or anythin'. I just wanted to – I don't know – be useful, or somethin'. A father – yeh know?

— Yeah. An' Mickey Rooney died as well.

— I know nothin' about him either.

— A child actor, by all accounts.

— Not fuckin' recently, but.

— He was in a lot o' fillums with Judy Garland. So they said on the radio.

— The only one o' hers I seen is *The Wizard of Oz*, an' he's not in tha', I don't think. Unless he was one o' the hobbits.

— Munchkins.

— Yeah. Or – now that I think of it – was he the friendly lion?

— The cowardly lion.

— Fuck off now. There was nothin' stoppin' him from bein' both friendly an' cowardly. It's easily managed.

— It wasn't him. Tha' was Bert Lahr.

— Okay.

— She had two kids.

— Saw tha'. Two little lads.

- - - - - -

- - - - - - - - - - -

193

22-4-14

— See David Moyes is gone.

— The wrong man at the wrong time.

— That's not wha' you were sayin' last year.

— No, I always had me doubts – in fairness. I never doubted his honesty or his work ethic—

— 'He'll be perfect for the job, wait an' see.'

— Are you fuckin' readin' tha'?

— 'He's mini-Fergie. A cranky cunt – and I mean that as a compliment.'

— A little black book? Where'd tha' come from?

— 'He's an excellent man motivator and his tactical acumen has long been under-fuckin'-estimated.'

— Yeh fuckin' prick.

— 'He'll be in the job for twenty years. That's the United way. We're not like other clubs.'

— Okay. Did yeh never hear of fuckin' irony, no?

— Goin' back a few pages. 'Whoever replaces Fergie, he'll be given the time to establish himself. We're not called Man Unitedski.'

— Yeh cunt.

— Here's another one. 'That's why we're the biggest club in the world. We have values.'

— Well, come here, yeh cunt. You're not the only one with a black book. Here's one from way back. 'There's no way I'd ever marry tha' one. She has a mouth on her like a fuckin' can opener.'

— I never said fuckin' tha'.

— 22nd of April, 1981.

23-4-14

— Well, the journalists got it right, annyway.

    — About David Moyes?

    — Yeah.

    — They're fuckin' brilliant, aren't they?

    — He was never the right man for the job.

    — Never.

    — We couldn't see it at first but – thank fuck now – the journalists could.

    — He wasn't even the righ' man at Everton.

    — He was shite there too.

    — For eleven years. Pulled the fuckin' wool over everyone's eyes.

    — It took Roberto Martinez to rescue them. To move them up from sixth to fuckin' fifth.

    — A genius, tha' fella.

    — Buyin' Aiden McGeady.

    — Stroke o' genius, tha'.

    — From Red Star Glasgow, or wherever the fuck he found him.

    — Changed the course o' the club's history.

    — World history.

    — Meanwhile Moyes bought Juan Mata.

    — A shite player.

    — A shite player who was one of the world's most exciting players, ignored—

    — Inex-fuckin'-plicably.

    — By José Mourinho.

    — Until Moyes bought him an' he became shite overnight.

    — Cos o' Moyes.

    — Arrives in Manchester in a helicopter an' immediately turns to shite.

— An' we never knew.
— But the journalists did.
— Cunts.
— What about Ryan Giggs?
— He's only temporary.
— Yeah, but—
— Wha'?
— Is the physio's wife safe, d'yeh think?
— I'd have me doubts.

— See using your phone while drivin's been made illegal.

— It's been illegal for years.

—Yeah, but it's really illegal now. A thousand-quid fine if you're caught.

— Yeah, but it's only for a few days. It'll be back to normal after the weekend.

— Shockin' though, isn't it? First the drink.

— Then the smokin'.

— Now yeh can't even drive up the quays an' do your online shoppin' at the same time.

— There's no pleasure left in life, is there?

— Last week – listen. I hit a woman with a pram – outside Artaine Castle, righ'. When I was havin' a quick gawk at the Paddy Power's website. But – and this is my point, this is why it's bad law. If I hadn't been choosin' a horse, I'd have been goin' way quicker and I'd have killed the poor woman. And, in fairness, she saw my point, once we got her down off the roof.

—What about the baby?

—Wha' baby?

— In the fuckin' pram.

—There wasn't a baby. It was her husband – her fuckin' life partner. She was bringin' him home from the Goblet.

—Was he hurt?

— Fuck'm. He was textin'. So he wasn't in control of his vehicle.

— See Bob Hoskins is after dyin'.

— Sad, tha'.

— Hadn't seen him in anythin' for a while.

— He mustn't have been well.

— No.

— He was one o' the lads, wasn't he?

— Brilliant. Just his face – the expressions, yeh know.

— Fabulous. From the very beginnin'. Fuckin' way back.

— *Pennies from Heaven*. D'you remember tha' one?

— I do, yeah. Brilliant. Your one, Gemma Craven, was in it as well.

— I used to like her.

— She was Irish, wasn't she?

— We won't hold that against her.

— *Mona Lisa*.

— There was no way *she* was fuckin' Irish.

— The fillum.

— Yeah, yeah – brilliant.

— I didn't like *Roger Rabbit*.

— Know wha' yeh mean. He was an irritatin' cunt. But Hoskins was good.

— Can't think of a bad one he was in.

— Cos he was in them.

— Probably, yeah – good point.

— The best, but. *The Long Good Friday*.

— Ah, Jesus. Magnificent.

— D'you remember the end, in the car, when he knows he's fucked?

— His face – yeah. Brilliant.

— He was frightened, grand, but he looked nearly happy as well. Impressed, like, tha' they'd snared him.

— D'yeh think he looked like tha' this time?
— When he knew he was dyin'?
— Yeah.
— I hope so.
— Me too.

3-5-14

— See Gerry Adams is after bein' arrested.

— No, you're wrong there. He went voluntarily.

— But—

— An' while we're at it, he was never a member o' the IRA.

— That's a load o'—

— And, in fact, he was never even called Gerry Adams.

— Wha'—?!

— An' there's no such thing as the IR fuckin' A.

— Hang on now—

— There never was a man called Gerry Adams. It's all a creation of the London and Dublin administrations, in cahoots with the media, to undermine Sinn Féin's election campaign.

— You've fuckin' lost me, bud.

— If there is such a place as Dublin – an' I have me doubts there as well.

— You're on your own.

— Not for the first fuckin' time.

— Gerry Adams isn't Gerry Adams. That's the theory, yeah?

— Stands to fuckin' reason. It's the only logical conclusion. He's all a myth. The beard an' the teeth. An' the trigger finger. Did I say tha'? I hope not. I fuckin' deny it.

— They've made him up?

— I think so, yeah. The only alternative is tha' he made himself up an' got a bit carried away.

— What abou' Mary Lou?

— What abou' her?

— Is she real?

— Big time.

4-5-14

— 'What A Wonderful World'.
  — Fuck off.
  — Louis Armstrong.
  — Fuck off.
  — Great song.
  — Fuck off.
  — Number one in May 1968.
  — Fuck off.
  — The last time Sunderland beat Man United at Old Trafford.
  — Fuck off.
  — It stayed at number one for four weeks.
  — Fuck off.
  — Ah now. Georgie Best scored for United.
  — Fuck off.
  — Good oul' Giggsy.
  — Fuck off.
  — An' the Class o' '92.
  — Fuck off.
  — Playin' the United way.
  — Fuck off or I'm leavin'.
- - - - -
- - - - -
- - - - - -
- - - - -
- - - - - - - -
- -
  — Biggest-sellin' single of 1968.
  — Fuck off.

9-6-14

— See Rik Mayall died.

— Sad.

— Desperate. Younger than us.

— Remember *The Young Ones*?

— Ah, for fuck sake. There was nothin' like it.

— 'His name's Rick. The P is silent.' Best line, ever.

— I always associate *The Young Ones* with me first video.

—Yeah – yeah. They both came at about the same time, didn't they?

— I'd tape *The Young Ones* an' watch it when I got home. There was once – when I got the video, like. A chap in work gave me a dodgy one. *Debbie Does—*

— Dallas.

— No – *Dungarvan*. It was Irish-made – made me proud. It was fuckin' rough, I'll tell yeh. But, annyway. I came in an' my ma was in the kitchen. She was stayin' a few days.

— She only lived around the corner.

—Yeah, but me da was howlin' at the moon.

— Grand.

— So, she says, 'You said you'd tape *Coronation Street* for me.' An' I thought, 'Oh, bollix – she's after seein' *Debbie*.

— Oh Jaysis—

— No, it was grand. I'd taped *The Young Ones* over *Corrie*. I made her watch it with me, an' the kids all got up to see, cos she was laughin' so much.

— That's nice.

— It is, isn't it?

11-6-14

— The mother and baby homes.

— Shockin'.

— That's the thing, but.

— Wha'?

— Yeh kind o' get used to it, don't yeh. The stories – all the fuckin' misery. It's been goin' on for years. Am I makin' sense?

— Kind of. I think so, yeah.

— I thought it was over, d'yeh know what I mean? All the inquiries, and the bishops an' tha'.

— Consigned to history, like.

— Exactly – spot on. An' then, when they're on about eight hundred babies dumped in a septic tank, or whatever the fuck—

— Nuns with buckets o' babies.

— Yeah – I mean, I haven't seen a nun in fuckin' years, with or without a bucket. They're like the fuckin' dinosaurs.

— Long gone.

— We'll only be seein' them in cartoons soon. But then— Yesterday, I'm readin' abou' the kids in the mother an' baby homes tha' were used for vaccine tests. In 1973. An' I think, 'Oh – my – Jaysis.'

— I was workin' in 1973.

— Me too. Or, I wanted to be. But those kids, like.

— They're younger than us.

— Much younger than us.

— So, it's not history, is it?

— No, it fuckin' isn't. It's current affairs.

23-6-14

— Three pints.

— One'll do me.

— No. Three pints is a binge.

— Says who?

— Heard it on the radio. Some fuckin' survey, or somethin'.

— That's fuckin' mad. I'd need three pints before I decide whether to go on a fuckin' binge or not.

— I worked it out earlier. I've been on a fuckin' binge since 1975. Three pints, two or three times a month, constitutes harmful drinkin'.

— So – wha'? You've been drinkin' yourself to death for nearly forty years?

— Apparently.

— Well, you're not very fuckin' good at it, are yeh? Yeh look grand.

— Thanks. I'll tell yeh wha' the problem is. An' it's not the drinkin'.

— Wha'?

— The drinkin's grand. I did me own survey an' most Irish people are happy enough with the amount they drink.

— How many did yeh talk to?

— Just the one.

— Fair enough.

— The problem is, the fuckers – the doctors – tha' do these surveys. They haven't a fuckin' clue what a good binge is. They've no righ' to use the word.

— It's ours.

— Exactly. So they can fuck off. Three pints in a row isn't a national crisis. It's a fuckin' necessity. It's probably the only thing tha' stops us from bein' Swiss.

25-6-14

—Yeh have to admire Suarez, all the same.

— Go on – why?

—Well, if yeh were goin' to bite an Italian—

— Sophia Loren.

— She wasn't playin' last night, I don't think. I didn't see her on the pitch.

— She was on the bench.

— Grand. You're Suarez.

— Okay.

— You feel the irresistible fuckin' urge to bite an opponent.

— Okay.

—You go down through the Italian team sheet.

— Like a menu.

— Exactly.

— Pirlo an' chips.

—There now – good man. You've put your fuckin' finger on it. You wouldn't go for Chiellini an' chips, sure yeh wouldn't?

— Too skinny.

— Too fuckin' hard. He'd knock the livin' fuck out of yeh. Pirlo wouldn't even notice if yeh bit him. He's too laid back.

— An' hairy.

— Movin' on. He – Suarez, like – he was the same when he was decidin' which o' the Chelsea squad he was goin' to sample. He didn't go for one o' the little lads. Oscar or Hazard. He bit a fuckin' Serb.

— A fuckin' warlord.

—I'm tellin' yeh. Suarez should have his own programme – on the telly, like.

— *Eat With Luis.*

205

— A football celebrity cannibalism quiz.
— With Robbie Savage.
— An' the other cunt.
— Jamie Redknapp.
— He'll do.

12-7-14

— See the last o' the Ramones died.

— Gabba gabba sad, tha'.

— They were brilliant.

— Fuckin' brilliant.

— Did you ever see them?

— I did, yeah. A fair few times, actually.

— Good man.

— The best was the TV Club. D'you remember the TV Club?

— I do, yeah.

— The floor – d'you remember the floor? You could feel the music in it. Specially the reggae.

— Yeah.

— But the fuckin' Ramones, m'n – they nearly broke me fuckin' legs. The bass comin' up out o' the floor. I forgot abou' me eardrums.

— Must've been somethin', alrigh'.

— Ah, man. Incredible. I thought I was goin' to fall over. I had to grab the nearest arm to me.

— A woman.

— Exactly.

— Your Ma.

— Fuck off.

— Your missis.

— Nearly. Her brother.

— Hang on. You got off with your wife's brother?

— No – Jesus. Keep your fuckin' voice down. Yeh fuckin' eejit – where's your imagination?

— You said it was a woman.

— She was with him an' she grabbed his other arm at the same time. It was fuckin' gas.

— A scene from a shite fillum in the middle of a punk gig. The Ramones must be vomitin' in their graves.

— Well, that's only right an' proper.

— True.

31-7-14

— Gaza.

— The footballer?

— Don't even start now—

— Sorry – okay.

— The place.

— Dreadful.

— Shockin'. It's tiny, but – yeah? Gaza, like.

— Yeah, yeah – really small.

— An' Israel itself is only a small little country as well.

— I saw that on the news, yeah. I never realised it was so small.

— Smaller than Ireland, like.

— Way smaller.

— An' Gaza's only a tiny bit o' tha' space, yeah?

— Yeah.

— So there can't be all tha' many people livin' there, can there?

— No – I suppose not.

— So. Are they going to keep bombardin' it till there's no one left?

— It's lookin' like tha', isn't it?

— It fuckin' is.

— It's desperate.

— Kids.

— Yeah.

— Fuckin' kids.

— Terrible.

— History doesn't matter here, or who fuckin' started wha'. Yeh can't kill children.

— Fuck the cause.

— Exactly. Fuck blame an' revenge an' reprisal an' fuckin' – whatever. Even security.

— Or freedom.
— Nothin' justifies killin' kids.
— I'm with yeh, bud.

12-8-14

— See Robin Williams killed himself.

— Hard to believe.

— Yeah.

— To accept, like.

— Yeah.

— *Mork an' Mindy.*

— Hated it.

— Me too. Fuckin' hated it.

— Nanu fuckin' nanu.

— A load o' shite.

— Of course, we didn't know he was a comedian.

— Not back then, no. There were no videos or internet.

— We'd no idea he was fuckin' brilliant.

— Then – d'yeh remember *Good Mornin' Vietnam?*

— GOOD MORN-*ING*—

— Shut up, fuck sake. You'll get us barred.

— VIET-NAAAM – ! Great fuckin' fillum.

— But it wouldn't've been great if he hadn't been in it.

— That's true.

— *Mrs Doubtfire.*

— Class.

— I ended up fancyin' him, a bit.

— Only in the fillum.

— 'Course – yeah. Only when he was a woman.

— He was in some great fillums an' a lot tha' weren't crap only because he was in them.

— The best but— Have yeh seen *Happy Feet?*

— Ah, Jesus. Lovelace.

— No – the other one. He played two different penguins.

— Ramon.

— 'Let me tell something to joo.'

— Brilliant.

— 'Let me tell something to joo.'

— You nearly have him.

— I watch it with the grandkids – Jaysis – once a week.

— All that happiness. But he didn't want to live annymore.

— 'Let me tell something to joo.'

25-8-14

— You're lookin' a bit pale.

   — The fuckin' ice bucket challenge.

   — Wha'?

   — One o' the grandkids challenges me. Grand. So I go out the back an' wait for me drenchin'. But yeh know those freezer bags for ice cubes?

   — Yeah—

   — They drop six o' those – rock fuckin' solid, like – from an upstairs window. Right onto me fuckin' head. I'm out cold.

   — Jaysis—

   — They get me into the van, straight up to Beaumont. I wake up when they knock me head off the path outside o' the A&E. An' inside! It's the fuckin' Alamo. Full of ice bucket casualties. There's a cunt with his head stuck in a bucket. There's seventeen women who've had heart attacks. There's a kid who's allergic to water – the fuckin' state of him. There's a lad who's attempted suicide cos no one's challenged him an' he feels left ou'.

   — Fuckin' hell.

   — So, I'm sittin' there – groggy, like. An' this sham asks if he can go ahead o' me. He's after cuttin' four of his fingers off. He holds up a Spar bag – full o' fingers, like. I ask him did he do it for charity, he says No. So I tell him to fuck off.

213

— See Jaws died.

   — Paisley?

   — Him too.

   — Sad abou' Jaws.

   — What abou' Paisley?

   — Don't know.

   — Yeah.

   — Hard to know how to feel.

   — He fuckin' hated us.

   — He mellowed a bit in the end, but.

   — That's true. But we all do tha'. Your man over there comin' out of the jacks. I used to think he was a complete cunt but now he's only a bollix.

   — Paisley, but. Granted now, he calmed down an' talked to the Shinners an' they got peace an' tha' up there. An' that's all great. But he went a bit fuckin' overboard, didn't he?

   — Grinnin' an' laughin' with McGuinness. He became Mother fuckin' Teresa.

   — Peace is overrated anyway, isn't it?

   — Borin'.

   — I'll tell yeh, but. I'm grateful to him for one thing. Remember when he said the Pope was the antichrist?

   — I kind of agreed with him.

   — No, yeh didn't. Anyway, I was watchin' it on the News with one o' the kids. An' he says, 'Da, is the Pope really tha' man's aunty?' An' I start to explain it to him, an' then I think, 'It's all a load o' bollix.' Religion. It was liberatin'. An' I've the Reverend Ian to thank for tha'.

19-9-14

— Wha' d'yeh think o' Scotland?

— He should play four at the back an' a holdin' midfielder.

— Wha'?

— That's just my opinion.

— I'm talkin' abou' Scotland.

— Yeah. Your man tha' trains the Under 14s.

— He's not called Scotland.

— Is he not?

— He's called English.

— That's righ'.

— Frankie English.

— What about him?

— Fuck him – I asked you about Scotland. Although why I bothered, I don't know.

— Well. I seen a picture. People delighted, cos they'd voted No. An' tha' looked a bit weird – unnatural, like. Bein' happy an' sayin' No at the same time. It must be a bit like tryin' to pat your head and rub your tummy at the same time – you know tha' thing the kids do.

— Yeah.

— But I'll tell yeh. It must've been brilliant. The whole referendum. A vote that actually meant somethin'. Fair fucks to them. We should have one of our own.

— We're always havin' referendums. Yeh can't fart without a fuckin' referendum.

— A real one, but.

— Wha'? Givin' ourselves back to Britain?

— Maybe, yeah. Or ISIS.

— The Muslems?

— Yeah, why not? A bit o' crack. The speeches — can you imagine? Fuckin' brilliant.

— The Shinners would be up for it. They're fuckin' Sunnis already.

29-9-14

— Is it quiet in your house?

— Jesus, man. It's like a morgue.

— Same in my place. I have to be careful about every little fuckin' thing.

— A pain in the hole.

— I even had to tell her the dinner was lovely – earlier, like.

— Wha' was it?

— Can't remember. But it was grand. So I wasn't lyin', but—

— Fuckin' Cooney.

— Clooney.

— Wha' the fuck was he doin'?

— What he's done – what he's after doin' – it's worse than fuckin' climate change, so it is.

— Wha'?

— The world needs at least one good lookin' bachelor that isn't actually gay. A man who's gettin' better lookin' as he gets older.

— You've given this some fuckin' thought, haven't yeh?

— Well, I'd nothin' else to do an' she was clutchin' the remote like it was Clooney's langer. So, yeah. The women need to know there's always someone else – a bit better, like – out there.

— And now there isn't.

— Exactly. Because tha' fuckin' eejit has gone an' upset the natural order o' things. Fuck knows what's goin' to happen now. War, famine—

— No ridn'.

— The end o' the fuckin' species.

— He's a thoughtless prick, isn't he?

— A bollix.

— I was talkin' to this sham in a jacks?

— A jacks.

— Pub jacks.

— Wha' pub?

— Never mind wha' pub. I'm washin' me hands an' I say, 'They'll soon be fuckin' chargin' us for this.' An' he says he works for Irish Water an' we've got it all wrong.

— Did you deck him?

— Just listen. Yeh know when you're runnin' the tap for a mug o' water an' yeh wait till it's grand an' cold. Well, they won't chargin' us for tha'. Just the water in the mug. An' the same with showers. They'll only start chargin' when yeh get in under the water.

— That's fair enough.

— I'm not finished. Yeh know when yeh use the jacks, one flush sometimes isn't enough?

— I do.

— Well, they won't be chargin' for the second flush – if you provide photographic evidence.

— A photograph of your shite?

— A jpeg – yeah. But it has to come from an independent source. That's why they need our PPS numbers.

— Why?

— To verify tha' the picture of the shite didn't come from anyone in the house.

— So we have to get one o' the neighbours to come in?

— That's it.

— Jesus.

3-11-14

— See Acker Bilk died.

— I'm still reelin' after Alvin Stardust an' Jack Bruce. I can't keep up.

— How come?

— Did yeh not notice I wasn't here?

— I thought you'd gone a bit quiet.

— I wasn't fuckin' here.

— Well, like – how come?

— Ebola.

— Wha'?!

— There was an outbreak in the house.

— Hang on— D'you live in fuckin' Liberia?

— Just listen.

— Go on.

— Halloween. All the gang are in the house. Great gas – brilliant costumes. Anyway. I take a swig from the granddaughter's Coke. Lovely kid – sixteen. An' she says – she's jokin', like – it'll be infected. I say it's Ebola – I'm jokin' as well. The younger ones love the word an' they run ou' the back, goin', 'Ebola, Ebola!' One o' the neighbours—

— Let me guess. Special Trevor.

— The dopey cunt phones the HSE. The Ebola team arrives.

— In their space suits?

— Half us are already in fuckin' space suits. It's Halloween. The missis is in her Lady GaGa dress—

— The one made out o' the rashers?

— The HSE lads decide she's got foot an' mouth. Pande-fuckin'-monium. We're in lockdown for four days. I'm only after escapin'.

— Why are yeh dressed like Barry White?

— I keep tellin' yeh. It was fuckin' Halloween.

— What's the difference between smilin' an' smirkin'?

— Wha'?

— The difference between smilin' an' smirkin'. It's a political issue.

— Why is it?

— Tell us first – what's the difference?

— Well – if yeh ask me—

— I just fuckin' did.

— Fuck off. I'd say, if yeh don't like the sham who's smilin', then he's smirkin'.

— Yeah, I'll go with tha'.

— Like, the wife said to me – last Sunday, 'What're yeh fuckin' smirkin' for?'

— Does she not like yeh?

— No, she does. She says she does. Now an' again. But she said it after she'd said tha' Nidge was goin' to kill Siobhan, in *Love/Hate*, like. An' I said, 'Don't forget abou' Patrick Ward', just before Patrick ran into the garden an' shot Nidge. An' Siobhan.

— You smiled an' she saw a smirk.

— Yeah. Why is it a political issue?

— Well. Maíría Cahill said Mary Lou McDonald smirked at her in the Dáil yesterday.

— Well, that's because Maíría Cahill wouldn't be tha' fond of Mary Lou. Seein' as Mary Lou denies quite a lot o' wha' Maíría Cahill is sayin'. The real question is – why was Mary Lou smilin' at her in the first place?

— Why?

— Guilt.

— Cos she knows Maíría Cahill is tellin' the truth.

— That's it.

— See they're goin' to pay us for usin' the water.

— Wha'?

— The Government. Announced it today. They've decided not to charge us for the water. It's all been a bit of a misunderstandin'. So, instead, they're givin' each house 160 euros if they agree to accept the water. An' a free face cloth.

— Yeh have it arseways.

— I know. But it feels a bit like tha', doesn't it? Bunch o' fuckin' schoolyard bullies, an' now they want to be our best friends.

— Smug pricks tellin' us we'll have to pay for the water tha' we've always fuckin' paid for.

— Tryin' to frighten people.

— It'd take more than a drop o' water to frighten me.

— I'm not so sure – I can fuckin' smell yeh from here.

— Fuck off, you. Fuckin' Noonan, an' his comment abou' leavin' the taps runnin' if we're not charged.

— Fuckin' eejit.

— They never explained it. Yeh know why?

— They didn't think they had to.

— Bang on. They always forget it's a democracy. But with the last crowd, at least it took about ten years before they forgot. This gang, though—

— They're fucked.

— They are.

— Who'll replace them?

— We're fucked.

— We are.

— See Jimmy Ruffin died.

— Ah, man – I'll tell yeh. Tha' one made me really sad.

— 'Wha' Becomes o' the Broken Hearted'. It's brilliant.

— No question. An' that's the thing. I had his greatest hits.

— The record?

— Vinyl – yeah. An' I decided to go up into the attic, to find it.

— Bit of a fuckin' adventure.

— Fuckin' stop. I had the grandkids with me. Did yeh ever go up a ladder with nine kids?

— Seven's my record.

— An' there's a four-year-old holdin' the ladder for yeh.

— Boy or girl?

— Does it matter?

— Yeah.

— Girl.

— Go on.

— The place isn't properly floored, yeh know. The kids goin' fuckin' mad in the dark. The dust an' fuckin' cobwebs. But I found it.

— Good man.

— An' the record player as well. One o' the old mono ones. I had it on me head. Back down the ladder – fuckin' hell.

— An' the little girl was still there?

— Yeah.

— See now.

— I had to change the plug – it was an ol' two-pronged. But then we got it goin'. The grandkids had never seen a record before. They were fuckin' mezmerized.

— Brilliant.

— First record they ever heard – 'Wha' Becomes o' the Broken Hearted'.
— Perfect.
— Isn't it?

— See Joe Cocker died.

— What a fuckin' voice.

— Ah, man— But the best thing about him – he taught me tha' Beatles were shite.

— Hang on – wha'?

— Me brother – he's three years older than me – he brought home Sergeant Pepper's. An' everyone in the house loved it. Me ma sang 'When I'm 64' and she always cried at 'She's Leavin' Home', and me sister said, 'Don't worry, Ma, I'll never run away like tha'.' But she did – to fuckin' London. She even met a cunt from the motor trade. But that's a different story. Anyway—

— What's this got to with Joe Cocker?

— I'm gettin' there – calm down. They all loved 'A Little Help from My Friends' – in the house, like. Even me granny – an' she hated fuckin' everythin'. An' I just thought somethin' wasn't right. But then he – me brother, like – he brings home Joe Cocker's version. The single.

— Brilliant.

— No question. An' me da shouts, five seconds in – 'Turn tha' shite down!' An' I knew it – in me heart. That's the way it should be. If the oul' lad reacts tha' way, it's good. If he hums along, it's shite.

13-1-15

— Were yeh ever up in Ikea, were yeh?

— Oh, for fuck sake.

— We got fuckin' lost up there.

— Same here. We went up for a desk for one o' the grandkids an' we ended up buyin' a fuckin' hammock an' three cocktail shakers. An' never found the fuckin' desks. Wha' about youse?

— We were lookin' for some Mohammed wallpaper.

— Wha'?

— Wallpaper with pictures of your man, Mohammed, on it.

— For fuck sake. Did yis find it?

— No, we didn't. It was the wife's idea. She was fuckin' outraged tha' the Charlie lads were shot just because o' those cartoons an' she said we should wallpaper one o' the rooms with Mohammed. As a mark o' solidarity, like.

— Come here, but. Does Ikea sell Mohammed wallpaper?

— No, but we just thought any sham with a beard would do us an' we'd just say it was your man.

— Any joy?

— No – none. We thought abou' paintin' beards on One Direction but it would've have been a bit obvious.

— So, wha' did yis do?

— We went for a different cartoon instead.

— Which?

— SpongeBob.

— Hold on – you're hangin' fuckin' SpongeBob wallpaper in solidarity with Charlie Hebdo?

— We are, yeah. Je suis SpongeBob.

— Wha' d'yeh think o' this 'out o' control' drinkin' campaign?

— Brilliant. An' abou' time.

— How d'yeh mean?

— Well, after all this bolloxology abou' binge drinkin' an' drinkin' sensibly. It's good tha' they're encouragin' us to go ou' an' get hammered.

— I like the ad.

— The drunk kid with the hurley waitin' to knock the head off her poor sick ma when she comes out o' the jacks? It's a fuckin' masterpiece.

— Every teenager's dream.

— Exactly. An' perfectly natural. So, yeah. It's a breath o' fresh air, the whole campaign. Get ou' o' your face an' fuck the consequences.

— No matter how young.

— It's part of our culture.

— The only part that's worth a fuck.

— And funded by Diageo.

— About time they gave somethin' back – all the money they've made off the people o' this country. And let's face it. The fuckin' government would never put money into somethin' as brilliant as this. Another pint?

— Can't – no. Sorry. I've to go an' collect the grandkids.

— Where are they all?

— Dollymount. They're diggin' worms to put into their tequila slammers.

— See now. Makes yeh proud to be Irish, doesn't it?

— It kind o' does.

10-4-15

— See Barry Manilow's after gettin' married.

— Seen that, yeah. To a fella.

— But, like – didn't he have a song called 'Mandy' years ago? A love song, like.

— I think so, yeah.

— Well, she must've wrecked his fuckin' head. Cos he's after marryin' a chap called Garry.

— Well, good luck to him.

— Definitely.

— An' it kind o' makes sense, doesn't it? Marryin' a man at that age.

— How d'yeh mean?

— Well, they can sit up in the bed with their Kindles an' chat abou' the football. Instead o' havin' to pretend to be listenin' to her goin' on about her health or the state we're leavin' the world in for our grandkids, an' all tha' shite.

— Yeah, yeah – I kind o' get yeh.

— It'd be relaxin'. Yeh know – after singin' 'Copaca'-fuckin'-'bana' for the last fifty fuckin' years. Where's he from, an' anyway?

— Barry?

— Is he Canadian, is he?

— Don't know. I always thought he was – like – from somewhere else altogether.

— I've a feelin' he's Polish an' they moved to Canada, or somewhere like tha'.

— Annyway, he's shite, wherever he's from.

— No question. But good luck to him.

— Absolutely.

— Barry an' Garry.

— That'll be a song – wait an' see.
— 'Decided to marry.'
— Told yeh.

15-4-15

— See Percy Sledge died.

— Seen tha'. 'When a Man Loves a Man'. What a song.

— An' Jimmy Ruffin dyin' there as well, a while back. It's like all the great songs are dyin'.

— I know what yeh mean. I met me missis durin' 'When a Man Loves a Woman'.

— Hang on – fuck off a minute. You say tha' nearly every time a great singer dies.

— Well, she never remembered me.

— What is she – a fuckin' goldfish?

— Don't start – fuck off. I just didn't make much of an impression. It was me own fault.

— How come?

— Ah, I was just a bit overwhelmed. Terrified she'd say 'No' when I asked her up.

— An' did she?

— Say 'No'?

— Yeah.

— Every fuckin' time.

— But you kept at it.

— I did.

— And – don't tell me. She said Yeah durin' 'When a Man Loves a Man'.

— Yeah.

— How come?

— Well, she said later it was because of the song. She'd never heard it before an' she loved it an' she just wanted to dance with someone.

— That's kind o' nice.

— An' then she got sick on me an' she felt a bit guilty.

— An' she even fuckin' married yeh?

— Basically – yeah.

— Which way are yeh votin' in the gay thing?

— The marriage equality referendum?

— Yeah.

— Yes.

— You're votin' Yes?

— Yeah.

— Why?

— Me sister's son – me nephew.

— He's gay, is he?

— Yeah.

— So you're supportin' him.

— Have you become Joe fuckin' Duffy or somethin'?

— I'm just curious.

— Then, no, I'm not supportin' him.

— But you're votin' Yes?

— Look it, he's a grand kid but he's an irritatin' little prick as well.

— So— I don't get yeh.

— I'm watchin' the football, righ'. He always comes to the house when I'm watchin' the football. An' he sits beside me – grand. But then – say it's Real Madrid. He'll go, 'Oh, I love Ronaldo', or 'Pass it to Ronaldo.' So – like, last night, I lost it a bit and I said, 'What's so special about Ronaldo?' An' he says, 'His pace, his accuracy, his leap, his ability with the dead ball, the way he can turn, his engine – the stats speak for themselves.' Never mentioned his fuckin' hair or his six-pack or whatever they're callin' muscles these days.

— An' that annoyed yeh?

— Well, he fooled me. No – he made me think like a fool. An' he's always doin' it – catchin' me ou'. So, I thought to meself, 'A few years o' marriage will fix tha' little fucker's cough for him.'

— That's why you're votin' Yes? It can't be—

— No. I'm just messin'. Look – fuck it, I love him. He's a great kid an' if he ever wants to get married, he should be able to. An' me sister can have her big day as well.

— An' he obviously knows his football.

— Oh, he does, yeah.

— What's he think of James Rodriguez?

— Same as meself. Gorgeous an' over-rated.

— There was a ring on the bell there earlier.

— At home?

— Yeah – earlier. I was watchin' *Game o' Thrones,* so me head was full o' swords an' tits.

— We live in a golden age o' television drama.

— We fuckin' do. Anyway. There's a woman there – at the door, like – an' she's talkin'. But I'm still thinkin', like, 'I wouldn't mind bein' a dwarf.' So it's a while before I notice the 'No' sticker on her jacket – and her leaflets.

— Oh fuck – leaflets?

— She hands one to me an' she says, 'All children deserve their mother.'

— So I say, 'She's only gone to the shops – for smokes. She'll be back in a bit.' I'm wide awake now, so I say as well, 'While you're waitin', you could go across to number 78 an' tell the kids there tha' they deserve their mother. Cos she's in Mountjoy, playin' Monopoly with the Scissors Sisters.'

— Is she?

— No – she was cuttin' the fuckin' grass. But I'm on a roll now, so I say, 'An' what's marriage got to do with children? I've seven brilliant grandkids an' none o' their parents are married.'

— An' is tha' true?

— I'm not sure, to be honest with yeh – I can't remember. But I say, 'D'yeh have the Sky Boxsets at home?' She says she thinks so. So I tell her, 'Go on home an' watch a few episodes o' *Game o' Thrones.* An' when yeh see wha' the mothers get up to in tha' thing yeh won't be so quick with your leaflets. An' don't,' I tell her, 'don't write it off cos it's foreign. Cos it isn't. It was made in Ireland.' An' she says, 'I know it was. In Belfast. By Protestants.'

13-5-15

— Remember Barry Manilow got married there a while back?

— Can yeh imagine the music at tha' fuckin' weddin'?

— Jesus— But I was thinkin' about it again. Cos o' the referendum comin' up. That it's not a bad idea for men our age to get married.

— To each other, like?

— Yeah.

— Walk out on the missis—

— No, no – not necessarily. Just—

— If the circumstances were righ'.

— Kind o', yeah. It definitely makes sense. Doesn't it? Sharin' the gaff with someone like yourself. With the same interests.

— The football—

— Exactly. An' not havin' to pretend yeh care abou' all the woman stuff. Their health an' tha'. It'd be – I don't know – nice. Wouldn't it?

— An' that's another reason for votin' Yeah, d'yeh think?

— Yeah.

— Come here, but. What if the man yeh married turned out to be gay?

— I never thought o' tha', mind you. So wha', but?

— Wha'?

— Well – as long as he has the same interests. Football an' war— How many men are gay, an' anyway?

— Is it one in five?

— I think that's the fruit an' veg.

— That's righ'. It's one in ten – I think.

— One in somethin'. We'll say ten. So, there's only a one in ten chance tha' the man yeh marry would be gay. I could live with those odds.

233

— Come here. Say if your missis died or somethin'—
— Wha'?
— Hang on. An' say mine did as well. They were both in a car crash or somethin'.
— Who'd be drivin'?
— Yours.
— Go on.
— Well, like – would yeh marry me?
— No.
— Would yeh not?
— No.
— Hang on— Are you seein' someone else?
- - - -
— Are yeh?
- - - -

— One of me sons came ou' there earlier.

    — Fuckin' hell. How d'you feel about tha'?

    — Wha'?

    — Your son, like. How did he come ou'?

    — Through the back door. Same as the rest of us.

    — Hang on. He came ou' the back?

    — Yeah.

    — You're fuckin' messin' with me again, aren't yeh?

    — No, I'm not. Me son came ou' for a chat. We were ou' on the deck.

    — Yis have a deck?

    — Yeah.

    — Since when?

    — Since one o' the grandkids took a pallet from behind the Spar an' threw it on top o' the fuckin' grass. But – come here. Isn't it fuckin' amazin' tha' we can even have a chat like this?

    — Abou' decks?

    — No – abou' comin' ou' an' our kids an' stuff like tha'. Not so long ago—

    — It would've been impossible.

    — Well – not impossible. But—

    — Fuckin' tricky.

    — Very fuckin' tricky. But – more. There was a fella in my class in school an' – words like 'gay' an' 'camp' didn't exist back then the way they do now. But he got a terrible fuckin' time. From the teachers an' the Brothers. Called him Twinkle-Toes an' stuff like tha'. They never let up – they battered him. An' we laughed. We had to – I remember thinkin' tha'. Or they'd've murdered us as well.

    — Wha' was his real name?

— Jim. I was thinkin' about him there. Wonderin', yeh know, how he was. An' that's another reason I'll be votin' Yes.

— Why?

— Well—

— Apologisin'.

— Yeah – yeah. I suppose so.

— Same as meself, so.

— D'you read much?

— Wha'? Books?

— Yeah.

— Well, I do. I'd always read a few pages in the bed. War – I like books abou' war.

— Same as meself.

— Hitler an' tha'. I fall asleep every nigh' readin' abou' Hitler an' Stalin. Fuckin' gas, really.

— I read a bit of one last night. The wife is in a book club.

— Mine as well.

— What is a book club, exactly?

— Well, far as I can make ou'. Yeh go to a pal's house an' get fuckin' hammered. An' yeh bring a book with yeh, if yeh remember it.

— Grand. Yeah, I thought tha', meself. Anyway, she was readin' one – *The Bend for Home*. An' she keeps sighin' and laughin'. Getting' on me wick a bit. Cos I'm tryin' to read abou' the siege o' Stalingrad.

— I fuckin' love Stalingrad.

— Yeah – but, anyway. She goes ou' to the jacks an' I pick up the book. *The Bend for Home*, like. An' I read a bit – and, ah man – I'm tellin' yeh. It's brilliant – fuckin' brilliant now. The bit I read – abou' a Thursday afternoon – in the town he grew up in, like. It was amazin'. You were there when yeh read it.

— Sounds good. Who wrote it?

— Dermot Healy.

— Played for Sligo Rovers back in the day.

— Tha' was Keely. Healy – Dermot Healy. So anyway, she said she was finished it an' I got dug in. 'The doctor strolls into the bedroom and taps my mother's stomach.'

237

— That's the start?

— Yeah.

— An' yeh remember it?

— Yeah. There's a photograph of him on the back—

— Ah, hang on, for fuck sake. Just cos we voted for the same-sex thing, doesn't mean yeh have to fall in love with him.

— Ah fuck off. Anyway, look it, it's the business – the book.

— Sounds great alrigh'.

— Will I pass it on to yeh when I'm finished?

— Is Hitler in it?

— No.

— - - G'wan then – okay.

Dermot Healy: 1947–2014

238

25-5-15

— See Bill O'Herlihy died.

— I can't believe it.

— I know. Same here.

— I can't— He was brilliant.

— The best – him and the other lads. The best thing on telly.

— He was one o' those people— Did yeh ever meet him?

— No, but I know wha' yeh mean. It was like we knew him.

— An' liked him.

— Loved him.

— He took the football seriously.

— Like politics.

— Exactly. He took us seriously.

— He'd have the lads riled up an' you'd flick across to ITV an' there'd be ads, and yeh'd flick back to Bill an' the lads would still be shoutin' – an' yeh'd flick to BBC an' they'd be analysin' Thierry Henry's fuckin' cardigan. An' back to RTE an' Bill an' the lads would still be talkin' abou' football.

— No shite or fashion statements.

— Except Bill's ties.

— D'yeh know what it is? He made me happy.

— Yep.

— After watchin' him. I might be shoutin' at the telly. But I was always happy.

— You can't say more abou' the man, really, can yeh? He made us happy.

— Okey doke.

— Good night an' God bless.

239

— See one of the fellas that's runnin' for President of America says it's a good idea to bring guns into cinemas.

— He's bang-on there.

— Wha'?

— It'd make life a lot easier – listen. I went to the new *Mad Max* – me an' the missis. And about an hour in, you can tell Max is tryin' to say somethin'. To your one with her arm missin'. But, like, it's been a hard oul' day. An' seeing those young ones climbin' out o' the petrol tank, or wherever they were hidin' – you'd be hard-pressed to string a fuckin' sentence together after tha'.

— Weren't they gorgeous?

— Lovely. But annyway. Max – your man who plays him – is just about to talk when a cunt behind me starts shovin' popcorn into his fuckin' gob. An' I missed it. An' I think I should've had the right to turn around an' shoot the fuckin' eejit in the face.

— But—

— Not only tha'. I got done for speedin' on the way home.

— Hate tha'.

— Well, you try drivin' under fifty after seein' tha' fillum. An' not only fuckin' tha'.

— Wha'?

— I'd forgotten to take off the fuckin' 3D glasses, so I got done for reckless drivin' as well.

2-9-15

— See the Monkees are Unionists.

— Wha'?

— The Monkees. The group, like – off the telly, in the '60s.

— They're fuckin' Unionists?

— Yeah.

— One o' them's dead, but.

— The other one. The one with the woolly hat.

— Mike Nesbith.

— He's the leader of the Ulster Unionist Party.

— Wha'?!

— I heard it on the radio there a few days ago. Mike Nesbith, the leader of the UUP, said they were pullin' out o' the Northern Ireland Executive. Cos o' the IRA.

— What about the IRA?

— They're playin' *Game o' Thrones* again.

— The IRA doesn't exist.

— Neither does *Game o' Thrones* but we still watch it every night.

— It can't be the same Mike Nesbith. Was he wearin' the woolly cap?

— It was the fuckin' radio – I told yeh.

— Well, did he mention anny of their hits?

— What – like? Mike Nesbith, leader o' the UUP, said he thought love was only true in fairy tales an' for someone else but not for him.

— But then he saw her face.

— Now he's a believer.

— The IRA in *Game o' Thrones*. That'd be good.

— They're in it already. The fuckin' Wildlings.

241

— Didn't see you over the weekend.

— I was at the Electric Picnic.

— Fuck off. Were yeh?

— I went up on Friday. It's in – what's the county that no one comes from?

— Laois.

— Yeah. So I drove the granddaughter up. An' I'm gettin' her gear out o' the van and this girl doin' security must've thought I was as well, cos she throws one o' the yellow reflective jackets at me. An', like, I put it on and next of all I'm searchin' the bags. An' there's this lad has a plastic bag full o' yellow tablets an' he says they're for this asthma. An' I say, 'D'yeh think I came down in the last shower?', an' I take one.

— Oh, fuck. Wha' happened?

— I ended up playin' drums for Grace Jones. Don't fuckin' ask me how. But, by all accounts, I was very good.

— What's Grace like?

— Well, there now. The bass player – a nice chap – he tells me it isn't Grace at all. It's just a big bird puttin' on the Jamaican accent an' Grace is actually back in her hotel with a mug o' Horlicks. But then, I might've been dreamin' tha' bit. Or all of it.

8-9-15

— Yeh know these Syrians?

— Yeah.

— Well, I don't think they should be let into the country.

— Wha'?

— Until they can speak American.

— Fuckin' wha'?!

— Your woman from tha' top bit of America—

— Sarah Palin.

— Yeah. Well, she's dead righ'. An' Trump as well. You should listen to him. All these years the Spanish have been tellin' us they speak Spanish, an' they've actually been speakin' Mexican. The shifty fuckers.

— Hang on – wha'?

— An' the Portuguese have been speakin' Brazilian.

— Hang on – I need a fuckin' map.

— But the worst – no surprise, really. The English.

— They haven't been talkin' English.

— No.

— They've been talkin' American.

— Yeah. Accordin' to Sarah.

— The fuckin' bastards.

— Shakespeare me hole.

— Hang on, but. What do we talk then?

— Shite.

— The Irish talk shite?

— Fluent.

— So we'll only let in people tha' can talk shite?

— Yeah.

— Well, there'll be no fuckin' shortage of candidates.

— We have to be generous.

— And you know who'll be at the front o' the fuckin' queue?

— Who?

— Trump an' Palin.

20-9-15

— See Putin an' your man, the Italian with the painted head, drank a bottle o' wine tha' was two hundred an' forty years old.

— Fuckin' hell. Were they in the jacks tha' long?

— Wha'?

— They open the bottle, then one o' them has to go ou' to the jacks. At their age, like – it's understandable.

— What is?

— Goin' to the jacks.

— For two hundred an' forty fuckin' years?

— Well, you were in there a fair while, yourself.

— Fuck off.

— No, but. I suppose not. It would make more sense if they had to go two hundred an' forty times after they drank it. It must've been fuckin' rancid, but – tha' fuckin' old. Can yeh imagine skullin' a pint tha' was that old?

— Wine gets better with age.

—Yeah. But two hundred an' forty years? Who actually knows? It might've been nicer when it was two. But there's no one alive now who'd know. 'Cept Cher an' John Terry.

— Shows yeh what a pair o' cunts they are, but, doesn't it? Putin an' Berlusconi.

—Well, would you not like to be doin' it? Demolishin' somethin' priceless in a country you invaded, while the rest of the world falls apart?

— Righ'. Let's get this out o' the way. Did you ever ride a pig?

 — Wha' part o' the pig?

 — Head.

 — No.

 — Grand.

 — What about yourself?

 — No.

 — No – same here. Nothin' tha' wasn't human.

 — An' female.

 — Probably, yeah. But—

 — Wha'?

 — No, it's nothin'—

 — Go on.

 — Well, I had this dog – when I was a kid, like. An' we were playin', on the floor in the kitchen. An' he stuck his tongue in me mouth an' I probably didn't shove him away as quickly as I should've.

 — Ah, that's harmless enough.

 — I was just relieved it wasn't a Christian Brother.

 — Were yeh ever a member of a private club?

 — Well, I have a SuperValu rewards card.

 — Did yeh have to fuck a pig to get it?

 — No. I filled in a leaflet.

 — It's gas, but. Wha' the English Tories have to do just to prove tha' they can become fully fledged cunts. D'you think our lads do the same?

 — Wha'? Like – stick it in a pig's mouth before you can join Fine Gael?

 — It kind o' makes sense when yeh think about it. There's no other reason why yeh'd join Fine Gael. Is there?

2-10-15

— D'you ever go to plays?

— In a theatre, like?

— Yeah.

— No.

— Meself an' the missis went to one – a while back. She was on about us doin' somethin' a bit different. Instead o' the pictures. So, it's her birthday an' her sister got her two tickets for this play.

— An' did she expect yeh to go with her?

— I was fuckin' dreadin' it – all the fuckin' fuss, yeh know. But anyway, we go along.

— An' it was brilliant.

— How did yeh know?

— Your face.

— Well, it was. It was brilliant. *Faith Healer*, it was called. Your man, the Nazi, was in it.

— Ralph Fiennes.

— Him – yeah. He was very good.

— He's good in everythin'.

— That's true. But the play itself. Man – the words. There was him an' two others. An' they just talked – just fuckin' talked. But – brilliant. Spellbindin'. It was like listenin' to really interestin' people, except way better.

— Wha' made yeh think of it?

— Well, your man who wrote it died today. Brian Friel.

— I heard tha', yeah – on the news.

— So – yeah.

— It made a big impact on yeh. The play.

— It did, yeah.

— Have you been to any since?

— Plays?

— Yeah.

— No. Fuck tha'.

— See Maureen O'Hara died.

— The most beautiful woman that ever lived.

— I'm with yeh there, bud.

— She was a Dub as well.

— She was. A Southsider, but.

— Ah well, she had to have one flaw.

— I suppose so. But d'yeh know wha' was really amazin' about her?

— Wha'?

— She was so fuckin' funny.

— Gorgeous an' funny.

— It's some combination. She didn't even have to say annythin'. We've this thing – at home, like. We all watch *The Quiet Man* at Christmas, the whole gang of us. The grandkids as well – the little ones. An' I'll tell yeh, when Maureen O'Hara—

— Mary Kate Danaher.

— Mary Kate. The minute she walks onto the screen, the kids start burstin' their little shites laughin'. Before she even opens her mouth. And then when she does, there's no fuckin' stoppin' them. We all know tha' fillum off by heart.

— 'Who gave you leave to be kissin' me?'

— Brilliant. But my favourite is when she tells her brother, 'Wipe your feet.' The fuckin' head on him.

— An' when she wallops John Wayne.

— 'You'll get over it, I'm thinking.'

— Brilliant. The whole fuckin' thing. We'll have a pint for Maureen, will we?

— 'It's a bold one you are.'

14-11-15

— Paris.

— Fuckin' hell.

— Unbelievable. Can you imagine? Out on a Friday nigh'. An' that happens.

— Fuckin' savages.

— Fuckin' terrible.

— Were yeh ever there?

— Paris?

— Yeah.

— No, I wasn't – not really.

— What's tha' mean?

— Well, like – I was never in Paris but I'd nearly feel like I was, yeh know. Cos o' the – yeh know – the images an' the songs an' tha'. They're just so well known an' brilliant. The fillums an' stories – Pinocchio.

— Fuckin' Pinocchio?

— The Hunchback of Notre Dame.

— Tha' wasn't fuckin' Pinocchio.

— Who was it then?

— The other fella – I can't remember. Pinocchio was the little wooden fucker.

— That's righ'.

— Italian.

— That's righ'.

— Irritatin' little bollix.

— That's righ'. Anyway. Thinkin' about it – wha' happened last night, like. Football, music, a bit o' grub on a Friday nigh', a few drinks. They don't like life, the cunts tha' did it. Sure they don't?

— Looks tha' way, alrigh'. Quasimodo.

— Good man. That's the Hunchback.

— I remembered. I was worried there for a bit.

— 'The bells, the bells.' He was brilliant, Quasimodo, wasn't he?

— One o' the lads.

— Je suis Quasimodo.

7-12-15

— See someone from the RTE News got wet?

— I've never seen annythin' like it, never seen such fuckin' courage. She didn't even have her hood up.

— And did you see the cars goin' past her? She could've been splashed. But fair play, she stuck at it.

— I'll tell yeh – I remember seein' news reporters in Vietnam—

— Yeah, yeah. An' Biafra.

— An' Palestine.

— An' the tsunami.

— An' Belfast, don't forget.

— Yeah, yeah. An' there was tha' photographer on the beach on D-Day when the lads were landin'.

— All sorts o' fuckin' bombs an' whizz bangs goin' off all around him.

— It wasn't rainin' on fuckin' D-Day though, was it?

— He had it fuckin' easy.

— But your woman.

— She just stood there, in the wind an' the fuckin' rain.

— An' she told us that it was windy an' fuckin' rainin'.

— An' to stay in.

— A hero of our fuckin' times.

— 'Don't make unnecessary journeys.' She could've stayed in herself an' looked out the window.

— Exactly.

— But no. She put on her coat an' went ou'.

— Personality o' the Year.

— Future president, I'd say.

— See they're bannin' the munchies.

   — The culchies?

   — The munchies – they're bannin' the munchies.

   — Wha'? Food?

   — The Health Minister – fuckin' Varadkar. He's bannin' cheap alcohol. Says it causes obesity cos it encourages us to drink at home an' to eat too much, cos we get hungry when we drink.

   — Well, he did his research – in fairness. He doesn't exactly look like he just escaped from Devil's Island, does he?

   — Why doesn't he just fuck off an' mind his own business? Look after his own fridge.

   — It's the nation's health he's worried about.

   — Fuck the nation. I get this thing on Saturday nights. A *Match o' the Day* Special. A tray o' beer an' a pizza. A Polish chap delivers it – Stan. Twenty euro.

   — That's not bad. What's the beer?

   — It's one he imports, himself. Bally-Gdansk. It's not too bad. An' he texts ahead to see wha' pizza we want. We usually go for the Five Seasons.

   — Five?

   — Yeah.

   — There's only four. Unless there's five in Poland, is there?

   — No. Only the one, accordin' to Stan. The soggy bit in the middle – that's Poland. He throws it in as a bonus. He only charges for the four.

— Where were yeh? Haven't seen yeh in a few days.

— Ah—

— José?

— Yeah.

— It hit yeh.

— I'm fuckin' devastated.

— He lost the dressin' room.

— Fuck the dressin' room. He was brilliant. An' a bit fuckin' mad. An' tha' made him even better. But I'll tell yeh what it is. There are two men I should've been.

— Wha'?

— Your man, Quinn, from *Homeland*. He's the man I'd be if I didn't have kids an' responsibilities an' tha'. Quinn would go down to SuperValu the same way he goes about killin' Moslems. Yeh wouldn't see him tryin' to make his mind up between Brennan's an' Pat the Baker. There'd be bread all over the shop.

— Grand. An' Mourinho's the other man, is he?

— Yeah – absolutely.

— Why?

— He was enigmatic.

— Wha'?

— An' charmin'.

— Fuckin' wha'? You fancied him.

— No – yeah. No – fuck off. No. I just— My last birthday, I told the missis I wanted a José coat – yeh know?

— Yeah.

— But she's not really into the football and she got me Tony Pulis's tracksuit instead.

— It's not bad.

— Thanks.

— I'm not sure about the cap, though.

— Fuck off.
— In the pub, like.
— Fuck off.
— See Chelsea won yesterday.
— The cunts.

23-12-15

— Where would I find a drone?

— Your man over there beside the jacks. He's a fuckin' drone.

— The little flyin' yokes, I mean.

— The things the Yanks use for bombin' Afghanistan an' tha'?

— He's promised he won't bomb anywhere.

— Who?

— One o' the grandkids. Justin. A great kid. He wrote to fuckin' Santy.

— For a weapon of mass destruction?

— He said he'll only use it for deliverin' medicine an' food supplies.

— In the letter to Santy?

— Yeah.

— What age is he?

— Five.

— Fuckin' hell.

— He's a bright little lad. No spellin' mistakes either.

— As far as yeh know.

— Fuck off.

— Santy will be impressed.

— That's what I'm fuckin' worried abou'.

— Wha'?

— That young Justin will get the drone an' I'll spend Christmas in the cop-shop explainin' to the fuckin' Guards that he didn't mean to bomb Cabra or Syria, or fuckin' wherever.

— The drones the kids are gettin' – they're only little ones. Kind o' harmless.

— No fuckin' way.

— Wha'?

— No way is one of my grandchildren gettin' some cheap oul' thing – a fuckin' toy, like. It's military standard or nothin'.

— I'm with yeh there, bud. Only the best for the grandkids.

— An' fuck the consequences.

31-12-15

— Did yeh do well this year?

— Not too bad.

— Wha' did yeh get?

— Pyjamas, a stab vest an' a book about the S.S..

— A fuckin' stab vest?

— Yeah.

— Who gave you tha'?

— One o' the daughters. They were two-for-one in Aldi. One for me an' one for the missis. It's nice enough. Black – with 'Belgrade P.D.' on the front.

— Nice. Are yeh wearin' it now? Or are yeh after puttin' on a few kilos?

— No, I'm wearin' it. The daughter was in the house an' I wanted her to see me wearin' it, yeh know. Annyway, it's New Year's Eve. All sorts o' mad cunts in here you never see any other time o' the year. An' I'm goin' to the chipper on the way home. So—

— Better safe than sorry.

— Exactly. It's a bit fuckin' tight, but.

— A bit strange, but. Isn't it? As a present, like.

— I'm happy enough with it. Wha' about yourself? Wha' did you get?

— Some socks, a suicide belt an' a book abou' the Gestapo.

— Fuckin' hell – are yeh wearin' it?

— The socks?

— The fuckin' belt.

— I am, yeah. One o' the grandkids made it in home economics.

— I brought some o' the grandkids to the new *Star Wars* there earlier.

— Wha' was it like?

— A load o' shite.

— I heard it wasn't too bad.

— It was shite, I'm tellin' yeh. It looked like it was made in the Phoenix Park with a load o' wheelie bins painted white. Absolute fuckin' drivel. It made no fuckin' sense.

— Was Princess Leia in it?

— Yeah – played by Angela Merkel.

— That's alrigh', isn't it? Yeh'd trust Angela to save the world.

— Only if she's playin' Angela in a fillum about Angela. Not in this fuckin' thing. She looks lost. She couldn't handle a fart, let alone the European economy. But the worst bit—

— Go on.

— They're tryin' to find that irritatin' little prick from the first fillum. Luke Skypilot. An' d'you know where they find him? In all the fuckin' Galaxy an' infinity or wherever – where do they fuckin' find him?

— Where?

— Kerry.

— Fuckin' Kerry?

— Not even Kerry. A rock off the side o' Kerry. He's been hangin' off a stone in the middle o' the fuckin' Atlantic. Not a Spar or a pub in sight. An' this cunt is goin' to save us? For fuck sake.

11-1-16

— See David Bowie died.

— See now – tha' makes no fuckin' sense. Wha' you just said.

— I know wha' you mean. How can Bowie be dead? He was never alive, like the rest of us.

— Tha' makes no sense either. But it's bang on.

— I remember once, I was havin' me breakfast. An' I saw me da starin' at me. So, I said, 'Wha'?' An' he says, 'Are yeh goin' to work lookin' like tha'?' I was still servin' me time and, like, I was wearin' me work clothes. An' me overalls were in me bag. So I didn't know what he was on abou'. 'Get up an' look at yourself in the fuckin' mirror,' he says. I did, an' I was still wearin' me Aladdin Sane paint. Across me face, like.

— You were ou' the night before.

— Not really. Only down the road. Sittin' on the wall beside the chipper, with the lads. Sneerin' at the fuckin' world. But that was what it was like. Bowie was our God.

— He has a new record ou'. Last week, just. Know how I know?

— How?

— Me granddaughter. She showed me his video. 'Blackstar'. Unbelievable. Brillant. Scary.

— Business as usual.

— Exactly.

— It's so fuckin' sad.

— Yeah.

— See Bruce's pal died.

— Alan Rickman.

— Yeah. Hans Gruber.

— He was brilliant.

— Fuckin' brilliant. The best. 'I am going to count to three. There will not be a four.'

— He was great in everythin' – the *Harry Potter*s. Everythin'. The fuckin' head on him.

— Like, Bruce is the man – no question. But he's only as good, really, as the baddie in the fillum. An' Hans was the best.

— Ever. Up there with Lee Marvin.

— When I was watchin' *Die Hard* – the first time, like – I knew there'd be a sequel. I just knew, like. And – swear to God now – I was hopin' Hans would win so we'd see him again in the sequel.

— Instead o' Bruce?

— Yeah.

— You wanted Hans to trounce Bruce?

— Yeah.

— Wait now – hang on. I know wha' you mean – kind of. I think. But you wanted Bruce to die?

— Only for a bit – a fleetin' moment, like. Hans was just so fuckin' great. Like, I know it's blasphemy an' tha', sayin' that I wanted Bruce to get killed.

— Says a lot about Rickman, but – doesn't it?

— The same age as Bowie.

— Saw that.

— Frightenin'. Will we have another pint?

— 'What idiot put you in charge?'

22-1-16

— The man in black.

— I was at a funeral. A man up the road.

— I'm sick o' funerals.

— Same here. But this one – it was a bit different. He was from Mayo or somethin'– somewhere over there. So it was a real country funeral. The coffin in the house.

— With your man in it?

—Yeah, yeah. He was a big man now. Hands like shovels, yeh know. He looked great, but – in the coffin. Like he was just pretendin' to be dead an' he was listenin' to the chat. Squashed into it, he was. A huge man. Larger than life. Reminded me of my own da. A bit.

— They gave him a good send-off, so.

— Jesus, man. The funeral itself – in the church, like. Packed. Loads of his kids and grandkids. An' all sorts o' culchies up from Mayo. Tryin' their best to look like Dubliners, God love them. But packed now.

— I haven't been in a packed church since I was a kid.

— Yeah, yeah – same here. An' the speech at the end. One o' the sons. Christ, it was brilliant. But the best bit. When they were carryin' the coffin ou'. A lad with one o' those things yeh put on your shoulder—

— A bag o' cement.

— A violin. He played 'The West's Awake'. Made me proud, kind of – the whole thing.

— Proud o' wha'?

— Don't know. Just proud. An' sad.

— You're not goin' to start writin' poetry, are yeh?

— No, I'm not – fuck off.

3-2-16

— Wha' d'yeh think of the election?

— Well, two things went through me mind. 'Oh fuck, no,' and 'Abou' fuckin' time.'

— Same here. Except I only thought, 'Oh fuck, no.' But you're righ'. It's about time. They're fuckin' horrible.

— An' we're stuck with them.

— D'yeh think?

— Yeah. They'll win again – the Blueshirts.

— Not Labour, though.

— No – probably not. An' it serves them righ' for forgettin' they're Labour.

— It's the lies on the posters that I hate. The fuckin' slogans, yeh know.

— I saw one there earlier. 'Making Work Pay.' Fine Gael.

— They've been in power for five years and suddenly they want to end slavery. Cunts.

— But – it's weird. Yeh know what's worse? The posters with no slogans. Just a big fuckin' head. 'Vote for me.' But, like, I'm all in favour of democracy. Votin' an' tha'.

— Will we have another pint?

— Show o' hands.

— Two for, none against. There yeh go. Democracy in action. Now all we need is a fuckin' barman.

— Who would yeh like to win the election?

— Well – in an ideal world. A coalition of ISIS an' the Greens.

— Wha'?

— 'Turn off the lights or we'll fuckin' behead yeh.'

— Well, that's clear.

— An' honest.

23-2-16

— See Joey The Lips died.

— The wife told me. She was cryin' – an' two o' the grandkids. They loved him.

— Wha' was his name again – his real one?

— Johnny Murphy.

— That's righ'. He had a real Dublin head on him, didn't he?

— He was brilliant. 'I get snotty with no man.' Fuckin' brilliant.

— I seen him in a play once.

— Did yeh?

— Yeah. The wife was goin' with her sister but then the sister smashed her foot kickin' a bowlin' ball – don't fuckin' ask. So I went instead. I was fuckin' dreadin' it – I didn't even know he was in it. But there he was, an' he was brilliant. *Waitin' for Godot.*

— Was it any good?

— Great – yeah. Mad. An' Joey was amazin'.

— You know what's really upsettin'?

— Wha'?

— Well, he was the oul' lad in the fillum. But he was the only one tha' got off with the girls.

— He made us think there was hope for us all.

— An' now he's dead.

— I met him – I just remembered.

— When?

— Years back. I missed me bus – kind of on purpose. An' I went into the Flowin' Tide. He was in there.

— Wha' did yeh say?

— 'How's Imelda?'

— Wha' did he say?

— Nothin'. He just grinned.

— You're in early.

— Had to get out o' the house. I wanted to watch *Soccer Saturday* but the wife's watchin' the election count an' she owns the remote.

— She fuckin' owns it?

— A couple o' weeks back. I told her it was hers forever if she put the brown wheelie out, an' she refuses to accept that I was only jokin'. She carries it around in her fuckin' bag.

— Great day for the telly, all the same. The football an' the politics. I brought me tenner into Paddy Power's. There's me bettin' slip, look. Chelsea to beat Southampton, West Brom to draw with Palace an' Fine Gael to get four more seats than Fianna Fáil. Look at the odds.

— Yeh have Chelsea down to beat Fine Gael.

— Do I?

— Look.

— Fuck. I forgot me readin' glasses.

— They would as well – Chelsea.

— D'yeh think?

— Diego Costa against Leo Varadkar? Poor oul' Leo would end up on a trolley in one of his own A&Es.

— Fair enough. The election's all over the place. Any predictions?

— A coalition of Fine Gael, Social Democrats, Sinn Féin an' Leicester City.

23-3-16

— Fuckin' terrible week.

— Another one.

— Jesus, though – tha' family in Buncrana. Can you imagine?

— No. No – yeah. I can.

— Puttin' the brake on but the car keeps slidin' into the water.

— I know. Desperate.

— Tha' poor woman.

— I know.

— Her mother, husband, sister – an' the two little lads.

— The heart ripped out of her.

— An' Brussels.

— Fuckin' hell, man. Another o' those days where I was countin' my kids an' grandkids. Makin' sure they were all safe an' sound.

— I rang me daughter – the youngest.

— Where was she?

— The kitchen. But I didn't know tha' till I rang her. Just wanted to hear her voice, yeh know.

— Yeah. I don't know much abou' Brussels. Do you?

— No. An' even tha' makes me feel a bit shite. Like, are any o' the footballers from Brussels? Or the teams?

— They'd have to be. The place – the city, like – is huge.

— D'yeh know who's Belgian, but? The little red-headed fella.

— Prince Harry?

— Tintin.

— Is he?

— Yeah. An' Snowy.

— Oh, well then.
— He's only a cartoon, but.
— He's still one o' the lads.
— Je suis Tintin.

24-3-16

— Are yeh doin' anythin' for 1916?

— I was wonderin' about tha' on the way up. You know – would I have been in the GPO, or wherever, back then?

— And?

— At the age I am now, no – I don't think so. The toilet facilities are important. I'd want to know there's a decent jacks nearby before I'd start shootin' innocent women an' children.

— The GPO would have a good jacks.

— What abou' Boland's Mills, though? Or Stephen's Green. Behind a tree? No fuckin' way.

— It's the GPO or nothin'.

— Seriously, though – the way I am now, I'd be fuckin' terrified. Worried sick abou' the kids an' the grandkids, yeh know. Like in Brussels. Annythin' like tha', I'm lyin' awake, I'm checkin' on the kids, makin' sure the doors are locked.

— An' we'd've been bang in the middle of it, back then.

— Only around the corner, yeah. Forty kids died in 1916.

— I was readin' there. One of them died from a bullet tha' went right through her father first. A little young one on Moore Street.

— There yeh go. Fuckin' shatterin'. But then, I look at my kids – an' they're Irish. Rock-solid Irish. An' I like tha'.

— Me too – I know what you mean.

— An' that's what the Risin' was about – I think, anyway. The right to be different. The things tha' make us Irish. The little things.

— So, all the killin' an' the executions – they were for our right to say 'Thanks' to the driver when we're gettin' off the bus?

— That's half it, yeah.

— What's the other half?

— The right to call him a cunt when the bus is movin' off.

21-4-16

— See Prince died.

— It makes no fuckin' sense – at all. Is it definitely true?

— Yep.

— Me an' the missis—

— Don't tell me you met your missis when Prince was playin'. Yeh do that every—

— I wasn't goin' to – fuck off.

— Wha' then?

— Fuck off.

— No – go on.

—Well – when our oldest was born an' we were bringin' her home from the Rotunda. We hadn't a fuckin' clue. I mean, it was brilliant, havin' the baby. But we were fuckin' terrified. I was, anyway. We didn't even have a car seat. Or a fuckin' car, for tha' matter. We were in the van, the missis had her on her lap. Fuckin' madness.

— Tha' was normal back then, but. When was it?

— 1983. January. There was ice on the roads an' all. We were nearly afraid to talk, yeh know. An' I stuck on the radio.

— An' it's Prince.

— '1999'. Fuckin' perfect. We knew we'd be grand. It's a brilliant piece o' music, tha'. It became her song. We'd named her already but we started callin' her Princess an' – well—

— Are yeh alright?

— No – no, I'm not. I'll be grand in a minute. It's just shite, though, isn't it?

—Yeah.

269

— See we've a new barman.

— Where?

— Over there – over beside the till.

— Oh yeah. Hang on, but. He looks like— It isn't, is it?

— Louis Van Gaal – yeah, it is.

— Fuckin' hell. He got another job quick enough, didn't he?

— Yeah. Although—

— Wha'?

— Well, manager of the world's biggest football club to pullin' our pints. It's a big fuckin' career shift, isn't it?

— The money probably isn't as good either, is it?

— Wouldn't think so, no.

— He's pullin' a pint now, look it. God, he's fuckin' slow, isn't he?

— It's probably the job he should've been doin' all along.

— Wha'? Pullin' pints o' Guinness?

— There's the time, tradition, the whole routine. Orderin' a pint should be slow and very fuckin' predictable. Like Man United have been for the last few years.

— Look at him now.

— Wha'?

— Your man there just ordered a pint from him. An' look at Louis. He has his fuckin' clipboard out an' – what's he writin' in it?

— He's probably drawin' the pint. Plannin' how much of the glass he'll fill early doors.

— An' his route to the tap.

— I told yeh. It's the perfect job for him.

— Until the place fills up.

— Then he's fucked.

— 'I am the greatest.'

— He fuckin' was.

— He was— Well, he was Muhammad Ali. The name's enough, isn't it? Says it all.

— I was thinkin' there, rememberin'. He was fightin' an English lad – Brian London.

— I remember tha'.

— My da let me an' me brothers stay up to watch it. I can't remember exactly, but I think we might've gone to bed for a few hours an' he came in an' got us, an' the lights were off an' we went in to the telly an' it was off as well. An' remember back then, the telly had to warm up after you turned it on?

— I do, yeah. There'd be no picture for a minute.

— So, he went into the kitchen to put on the kettle an' he poured us cups o' milk and me ma had left a couple o' Clubmilks for us. So we gathered up the cups and went back in an' Brian London was on his back. The fight was fuckin' over.

— Brilliant.

— Me da was bullin'. For a minute, just. But I could see it on his face. This was better. The story, like. An' he told it all his life.

— And you were in it.

— I was.

— Tha' was nice.

— Yep.

— See Robbie Keane's retirin'.

— It's weird.

— Why?

— Well, like – he used to be a teenager.

— I think I know what yeh mean.

— I'll tell yeh – when you measure your life in football, it goes past very fuckin' quickly. One minute he's a kid, the next he's retirin'.

— He was great but, wasn't he?

— No question. Brilliant. An' the best thing about him – he had a real Dublin head on him.

—Yeah, yeah – I know what yeh mean. Richard Dunne, Duffer—

— Dublin heads.

— John Giles, Stapleton, Paul McGrath, Brady. You just see them an' you think—

— Dublin. They couldn't've been from anywhere else.

— But then yeh look at Roy Keane an' yeh think—

— Cork.

— Exactly. You might wish he was from Dublin but he wouldn't have been Roy if he'd come from anywhere else.

— You look at Shane Long an' yeh think—

— The sunny south-east.

— Shay Given?

— Donegal – no question. Seamus Coleman the same.

— Kevin Kilbane?

— Da from Mayo – his fuckin' ears.

— Robbie Brady?

— Northside.

— Stephen Ireland?

— Argos.

— D'you remember that goal Robbie – Robbie Keane, like – scored against Germany?

— Ah, man.

— Still makes me want to punch the air.

— Thank you, Robbie.

— Thank you very much.

— See Young Frankenstein died.

   — Gene Wilder – yeah.

   — Terrible, isn't it?

   — Some o' those fillums he was in.

   — Brilliant.

   — Fuckin' brilliant.

   — *The Producers*.

   — 'I'm wet – an' I'm hysterical.'

   — *Blazin' Saddles*.

   — 'Little bastard shot me in the ass.'

   — I met him once.

   — Fuck off – where?

   — Here.

   — Fuckin' here?

   — Dublin – yeah. When I was a kid. He was makin' a fillum. *Quackser Fortune Has a Cousin in the Bronx*.

   — I'd forgotten tha' one.

   — It wasn't his best. But annyway. They were filmin' on the street outside me house. Vans an' lights an' all – loads o' people. An' Gene Wilder was leanin' against the railings just down from me house. I didn't know who he was back then. An' I said to him, 'Are yis makin' a fillum, mister?'

   — Wha' did he say?

   — He smiled an' told me to say it again. He liked the way I said 'fillum'. It was better than 'movie', he said.

   — That's nice.

   — The first time I ever felt intelligent.

   — An' the last.

   — Fuck off.

   — I told the grandkids there, when it was on the News. I told them Willie Wonka was dead. An' they were all cryin'.

   — Says it all, really, doesn't it?

20-9-16

— See Angelina an' Brad have broken up.

— I couldn't give a shite.

— Ten years together, they were.

— I couldn't give a fuck.

— She wasn't happy with his parentin' style.

— I don't fuckin' care.

— Wha' does tha' mean – parentin' style?

— Don't know. His aftershave or his shirts or somethin'.

— I think there might be more to it than tha'. The whole package, I'd say.

— I'll tell yeh one thing, and it's the only thing I'll say on the matter. My missis has never complained abou' my parentin' style.

— Same here.

— Everythin' else, she's slaughtered me. But not tha'. Which makes me think.

— Wha'?

— She just doesn't like him. She's copped on – that's all. Brad's only a cunt, like the rest of us. He's human, like.

— So she might as well have married one of us.

— There yeh go. It's the good thing about gettin' old. See, the older he gets, the more he looks like us. An' the older we get—

— We look like Brad.

— Exactly. We all end up lookin' like Brad.

— Except Brad. What'll they do with the kids?

— Don't know.

— They've hundreds of them.

—They could give some o' them to Madonna, I suppose.

23-9-16

— You know *The Great British Bake-Off*?

— You're not still goin' on about 1916, are yeh? It's time to move on.

— The television programme. Have yeh seen it?

— I fuckin' hate cakes.

— Have you fuckin' seen it, I said?

— Yeah.

— An' it's a load o' shite, isn't it?

— It's the most popular thing on the telly.

— An' it's still a load o' shite. Fuckin' eejits makin' cakes. Who'd want to watch tha'?

— Millions o' people watch it.

— Fuckin' eejits watchin' fuckin' eejits makin' cakes. It was the main thing on the news. Just cos they're movin' to Channel 4.

— They're just worried – because it's Channel 4, like – tha' they'll make the contestants flash their tits or stir the cake mix with their langers.

— I just think it's fuckin' mad. An' today they're tellin' us tha' we're becomin' the fattest nation in the world.

— Fuck them.

— Who – the fat people?

— No – the fuckin' eejits who measure these things. The scientists an' tha'.

— At least we're good at somethin'.

— Wha'? Bein' fat?

— Well, it's a skill. It takes dedication.

— Some gobshite on the radio said fat should be a Leavin' Cert subject.

— Well, you'd get an A.

— Fuck off.

— See Bob Dylan won the Nobel Prize.

— Which one?

— Wha'?

— There's loads o' them. Bukes, science, accountancy – there's rakes o' the things. There's even one for fuckin' peace.

— Science then – I think.

— Fuckin' science? He won the Nobel Prize for science?

— Has to be, I'd say. That song, 'Mister Tambourine Man'.

— What about it?

— Well, how can one sham play a song with only a fuckin' tambourine? It can't be done. It's like givin' some poor fucker one o' them Irish yokes—

— A bodhrán.

— Exactly. An expectin' him to play 'Bohemian Rhapsody' on it. It's just not possible.

— But Dylan cracked it.

— That's me theory. But seriously—

— Go on.

— He deserves it. The buke – the literature – prize.

— I'm with yeh.

— I remember when me brother brought home *Highway 61 Revisited*, when it came ou', like. Now, I love me music – always did. But The Beatles, like – 'Love Me Do' an' tha'. I mean, there wasn't much in the lyrics of any o' the songs back then. An' then I heard Dylan singin' about the postcards an' the hangin' an' tha'. 'Desolation Row', yeh know. An' it was amazin'. The start of me life, nearly. Even me da stopped complainin' about the noise. For a minute.

9-11-16

— For fuck sake.

  —Wha'?

— Did you ever think it would happen?

  —Wha'?

— He'd get elected.

  —Who?

  —Trump.

  —Who?

— Trump – Donald fuckin' Trump.

— What about him?

— Did yeh not see it?

— See wha'?

— The election – last night.

  —What election?

— The American election – where were yeh? He's after gettin' elected.

  —Who?

— Trump – I told yeh.

  —Wha'?

— No, hang on – fuckin' hang on. How long are yeh goin' to keep goin' on like this?

— Four years.

— Ah, Jesus—

— Maybe eight.

10-11-16

— You know over in the States, the blue-collar workers tha' they say voted for Trump?

— What abou' them?

— Well, that's us, isn't it? We're blue-collar, aren't we? If we were over there.

— S'pose so.

— Even though your collar's a bit grey an' I've no collar at all. Unless a hoodie has a collar, does it?

— No, a hoodie has a hood. That's the fuckin' point.

— Thanks for the fashion tip, Melania.

— Fuck off.

— Annyway. We're blue-collar. Workin' class.

— So, you're wonderin' if we'd have voted for Trump if we were over there.

— Kind of.

— No fuckin' way.

— Are yeh sure, but?

— Yeah. I think so. Anyway, it's different here.

— How is it?

— Well, are you angry?

— No – sometimes, just. The water charges. Things like tha' – unfairness. But, like, the gays are grand and the women I know are brilliant an' I've no problem with the Africans. I'm a bit miserable but, generally, I'm grand.

— Maybe it's just America.

— That's wha' I was thinkin'. But then I heard abou' this letter that's been doin' the rounds in the HSE. Old people who take up hospital beds bein' referred to as 'trespassers'.

— An' your collar started to feel very blue.

— Yeah.

— See Trump killed Leonard Cohen.

— Saw tha'.

— He doesn't only hate women. He hates the men tha' women love. 'Specially older women.

— Fuckin' Clooney's gone into hidin'.

— Fuck him an' his Nespresso.

— And the Pope.

— Fuck the Pope?

— No. Women – they love him. Mine does, an' anyway.

— Poor oul' Leonard. He was good, but. Wasn't he?

— Ah, he was. You should hear me grandkids singin' 'Hallelujah'.

— Good, yeah?

— Fuckin' hilarious.

— The wife loved him.

— Leonard?

— She even became a Buddhist cos o' Leonard.

— Is tha' righ'?

— For a few weeks, just. Then she saw me eatin' a quarter pounder an' she said, 'Fuck the Eightfold Path.' But she's always on at me to wear a hat like Leonard Cohen's.

— Well, he won't be needin' it any more – in fairness.

— The thing is, but. If Leonard walked in here – if he wasn't dead, like – they'd all go, 'There's an interestin' man with a hat on him.' If I walked in, it'd be, 'Will yeh look at tha' fuckin' eejit with the hat.' An' that's the big difference between us an' Leonard Cohen. We couldn't even start bein' cool an' Leonard never even had to try.

— Will there be many in your place tomorrow?

— The whole gang, yeah. Can't remember how many exactly – it's into the hundreds.

— Jesus. How will yis manage?

— It's not too bad. We stick on *The Sound of Music* in two o' the rooms an' all the females an' two nephews bail in an' watch tha'. Then we assemble the cage.

— The cage?

— Yeah, yeah – Hell in a Cell. We started a few years back. All the men an' lads, four nieces an' a granddaughter.

— Yis fight?

— Yep.

— On Christmas Day?

— First thing – before the grub. We did it after the dinner once but it was a fuckin' killer – puke an' sprouts everywhere.

— Yis all get into a cage – where?

— The kitchen. Down to the kaks and covered in brandy butter.

— For fuck sake.

— It makes sense when you think about it. A year's worth of rage an' bitterness – get it out o' the system. Knock fuck out of one another, then it's good will to all men for the rest o' the day.

— What abou' the women?

— It's their turn after *The Sound o' Music*. An' I'll tell yeh, man – the hills are alive with the sound of envy.

—There's three generations o' women mournin' at home.

— Princess Leia?

— Yep.

— Same as my place.

— There's bit o' George Michael in the mix as well.

— Yeah.

— The *Star Wars* music an' '*Careless Whisper*'.

— But mostly it's Carrie.

— Mostly Carrie – yeah. I mean, the daughters liked George, an' the wife – yeh know the way women, when they hit a certain age, they start to like gay men?

— No.

— No? Is it only in my house?

— Must be.

— Movin' on. Princess Leia.

— She was iconic.

— I don't know wha' tha' means, exactly, but you're bang on. I knew it after we got our first video. Back in the day, d'you remember?

— You had to throw turf into the back of ours.

— As big as a fuckin' cooker, ours was. Anyway, we got *Stars Wars* an' put it on. Our eldest daughter was only a little thing at the time an' she wasn't payin' tha' much attention. But then Princess Leia came on.

— An' she sat up.

— She fuckin' did. An' she's been sittin' up ever since.

— An' Carrie's mother's after dyin' as well.

— Fuckin' unbelievable.

— That's why they're stars, I suppose – is it? They're spectacular.

— George as well.

— Definitely – George as well.

27-1-17

— Was Hitler funny?

— Wha'?

— Before the war, like – say, 1937. Did people think Hitler was funny?

— Don't compare Trump to Hitler – please.

— I'm not.

— I'm fuckin' sick of it. Anything yeh say or do gets you called Hitler these days. At home, like. Even callin' the dog an eejit – I'm told I'm a fuckin' fascist.

— I know—

— And all dogs are eejits, by the way. It's a big part of the fuckin' job.

— I know – I'm with yeh. Hitler, but. Not Trump. Was he funny? Did people think he was just fuckin' ridiculous?

— Well, there was Charlie Chaplin.

— Yeah, yeah – *The Great Dictator*. Good fillum.

— Not tha' good.

— Okay. But they all went to it an' laughed an' came ou' thinkin', 'Well, that's Hitler nailed. What a silly little cunt.' An' then he went ahead an' did everythin' he did. It didn't matter if he was ridiculous. D'you get me point?

— Think so.

— So, Trump. I can't walk in the fuckin' door but there's a kid or a grandkid showin' me a funny Trump thing – on YouTube or whatever. But he's not fuckin' funny.

— No.

— An' the fuckers behind Trump – they're not funny either.

— No.

— See John Hurt died.

   — Yeah, but did you see how many times he died?

   — Wha'?

   — One o' the kids showed me this thing on YouTube – 'The Many Deaths of John Hurt'. He started dyin' in 1962 an' he was still doin' it right up to the end.

   — He was brilliant.

   — Ah, man. I met the wife durin' *Alien*.

   — Wha'?

   — She grabbed me knee – when the yoke came out o' John Hurt's stomach. She nearly fuckin' knee-capped me and then her boyfriend wanted to box the head off me. So she gave him a box, decked the poor fucker. An' then we kind o' fell into each others arms.

   — Yeh must've missed most o' the fillum.

   — We went again the day after. She told me that when she felt my leg, she just knew I was the chap for her. An' the fact that I didn't object. She wanted to spend the rest of her life with me. So she said, an' anyway.

   — When?

   — An hour ago. When we heard it on the News.

   — So John Hurt introduced yis, really.

   — Yep.

   — An' when did you get to feel her knee?

   — Half an hour into *The Elephant Man*.

19-3-17

— See Chuck Berry died.

   — I didn't know he was still alive.

   — Same here. But he was. Till yesterday.

   — It's a bit sad, tha'.

   — It is. Kind o' forgotten abou'. Cos he was brilliant.

   — Yeah.

   — A brother o' mine – he was way older than me. He was out o' the house before I started school, nearly. Annyway, I used to love goin' to his flat. He was mad into Chuck Berry. An' the flat – it was like walkin' into America.

   — Brilliant.

   — Ah, man. There were road signs on the walls, for all the places in his songs. Memphis, Tennessee an' tha'. An' his wife – come here, listen. His wife – me brother's wife, like. She always called him her brown-eyed-handsome man.

   — Were his eyes brown?

   — One o' them, yeah. An' he called her Maybelline.

   — An' her real name was—?

   — Bernie. But they lived – the both o' them – inside Chuck Berry's music. An' I never met a happier couple.

   — They still happy?

   — They're dead – these years. Maybelline died a month after him.

   — Heartbreak.

   — She tripped over the record player.

29-3-17

— What abou' Brexit?

    — Ah, fuck off – please.

    — No – come on. Brexit.

    — Can we talk abou' Trump instead? At least tha' cunt has a face.

    — A chap on the radio this mornin' said it's the most important day since Dunkirk.

    — Wha'?!

    — So he said.

    — Who?

    — Didn't hear his name – an economist.

    —The fuckin' eejit. Can yeh see the economists runnin' onto Omaha Beach, into enemy fire? Band o' brothers, me hole.

    — Tha' was D-Day. He said Dunkirk. The retreat, like.

    — Same thing – backwards. I'll tell yeh, but.

    — Wha'?

    — When yeh hear things like tha' – spoofers on the radio an' the telly. You can be sure o' one thing. They haven't a clue. An' when yeh hear Enda Kenny sayin' that Ireland will be negotiatin' from a position o' strength, you know for certain we'll be negotiatin' from a position in a galaxy far, far away. And when they use words like 'frictionless' an' 'seamless' to describe the new border, you can tell for a fact tha' the border will be a solid wall with razor wire an' cunts with rifles. It's goin' to be the worst kind o' nightmare.

    — What's tha?

    — A borin' one.

— Did you ever see *The Righ' Stuff*?

— Brilliant fillum.

— Your man from it died.

— Chuck Yeager.

— Sam Shepard – yeah.

— He was brilliant.

— I mean – I didn't know he was in so many things. But one o' the granddaughters is doin' a thing in college abou' fillums. Watchin' them, like.

— Can yeh do tha'?

— Yeah – she loves her fillums. A great young one, by the way. Anyway, she was in the house an' she tells us abou' this one. *The Assassination of Jesse James by the Coward Robert Ford*. I think that's the name of it, an' anyway.

— An' Sam Shepard's in it?

— Jesse's brother, yeah.

— Frank.

— Exactly. So we watched it.

— Good?

— Brilliant. Like, he was just brilliant in everythin', wasn't he? An' then she tells us abou' this one. *Paris, Texas*.

— Seen tha' one years ago. He's not in it, but.

— He wrote it.

— Fuckin' wrote it?

— Yeah.

— Jesus. He was married to Jessica Lange as well.

— There was no end to his fuckin' talents. So, we watched it.

— *Paris, Texas*?

— Brilliant again. They were bawlin' at the end. The wife an' the granddaughter.

— My wife says he was one o' the great handsome men.

— Same here.
— Bastard.
— Yeah.

9-8-17

— See Glen Campbell died.

— I was readin' a list of his songs this mornin'. Jesus.

— He was big in our house when I was a kid.

— Same here.

— Me father hated music – any o' the records me an' me brothers brought home.

— Same here, yeah.

— It was his job, like. I can see tha' now. A big part o' bein' a da.

— A pain in the arse back then, but.

— Every record we tried to play. 'Turn down tha' bloody noise!' Before we'd have the thing out of its fuckin' sleeve. It was fuckin' terrible. But then – one Saturday. One of us brings home 'Witchita Lineman'.

— What a song.

— Well, there yeh go. We put it on, and I look at me da, expectin' the roar. But his face—

— Transfixed.

— Fuckin' spellbound. He loved it. And then last nigh' – when we found ou' Glen Campbell was dead. We've one o' the grandkids stayin' with us – for a few nights, just. A lovely kid – she's sixteen. Anyway, she says, 'Who's Glen Campbell?' An' the wife tells her to look up 'Witchita Lineman' on YouTube.

— An' she was spellbound.

— She was, yeah. Exactly like me da.

— Come here – did you see that ad? The Marks an' Spencers one.

— With Paddin'ton Bear in it.

— That's the one.

— He's sound, Paddin'ton Bear. He's a nice, harmless fella. You could have a pint with Paddin'ton. An' that's more than yeh could say abou' most o' the others.

— What others?

— The fuckin' cartoons.

— I don't know. Bugs Bunny. You'd have a pint with Bugs, wouldn't yeh?

— Okay – yeah. He'd wear yeh out, but, wouldn't he? After a while. With all the fuckin' 'What's up, Doc', an' tha'.

— Good point – yeah. But the ad.

— What about it?

— You've seen it, yeah? Paddin'ton mistakes the burglar for Santy.

— It took me a while to cop on to tha'.

— Same here. But annyway. He brings the burglar back over the town, puttin' back all the presents tha' he's after robbin'.

— It's fuckin' gas, tha' bit.

— Well, it's mildly amusin'. But at the end, after the sham has seen the error of his ways. He leans down to Paddin'ton and he gives him a hug, an' he says, 'Fuck you, little bear.'

— I think it's, 'Thank you, little bear.'

— No, it's 'fuck you' – definitely. But why would he say tha'? To Paddin'ton, of all people.

— Well, he's after deprivin' the poor man of his liveli-hood – in fairness.

— Well, that's true.

1-3-18

— Fuckin' snow.

— The snow can fuck off with itself. I got home there at about four an' it was drifted up against the front door. I had to go round the back – had to climb over the gate. I haven't done annythin' like tha' since I was abou' ten – nearly broke me bollix.

— Hate tha'.

— Me hands were fuckin' numb. I could hardly hold the fuckin' key. An' then I couldn't get the door open.

— How come?

— Bread – there was a wall o' Brennan's bread up against the back door. The kitchen was full o' sliced pans.

— That's a bit fuckin' excessive – is it?

— Well, she – the wife, like – she was down in SuperValu an' she saw people grabbin' the bread and she doesn't know wha' came over her – some primitive urge or somethin'. She got into the ruck. She says she gouged some poor young lad's eyes ou' an' all he wanted was a cream slice. Anyway, she went back five times for more.

— For fuck sake.

— The best bit, but. She asks me what I want for me tea an' I say a toasted sandwich. Cos, like, we have the fuckin' bread. An' she says, 'No – fuck off – we're keepin' it for an emergency.'

— We're both a bit sad tonight.

— We are.

— Ray Wilkins.

— What a player.

— I'll tell you – Chelsea were never the same after he left. It's goin' back, I know. 1979, I think it was.

— You're righ'. That's when he came to United.

— If he wasn't dead I'd be callin' him a fuckin' traitor. Fuckin' United! But, anyway—

— He was brilliant.

— Brilliant – no question. One of the few brilliant things about Chelsea back then.

— A great passer o' the ball.

— His vision, man – Jesus. He knew where to put the ball two days before the fuckin' match. He was only eighteen when they made him the captain.

— That's the thing now – that's why it's so fuckin' sad.

— Wha'?

— His age. He was the first great player tha' was the same age as us.

— You're righ'. I remember, it was hard to accept at the time. I was askin' me ma if I could go out on Sunday night an' he was the captain of Chelsea.

— Here's somethin'. Ray Wilkins played against both George Best and Ryan Giggs.

— Is tha' true?

— It is, yeah.

— That's amazin'.

— Says a lot about the man, I think. A fuckin' giant.

27-4-18

— See Abba are back.

    — Ah, that's sad.

    — Wha' – why?

    — Well, they were so – I don't know – iconic.

    — Hang on – I didn't say they were dead.

    — Oh.

    — I said they're back.

    — Oh – grand.

    — Did yeh think they all died at the same time – all four o' them?

    — Some sort o' suicide pact, yeah. They're Swedish. It wouldn't be tha' weird up there.

    — In a fuckin' sauna.

    — Listenin' to 'Dancin' Queen'.

    — Well, I'd fuckin' kill meself if I had to listen to tha' shite too often.

    — They've recorded some new songs.

    — Ah, Jesus. I mean, they must be a fair age by now. Older than us, like.

    — Yeah.

    — Do you want to see a pair of oul' ones on zimmers singin' 'Take a Chance on Me'?

    — It's a bit frightenin', alrigh'. But the new numbers might reflect their age.

    — Here – 'Gimme gimme gimme Complan after midnigh'.'

    — Good one. Annyway, I think it's kind o' nice.

    — Tha' they've reformed?

    — Yeah – it's nice.

    — Is it?

    — Ah, it is.

— They must've broken up – when? Must be nearly a hundred years ago, is it?

— Close enough, yeah. So, it's a good thing, is it?

— Ah, yeah.

— As long as we don't have to listen to them.

— Absolutely.

4-5-18

— Would you ever have an abortion?

— I only came in for a fuckin' pint.

— Would yeh?

— Look at me, for fuck sake. I'm not gettin' pregnant any time soon.

— Come on – the time has come. What's your opinion?

— Well – okay. Right— I've never told this to anyone outside o' the family.

— I'll tell no one.

— Doesn't matter. Years ago, one o' the daughters – she was sixteen. Just about.

— Pregnant.

— There yeh go. She hadn't a clue, God love her. An' the fella, he was sixteen as well. Clueless, the pair o' them. We asked her did she want it. She hardly knew wha' we meant. She just wasn't ready, like. So, anyway, the missis gets a number in London. She makes the appointment. Explains it to the daughter – is this what she wants? She says yeah, she thinks so. This is goin' back now – early '90s. So we book the flights – into town to book them. We half-expected to be arrested just for buyin' the tickets. Anyway, the wife goes over to England with her and I stay here. They were gone for three days.

— What was tha' like?

— Fuckin' dreadful. There were no mobiles or anythin'. I didn't know how it was goin' – how she was, like. Until the wife called. An' she was grand.

— Good – great.

— It was the secrecy I hated, but. Like we were ashamed. Cos we weren't – not really. It was like we were breakin' the law, an' I'm not even sure if we were. Just cos we loved our child.

— But it worked out okay, yeah?

— Yeah, but it was wrong. Smugglin' her out o' the country.

— You'll be votin' Yes, so.

— I'll be waitin' for the fuckin' doors to open.

14-5-18

— You know all the posters with the foetuses on them – the No ones?

— They're all over the fuckin' place.

— I seen a new one earlier.

— Another one?

— It says, 'I am only 9 weeks old. I can hack into your bank account.'

— Are yeh serious?

— It's outside Paddy Power's.

— Hang on – is it a Paddy Power's poster? One o' their ads?

— No – no. Calm down, for fuck sake.

— You're havin' me on, aren't yeh?

— I am, yeah. But yeh know the real one – 'I am 9 weeks old. I can yawn and kick'?

— Yeah.

— Well, yawnin'. It's not that impressive, is it? We can all do tha'.

— An' if he's yawning when he's nine weeks what's he going to be like when he's twenty-nine?

— Fuckin' unbearable.

— There yeh go.

— Come here, but. Your grandkids. Would yeh be worried abou' them seein' all them posters?

— Well, there now – I asked one o' me sons the same thing. He has two lads, like – two sons. An' he says not at all. They don't even notice the pictures. They're too busy countin' all the Yeses an' the No's.

— Brilliant.

— There's one o' the posters, but. The woman's body seems to be real but the foetus is definitely a drawin'. Have yeh seen tha' one?

— I have, yeah.

— Tha' one worries me.

— Why?

— Tha' poor young one – she needs to be warned. She'll be givin' birth to a cartoon.

— Barney Rubble.

— Exactly. Or SpongeBob.

16-5-18

— Does your missis ever drag you to plays?

— No. I mean – she made me go with her to the snooker in Goff's once, an' it wasn't too bad. An' a weddin' there recently. I can't remember who – it might've been one o' the kids. But not plays. Never.

— My one loves plays. An' she started gettin' me to go with her after she had tha' row with her sister.

— When was tha'?

— 1977.

— Jesus.

— They haven't spoken since. So, anyway, I've seen a fair few fuckin' plays in my time.

— There was a thing in the News this mornin'. Some playwright died.

— Tom Murphy.

— You've seen some o' his, have yeh?

— Loads o' them, yeah. There was one, but – in particular. *Bailegangaire*.

— Good?

— Ah, man.

— Wha' was it abou'?

— Women.

— Women?

— Women talkin'.

— It must've been fuckin' long, so.

— Don't start now – don't fuckin' start. There was a big bed in the middle o' the stage. With this oul' one in it. An' her two granddaughters comin' and goin' around her. It was amazin' – fuckin' mesmerisin'. An' I'll tell yeh, I've loved listenin' to women ever since. It was fuckin' brilliant.

— Come here – you're sad, aren't yeh?

— I am, yeah.

— Will yeh be watchin' the Royal weddin'?

— I will in me hole.

— Ah, come on – they seem like a nice enough couple.

— Me an' the missis, we're a nice enough couple. Will annyone be watchin' us?

—Well, like – first, yis aren't gettin' married, an' you're not a prince an' your wife, as far as I know now, isn't a fuckin' fillum star.

— It's a load o' shite.

— An' on top o' tha', yis aren't even a nice couple. You're a cranky pair o' cunts.

— At least we're interestin'.

— Fuckin' interestin'?

—Yeah – interestin'. The prince fella – what's his name? Harry. Name one single interestin' thing he's ever said or done. Go on, I'm right. Fuckin' nothin'. He's just like the rest o' them, a square-headed fuckin' dope.

— What about Meghan? She's been in fillums an' the telly.

— That's not interestin'. That's just actin'.

— Jesus, it's like sittin' beside fuckin' Death.

— Sit somewhere else then. Fuck off – go on.

— Here – listen. There's one really interestin' thing about Meghan.

—Wha'?

— Her ma.

— Her ma?

— Yep.

— - - - Wha' time is it on?

1-7-18

— Oh, Jesus – look over there.

— Where? Oh, fuckin' hell—

— Is that who I think it is?

— I think so.

— It's Lionel Messi.

— Yeah.

— An' that's—

— It's fuckin' Ronaldo. Sittin' there with him.

— What're they doin' in here?

— Well, they both got knocked out yesterday.

— So, they're on their fuckin' holidays?

— Yeah.

— In here?

— A bit of ordinary livin'. It has its attractions, I'd say – the pressure they're always under.

— In here, but. It's not exactly the Cliffs o' Moher.

— Messi's havin' a pint.

— I'd have expected tha'.

— An' what's tha' Ronaldo's drinkin'? It looks like gin – there's fuckin' cucumber floatin' in it.

— I'd have expected that as well.

— I felt sorry for them yesterday.

— A great World Cup, but, isn't it?

— Fuckin' sensational. Tha' kid, Mbappe.

— What a player.

— I've got grandkids that are older than him.

— It's funny tha', isn't it? How we age durin' the World Cup.

— Messi's gettin' up – look. He must be goin' to the jacks.

— He's headin' straight to the women's – look.

— Yeah – no. Jesus, what a swerve.

— Brilliant – amazin'. He had us all fooled. Fuckin' hell – did yeh see tha'?

— He got into the men's without openin' the door!

16-8-18

— See Aretha Franklin died.

— All those songs. Jesus, man, she was amazin'.

—Yeah, yeah. I met the missis when there was an Aretha song playin' – did I ever tell yeh?

— Hang on now – fuck off. Every time a singer dies you tell me you met your missis at one of their gigs or a dance.

— Well, I did.

— I'm not listenin'.

—You don't really know my wife. But I'll tell yeh. You're never goin' to woo a woman like tha' in one three-minute song.

— Woo?

— Yeah – fuckin' woo. It was never love at first sight, like. It was more like love at twenty-seven fuckin' sights. I had to win her over. An' that's where Aretha comes in.

— Okay – wha' happened?

— There was a club, a room over a pub, like – just off Capel Street. I can't remember wha' it was called. But they only played soul.

— Sounds good.

— It was. An' anyway, they're only playin' Aretha songs this nigh' an' I boogie up to the missis, an' I shout, 'R.E.S.P.E.C.T.'. Right in front of her, like.

— Wha' did she do?

— Well, there – she sang back.

— Wha'?

— 'F.U.C.K.O.F.F.'

— Tha' doesn't sound all tha' encouragin'.

— Ah, but – she was smilin'.

— It's sad about the Spider-Man fella, isn't it?

— Bruce Lee.

— Stan.

—That's him. Were you into Spider-Man an' all o' them when you were a kid?

— No.

— Same here. But my kids—

— Fuckin' mad abou' them.

— An' the grandkids. I hardly noticed the man had died until last night. One o' the daughters came over with her gang. An' they were all over me, tellin' me all abou' the different characters. It was like doin' the fuckin' Leavin' Cert.

— The *Spider-Man* fillums were great.

— Class. I liked his mott.

—Yeah.

— What was her name, the actor?

— Dunsten something. I had me own Spider-Man moment a few years back.

— Go on.

— In the son's house. The hall – they don't go for carpets. Bare floorboards, yeh know.

— Fuckin' eejits.

— I'm with yeh. But anyway, there's a Spider-Man mask on the floor an' I slip on it. The legs are gone an' I land right on me fuckin' back. An' the mask lands on me face. An' they're all there – the grandkids. They're lookin' at me an' the mask, then up at the ceilin'.

— They thought you were fuckin' Spider-Man.

— The happiest few seconds of my fuckin' life.

— Are you growin' a moustache?

  — I am, yeah.

  — At your age – for fuck sake.

  — It's a disguise – fuck off.

  — Disguise?

  — Yeah.

  — Why?

  — I'm dead.

  — Wha'?!

  — I'm dead – officially.

  — What's the story?

  — Listen. One o' the granddaughters plays for the Under-11 girls. An' – don't ask me how – I've become their fuckin' manager.

  — How come?

  — Their regular coach eloped with a referee.

  — Not Jimmy the Whistle?

  — His brother. They've a whole family o' fuckin' referees. But anyway, she's a useful little player, the granddaughter. But our goalkeeper. Ah man, she's fabulous. She's six foot, three.

  — What age is she?

  — Ten. Hands like shovels. A lovely kid as well. But anyway, she couldn't make the match at the weekend. She had to go to a weddin'. An' the game was against the Arklow Amazons.

  — They sound useful.

  — Unbelievable. They've a young one playin' for them tha' they're already callin' the Hacketstown Neymar. So, there's only one option. Get the game postponed. But the weddin' isn't a good enough excuse. We looked up the rules, like.

— A death.

— Exactly. So I phone the league an' I tell them the manager's after dyin'. But I forgot I was the fuckin' manager.

— For fuck sake—

— They're all comin' to the fuckin' funeral – all the heads from the FAI. Mick McCarthy an' all.

— When's the funeral?

— Tomorrow mornin'.

— Yeh fuckin' eejit.

— I know.

1-2-19

— D'you have your breakfast every mornin'?

— I do, yeah. Although it depends how you define 'mornin''.

— Wha' d'you mean?

— Well today, like, I had me breakfast last nigh' – if tha' makes sense. Before I went to bed. I just thought I'd get it out o' the way. But, yeah, I'd always have a good breakfast.

— The most important meal o' the day.

— Absolutely.

— It isn't.

— Wha'?

— The most important meal of the fuckin' day.

— Says who?

— The scientists – the fuckin' experts. Again.

— Tha' can't be righ'.

— So they're sayin', an' anyway. It was on the News earlier – before Brexit an' all.

— My Ma used to say it.

— Same here.

— Eat all o' it now. It's the most important—

— Meal o' the day. Same here, yeah.

— So. The scientists – they're sayin' my Ma was a liar.

— More or less.

— The woman who gave birth to me, mind. She was just havin' us on?

— That's wha' they're implyin'.

— I'd imply their bollixes if I met them. What is the most important meal then? If it isn't the breakfast.

— They didn't say.

— An' that's typical as well, isn't it? An' I'll tell yeh one thing. I bet it's not the dinner.

— That'd be too fuckin' obvious, wouldn't it?

— See Georgie Burgess died.

— Pat Laffin.

— That's him – Georgie.

— He was brilliant in *The Snapper*, wasn't he?

— Brilliant – yeah. 'Are yeh alrigh', Sharon?'

— The head on him. 'Did yeh not see me at the vegetables?'

— It must be hard, though, sometimes. For actors, like.

— Why?

— They become known as the character they play in the fillum or the television thing. I'd say even their fuckin' families forget who they really are.

— Pitfall of the job, I'd say. Or a blessin'.

— He was Pat Mustard as well – in *Father Ted*.

— Well, there yeh go. It's like he played for both Barcelona *and* Real Madrid.

— 'I'm a very careful man, Father.' My gang are devastated – at home. They all grew up with Georgie Burgess an' Pat Mustard. Even the ones tha' weren't born when they came ou'. They're goin' around quotin' all the lines.

— Same with us. Come here – we've one o' the grandkids stayin' the nigh'. He's only four – a lovely kid, he's fuckin' gas. We're all sittin' around the table – havin' the dinner, like. An' he finishes his last chip an' he gets up. 'Now to ride Mrs O'Reilly,' he says an' he walks out into the hall.

17-10-19

— See your man, Doyle, has a new buke ou'.
— What's it abou'?
— Two fuckin' eejits talkin' shite in a pub.
— Are yeh serious?
— Yeah.
— Two shams like us?
— Yep.
— Talkin' shite.
— Yeah.
— Who'd want to read tha'?
— No one is my bet.
— Would you want to read a fuckin' buke with you in it?
— I'd only be half the buke.
— Wha'?
— The other half would be the other cunt.
— What other cunt?
— The cunt talkin' to the other fuckin' eejit.
— Hang on – me?
— Spot on.
— Fuck off now – wha' do they talk abou'?
— Well – the ice-bucket challenge.
— Ah, yeah.
— An' David Bowie an' Prince.
— Ah, yeah.
— An' Robin Williams.
— Poor oul' Robin.
— An' Bill O'Herlihy.
— Ah, Bill.
— An' the same sex marriage thing.
— Ah yeah.
— An' the football an' tha'.

— Just like us.

— Yeah.

— Hang on, but. Is it actually us?

— The wife picked it up there – in Eason's. An' she had a flick through it. An' she says, Yeah – she recognised me.

— It's us?

— Yeah.

— It mightn't be tha' bad, so. Did she buy it?

— No, she didn't. She says she already has me on audio – why would she want the fuckin' buke?

4-11-19

— See Gay Byrne died.

— Gaybo – yeah. Hard to imagine, really – him dead, like.

— Was he big in your house?

— Ah, man – the old Late Late.

— Saturday nights – yeah.

— I'd forgotten tha'. Black an' whi'e.

— Yeah, yeah – years before the colour.

— The best way to watch it, I'd say – black an' whi'e. Like Humphrey Bogart.

— Are you sayin' Gay Byrne was Humphrey Bogart?

— Well, he kind o' was, in fairness – in Ireland back then, like.

— Did your Ma like him?

— She loved him – she absolutely fuckin' loved him.

— Same here. Me Da hated him.

— Well, there yeh go – the key to every successful marriage in Ireland back then. The woman loved him, the man hated him, an' the sparks flew.

— You might be righ'.

— I'm fuckin' tellin' yeh – half the children in Ireland were conceived straigh' after the Late Late Show.

— D'you think?

— Or durin' the ads – yeah.

— What abou' yourself? Were you a Late Late baby?

— No, no – I was born years before the telly.

— Same here. We were wireless babies.

— It's sad, but, isn't it?

— It is.

— It's kind o' like an uncle dyin'.

— Exactly. The nice one – the uncle who was always a bit o' crack.

311

— D'you ever have dreams?

— I do, yeah. I had one there a while back – abou' Nigella.

— Were you asleep?

— No.

— Good man. I had a horrible one there tonigh' – before I came ou'.

— Were you in the scratcher before you came here?

— No – no. I fell asleep in front o' the telly.

— I hate tha'.

— Same here – but I couldn't help it. *Nationwide* was on.

— Oh, for fuck sake.

— Ou' for the fuckin' count I was. Slept righ' through *The Kids Are Alrigh'* and *Eastenders*. An' I wake up in the middle o' the News – an' there's Boris fuckin' Johnson, righ' in front o' me.

— Yeh poor cunt.

— The problem – the fuckin' problem. Was. I didn't know where I was. I thought he was one o' me kids.

— A nightmare.

— An absolute fuckin' nightmare. You know the way — Johnson, like – the way he holds his fists, kind o' punches them in front of himself?

—Yeah.

— Well, one o' mine did that – when he was a toddler. Whenever he wanted somethin'. A biscuit or a tractor or whatever. An' – fuckin' hell – I thought he'd turned into Boris Johnson.

— D'you want a small one with tha' pint?

— I think I fuckin' need one.

6-2-20

— I am Spartacus.

— See he died.

— I was Spartacus.

— He was brilliant, but, wasn't he?

— He was. Even his name was fuckin' brilliant.

— Tha' wasn't his real name, but.

— Was it not?

— Issur Danielovitch.

— Tha' was Kirk's real name?

— Yep.

— How did yeh fuckin' know tha'?

— He was one o' the Tallaght Danielovitches. The wife's cousins.

— Ah, fuck off.

— My favourite, but – my favourite fillum o' Kirk's.

— Go on.

— *The Vikings.*

— I don't think I remember tha' one. What's it abou'?

— The fuckin' Vikings. Wha' d'yeh think it's abou'? The nuns?

— Fuck off. I meant the story – the plot. What's it abou'?

— I can't really remember, to be honest with yeh. I was only a kid. But I'll never forget it.

— You did fuckin' forget it.

— Fuck off – yeh know what I mean. It was fuckin' amazin'. All the fights an' tha'. There was a gang of us. In the Corinthian, the cinema. D'you remember the Corinthian – on Eden Quay?

— I do, yeah.

— Anyway, there was a Viking funeral in the fillum. They burnt the boat, yeh know. And after the fillum we

313

ran straight over to the river an' we had our own Viking
funeral.

— Did yis?

— Yeah, yeah. We picked up Leggy O'Hara an' fucked
him into the Liffey.

20-2-20

— Fuckin' VAR.

   — It's ruinin' the game o' football.

   — All those disallowed goals.

   — Fuckin' desperate.

   — Someone said—. I think it was George Best. He said scorin' a goal was like havin' an orgasm.

   — It was definitely George Best.

   — Probably, yeah. But now – listen. Yeh score your goal, yeh have your orgasm—

   — In front o' millions o' people.

   — An' a few minutes later, a gang o' referees tell yeh it wasn't an orgasm at all.

   — For fuck sake.

   — Not even one o' the interrupted ones. Can you imagine the psychological damage that's doin' to the players?

   — An' the fans.

   — It could be the end o' the human race – as we know it.

   — Ah Jesus—.

   — And now the missis—

   — Wha'?

   — She's after introducin' VAR.

   — In your bedroom?

   — No – God, no. The fuckin' kitchen.

   — Wha'?!

   — On Sundays – durin' the dinner. To guarantee fair play.

   — Hang on – wha'?!

   — She says it killed her mother.

   — The dinner?

   — No – just listen. This is years ago, mind. Her ma went up to the jacks an' when she came back half the spuds were gone off her plate. An' she never recovered from the hurt.

— So, there's a gang o' referees in Stockley Park watchin' you eat your dinner every Sunday?

— Yep.

26-2-20

— All set for the coronavirus?

— Yeah, yeah. We've the freezer full o' Brennan's bread an' we got a couple o' the big yokes o' Bisto. We'll be grand.

— It's not the weather that's comin' at us, man. It's a virus – it's the fuckin' plague. Yeh can't fight the plague with Bisto!

— Calm down, for fuck sake.

— It's in Italy!

— Is it here? Look around you. Wait –! Now look.

— Wha'?

— Look.

— I am lookin'.

— Is it here? The virus – your fuckin' plague?

— Well, like—

— Wha'?

— How can I tell?

— Exactly. I'm tellin' yeh, man. A good dose o' the plague would improve this place no end. Look at Denis the Disaster over there. Is he even alive?

— Wha'?

— The colour of him – look it. A good scrap with the corona thing would give him somethin' to live for.

— It's not a bad theory.

— I'm tellin' yeh. The best fight he's been in since his missis ran off with his ma.

— She wasn't his ma.

— That's another fuckin' story. An' anyway – the country's ready.

— D'yeh think?

— A bottle o' Benylin in every Garda station.

— An' a plastic spoon.

— Bring it fuckin' on.

— It's like winnin' the Eurovision again, isn't it? After all these years.

— Wha'?

— The coronavirus case.

— In here?!

— No, no – calm down. Belfast – up the road.

— Today?

— It was on the news there. Before I came ou'.

— Jesus.

— It's kind o' nice, I think. Bein' included. In the list o' countries, like. The nations o' the world.

— Jaysis – I don't know abou' tha'.

— Come here, but. They say 2% of people who get it – contract it, like – die from it.

— Still a lot o' bodies.

— Yeah, but there's only the pair of us left in the house – officially, like. Me an' the missis.

— Okay.

— So, what's 2% of the two of us? A toe? I mean, I'd happily sacrifice one of me toes. She probably needs hers more than I'll be needing mine.

— Why d'you think that?

— I'm not sure. An opportunity to be noble, I suppose. An' it's no big deal, really. A toe – is it? I'm not even sure what your toes are for.

— Balance or something.

— Balance – at our age?

— Women's toes, but.

— That's different.

— Works of fuckin' art.

— Is tha' another o' the symptoms?

— Wha'?

— Talkin' about toes.
— Might be.
— One last pint?
— Okay – yeah. To be on the safe side.

—You were fuckin' ages in there.

— I fell asleep.

— In the jacks?

—Washin' me hands. Countin' to twenty, yeh know – it takes for fuckin' ever. An' I dozed off.

— They said you should sing 'Happy Birthday' twice – it takes twenty seconds.

— It's so fuckin' boring but, tha' song – there's no story in it. It's fuckin' mayhem in there, by the way.

— In the jacks?

—You know your man with the head tha' looks like it's made o' Lego?

— I do.

— He's in there washin' his hands, singin'.

— 'Happy Birthday'?

— No. He says it's not nearly long enough. So he's singin' 'Bohemian Rhapsody'. All of it – there's a fuckin' queue behind him.

— Is he anny good?

— It's dramatic. But – this is tragic.

—Wha'?

—You know your man tha' had the cancer?

— Prostate Pat.

— That's him. He only half-heard the information on the radio an' he thinks you're supposed to have your piss in twenty seconds. An', like, it takes him twenty minutes to have a decent slash these days. He's in bits – he's convinced he's after bringin' the virus into the pub. There's a team from the HSE in there, tryin' to persuade the poor bastard to go back to his pint.

— I don't like this remote control drinkin'.

— It's not remote control, for fuck sake. It's Skype. That's a real can in your hand – look it.

— It's thick.

— It's better than nothin' – stop whingin'.

— What'll we talk abou'?

— The football.

— There's no fuckin' football.

— Old football.

— - - -

— - - -

— The 1970 World Cup was brilliant, wasn't it?

— Yeah.

— I'll never forget it.

— No.

— This is ridiculous. Havin' to stare at yeh while we're talkin'. It's not natural. Is tha' your fridge behind yeh, by the way?

— Never mind me fuckin' fridge. We're supposed to be pretendin' we're in the boozer.

— Did a child just walk past there?

— One o' the grandkids, yeah.

— Ah, for fuck sake.

— Hang on—If I shift me phone here a bit—Now. It's a bit more like we're sittin' beside each other. In the boozer, like.

— That's better – yeah. More realistic. How're yis doin' for jacks paper?

— We're grand – we've loads. Unless it starts rainin' arses.

— Nothin' would fuckin' surprise me annymore. What abou' food?

— Well there—. We're down to catfood or the fuckin' cat.

— Would yis eat your own cat?

— Moggy in Bisto? 'Course we would.

24-4-20

— You're not lookin' the best there. You're a bit pale. Is it the light over your head?

— Fuck the light over me head. It's the Dettol.

— Wha'?

— Well, we were ou' the back earlier – me an' the wife. On what's left of the deck, like. An' the radio was half on.

— Half on?

— The fuckin' volume was down – fuck off. We were only half listenin' – that's what I mean.

— Okay.

— An' anyway. Trump was sayin' somethin' abou' sunlight an' disinfectant bein' good for killin' the fuckin' corona. So, we—

— Wha'?

—Well, we already had the sunlight. It was lovely out earlier – remember?

— Like the fuckin' Sahara.

— Exactly. So, anyway, we got a bit carried away an' the wife went in an' made us a jug o' Dettol an' blackcurrent.

— Hang on – you drank Dettol?

— An' blackcurrant, yeah. Way more blackcurrant than Dettol now – in fairness. Five to one – like the Robinson's Barley Water, yeh know.

—Dettol, but.

— I know.

— What was it like?

— Well, it was so fuckin' disgustin', it was funny. An' we were laughin' at the same time we were pukin' – you should see the fuckin' deck, m'n.

— Filthy?

— No – spotless. We were not listenin' to me? We were pukin' fuckin' Dettol.

— Are yeh all set for Stage 2?

— Fuck Stage 2.

— We're allowed to go shoppin' on Monday.

— I don't want to go shoppin'. I've no interest in fuckin' shoppin'.

— Are yeh not even a bit curious?

— Listen. Men our age. Why would we go shoppin'? Unless we're fuckin desperate, tell me one good reason why we'd go shoppin' – why we'd endure it. Honest answer now.

— So we can go for a pint after.

— An' will we be able to go for a pint after?

— No.

— Then fuck it.

— Well, the wife's quite excited.

— No – come here. I don't begrudge her tha'. Or anyone else.

— She's downstairs ironin' her mask.

— Great – brilliant. Good luck to her. My one's goin' into town with her sister. So – grand. Just don't expect me to be giddy cos I can buy a fuckin' shirt.

— We can go 20k.

— Not interested.

— We can visit the old folks' homes.

— That's a fuckin' conspiracy. Be very careful. They'll let us in but – men our age, cranky cunts like us — will they let us back ou'?

— Ah, come on—

— I'll leave it at tha'. The whole fuckin' country might think we've won the War of Indendence again but – look it. We're still stuck in this Zoom prison, aren't we? Are yeh still there – ?

— - - - Yeah.

— See Tony Holohan's steppin' back.

— I'll tell yeh – he's been brilliant.

— That's puttin' it fuckin' mildly.

— I've a brother – me oldest brother. He's nine years older than me, like. And – this is true; I'm not bein' sentimental. He wouldn't be alive if it wasn't for Tony. Sorry – I'm a bit tearful. Can you imagine what I'd be like if I even liked me brother?

— There's a story like tha' in every family, I'd say.

— He was just so good at the job. Clear an' calm, an' none of the 'I'm an expert' bolloxology.

— Plain English.

— Exactly. An' d'you know wha'?

— Go on.

— I was thinkin' abou' this last nigh' – when it was on the news. Tony has made me proud o' two things. The first – I'm Irish.

— I'm with yeh.

— I never felt tha' before – only with the football an' when Katie won the boxin'.

— What's the other?

— I'm a man.

— I think I get yeh.

— Because – let's face it – a lot o' the men have been fuckin' disastrous. Not just Trump, but tha' fuckin' dope, Johnson, over there as well. It's the women who've been the leaders. Angela in Germany – an' Jacinda.

— I love her.

— Same here – yeah. But Tony, like – he's been a good, decent, competent man. The way a man should be.

— He's one o' the lads.

— There's no bigger compliment.

11-7-20

— See Big Jack's gone.

    — It's hard to believe.

    — I feel like me da's after dyin'.

    — I know what yeh mean.

    — The impact tha' man had on us.

    — An' it wasn't just the football.

    — No – but the football as well. Remember when we beat England – Ray Houghton's goal?

    — I proposed to the wife at half-time.

    — And Italia 90.

    — The country was never the same after it.

    — Thank fuck.

    — We had somethin' to celebrate.

    — The fact tha' we were Irish.

    — Exactly – the fact tha' we were fuckin' Irish. We took the flag back off the Provos.

    — We were proud to be Irish.

    — Because of an Englishman.

    — There yeh go. It seemed like the end o' the bad ol' days, didn't it? The economy picked up. Everythin' seemed to get better.

    — I don't think the economists would see it tha' way.

    — Fuck the economists – we know the truth. Packie Bonnar saved a penno an' we became a modern European country.

    — Cos o' Jack.

    — Cos o' Jack – exactly.

    — The biggest thing he did, though – the most important thing.

    — Wha'?

    — He made us look differently at England an' the English.

— That's very true.
— Jack Charlton started the peace process.
— An' he made us proud an' very happy.
— That's some legacy, isn't it?
— Considerin' he played for fuckin' Leeds.

1-8-20

— Were you in *The Commitments*?

— Stupid question. Do you know annyone our age who wasn't in the fuckin' *Commitments*?

— Exactly – yeah. Our grandas were all in the GPO in 1916, our das were there the night the Germans bombed the North Strand, and we were in *The Commitments* – every fuckin' one of us.

— Where are you in it?

— Sheriff Street. Behind one o' the horses. Yourself?

— On the DART. When they're singin' 'Destination Anywhere'.

— I don't remember yeh.

— I'm there – in the back. It was actually me tha' suggested the song.

— Wha'?

— They were all set to start singin' 'Is This the Way to Amarillo', an' I went up to the director – Alan Parker, like – an' I said, 'Here, Al, what abou' this one instead?' An' I sang it for him.

— An' wha' did he say to tha'?

— He told me to fuck off an' mind me own business. But he was smilin'.

— An' he took your advice.

— He did.

— See he died there, yesterday.

—Yeah – yeah. That's what I remember most abou' tha' day, anyway. He had a big smile – a very nice fella.

— Jack Charlton an' Alan Parker – the two Englishmen who changed the face of Ireland.

— It's gas, isn't it?

— See Johnny Nash died.

— I got a shock when I read it. I thought it said Johnny Cash.

— Tha' Johnny died years ago.

— Tha' was the shock. I thought he was after dyin' again.

— To outdo Elvis.

— Then a suicide pact – I thought for a minute. The two Johnnys bowin' out together.

— That'd be some fuckin' funeral.

— Johnny Nash but.

— Brilliant.

— I mean, I hadn't thought o' Johnny Nash in fuckin' years but then when I seen he died – well—.

— He'd some great fuckin' songs.

— 'Tears on Me Pillow', 'There Are More Questions Than Answers'.

— 'Stir It Up'.

— I always thought he was Jamaican – cos o' the reggae. But it turns ou', he was a Yank.

— He was brilliant wherever he fuckin' came from.

— His masterpiece, but – 'I Can See Clearly Now'.

— He was singin' tha' one when I asked the wife up to dance – the first time, like.

— 'I Can See Clearly Now'?

— It was ironic, really. She told me later. She was pissed out of her head an' she could see fuck-all.

— An' she married you.

— She should've gone to Specsavers – I've no fuckin' sympathy for her.

— Come here, but. Will the pubs ever open again?

— No.

— Another lockdown.

— Another fuckin' lockdown.

— Were yeh ever in jail?

— Not that I remember – no.

— It has to be better than this shite.

— How can it be? We're not in fuckin' jail, m'n. We can go for a walk, for fuck sake.

— That's wha' appeals to me about jail.

— Wha'?

— I wouldn't have to go for a fuckin' walk. I'm sick o' fuckin' walkin'. I'll tell yeh what I'm really sick of, but. I'm sick o' walkin' past places that are shut.

— We could meet for a coffee.

— Coffee?

— Or tea – yeah.

— Fuckin' tea?

— Bring a fuckin' can – it doesn't matter.

— Where?

— I don't know – St Anne's or Dollymount. They're both inside our permitted 5K.

— What if it's rainin'?

— So wha'? Come here – we can pretend we're mitchin'.

— Good idea. I'll borrow a school uniform off one o' the grandkids.

— You might be a bit big for it.

— She's a big girl – in fairness.

— Did I hear you laughin' there?

— No, you fuckin' didn't.

— When'll we do it?

— Hang on – I'm lookin' at me diary here.

— Now?

— Yeah.

— See yeh at the Red Stables in half an hour.
— Grand.
— It's pissin' out.
— Even better.

TWO PINTS

The Play

TWO PINTS was produced by The Abbey Theatre and received its premiere on July 11th, 2017, at The Foxhound Inn, Greendale Road, Kilbarrack, Dublin 5.

Cast:
ONE: Liam Carney
TWO: Lorcan Cranitch
RAYMOND: Brendan Galvin.

Director: Caitríona McLaughlin
Designer: Kate Moylan
Producer: Kelly Phelan
Stage Manager: Brendan Galvin
Lighting and Sound: Alan D'Arcy

Later Productions:

Cast:
TWO: Philip Judge
RAYMOND: Laurence Lowry

Stage Manager: Emma Doyle

Act One

Suggested music: "Just a Little Lovin", by Dusty Springfield.
A pub counter; a line of stools. TWO occupies a stool, his back
to the audience. He's alone, but there's a half-full pint glass at
the empty stool beside him, to his left. The barman, RAYMOND,
is pouring pints etc. for other, unseen, customers. ONE enters,
from the gents. He talks and checks that his fly is shut as he
moves to his stool.

ONE: Annyway, I'm there, righ'. An' the barrier won't go up. With me ticket in the fuckin' thing. So I press the button for the voice – the fella behind the wall, like. An' I tell him the story an' he says it's the wrong ticket. I'm after puttin' in the wrong ticket.

TWO: Wrong ticket?

ONE: So he says. But it can't be. I'm only after payin' for the thing. Luckily now, there's no one behind me, no other cars, like. So there's no one leanin' on the horn. But your man comes ou' an' sorts it.

TWO: That's good.

ONE: Well, I'm not sure. He was wearin' – yeh know them grey trackie bottoms?

TWO: I do, yeah – like pyjamas.

ONE: Exactly. Under his jacket, like. It's a bit fuckin' casual, yeh know.

TWO: But—.

ONE: Wha'?

TWO: It's a car park.

ONE: It's a hospital car park. A fuckin' hospital.

TWO: So—. Wha? He should be wearin' a white coat an' a fuckin' yoke – a stethoscope?

335

ONE: No – fuck off. I'm just sayin'. It's a fuckin' hospital. On the grounds, like.

TWO: The campus.

ONE: A bit o' fuckin' respect wouldn't go amiss. He doesn't know wha' sort o' state I'm goin' to be in. I could've just witnessed a death. I'd be upset. An' he comes ou' dressed for bed or a fuckin' bank raid. The shiftless prick. D'you see me point? A bit o' fuckin' sensitivity.

TWO: Grand – yeah. They found your man, Richard the Third, in a car park, didn't they?

ONE: Hang on – who?

TWO: Richard the Third.

ONE: Who was he?

TWO: The King of England.

ONE: Wha' happened the fuckin' Queen?

TWO: Before her.

ONE: He was her da?

TWO: Grandda – I think. Maybe older. Anyway, they found him.

ONE: They took their fuckin' time.

TWO: Yeah – yeah. I'd like to think that if I got lost, my gang would try a bit fuckin' harder.

ONE: He was probably a bit of a cunt.

TWO: Safe bet. They're all cunts.

ONE: Wha' happened him, annyway?

TWO: He couldn't find his car.

ONE: So he just lay down an' fuckin' died?

TWO: Well, like. If you're used to people doin' everythin' for yeh—.

ONE: Ah, fuck off.

TWO: I'm only messin'. He was in a fight. Swords an' all.

ONE: The car park was in fuckin' Swords?

TWO: No – the fight. There were swords. He was brutally hacked – accordin' to the English cops.

ONE: How do they know it was him? He must've been there for ages.

TWO: His DNA.

ONE: What about it?

TWO: It was forty-five per cent horse.

ONE: Ah well, then he was definitely one o' the British royal family.

TWO: Anyway, they buried him.

ONE: Hang on – say nothin'. Fuckin' Wikileaks.

They wait as WIKILEAKS, *unseen, crosses the stage behind them, from the gents.*

ONE: Okay – we're grand. He doesn't look like a man whose missis is ridin' the fella tha' did their deck, does he?

TWO: Wikileaks?

ONE: Yeah.

TWO: Who told yeh tha'?

ONE: Your woman in Paddy Power's.

TWO: Which one?

ONE: Your one with the back.

TWO: Never mind her. Wha' did she say?

ONE: I don't know if she *said* annythin'. More, hinted, is how I'd describe it. Insinuated.

TWO: Wha'?

ONE: Well. She muttered somethin' abou' sluts an' cedar wood.

TWO: When he was walkin' ou'?

ONE: Yeah.

TWO: With his winnin's?

ONE: Yeah – possibly.

TWO: Well, then. He fixed it, anyway.

ONE: Sorry – wha'?

337

TWO: The young lad in the car park. He sorted it ou'.

ONE: How do *you* fuckin' know?

TWO: Well, you're fuckin' here, like. In fairness.

ONE: Yeah – okay. He fixed it.

TWO: What was wrong with it?

ONE: Wha'? Oh – wrong ticket.

TWO: So he was righ'.

ONE: Half righ'. It wasn't a ticket at all.

TWO: Wha' was it?

ONE: A loyalty card. SuperValu.

TWO: Wha' were you doin' with a SuperValu loyalty card?

ONE: Buyin' stuff in fuckin' Tesco's. Wha' d'yeh fuckin' think?! Look it – sorry. It was just—. Yeh know the leather yeh get around the gearstick? In the car. Yeh know it. Like a – wha' d'yeh call it? – a scrotum?

TWO: Not fuckin' mine.

ONE: Yeh know what I mean. The leather with the wrinkles an' tha'. Around the fuckin' gearstick.

TWO: Go on.

ONE: Well, I'd put the ticket there, like – the car park ticket. An' the loyalty card was there already. So when I got to the barrier—

TWO: Yeh picked up the wrong one.

ONE: Exactly.

TWO: But one o' them's plastic an' the other one's made o' paper. How did yeh mix them up—?

ONE: I was only after leavin' the hospital. That's my point. Why I brought up the subject in the first fuckin' place. Yeh can't be expected to be – I don't know – fuckin' car park fuckin'-friendly, when you've just come out of a hospital. (*to* RAYMOND) Two more, Raymond – good man.

TWO: I had me own car park experience up there. In Beaumont. Did I tell yeh? I must've.

338

ONE: Remind me – go on.

TWO: A few Christmases back. The mother-in-law.

ONE: Your mother-in-law? I thought she'd died.

TWO: The new one.

ONE: Oh, fuck.

As they speak, below, ONE *takes money from his pocket and leaves it on the counter for* RAYMOND, *who takes it when he delivers the pints.*

TWO: Annyway. They all come to the house – the whole gang, like. An' she reacts badly to the stuffin'. A Nigella recipe, as it happens. Sausage meat an' Red Bull.

ONE: Sounds lovely.

TWO: Ah, fuckin' massive now. Lovely. But, anyway, she starts expandin'.

ONE: It was the Christmas dinner. We all fuckin' expand.

TWO: Really quickly, but. Like a thing in a fillum.

ONE: Fuck.

TWO: Exactly wha' I said. But anyway, then there's the lotto – who'll bring her up to the A&E? An' they're all lookin' at me. But I want to stay at home with me family. And, as a matter of principle, like – I'm not willin' to bring anyone to Beaumont Hospital until I'm assured tha' the car parkin' charge isn't goin' to top up some chief executive's salary. Cos it was in the news at the time, d'yeh remember?

ONE: Yeah, yeah. The secret top-ups. The bosses of all the charities an' tha'.

TWO: But, anyway. Then I couldn't find the fuckin' van. Hadn't a clue where I'd left it. In the car park, like. An' by the time I found it, the money I'd paid didn't cover the charge. So I'm stuck – like yourself. But your man lifts the barrier for me—.

ONE: A little cunt in tracksuit bottoms?

339

TWO: Don't know – didn't see him. He did it automatically. He seemed alright, but. He wished us a happy Christmas.

ONE: For fuck sake—. There's a thing now, but – Nigella.

TWO: What about Nigella?

ONE: There's no pictures in her books. Of Nigella, I mean. There's only pictures of fuckin' cakes an' tha'.

TWO: I'm not tha' keen on cakes.

ONE: No – me neither. Fuck them.

TWO: Nigella, but.

ONE: She's a great young one.

TWO: She's fifty-eight.

ONE: Exactly.

TWO: She took cocaine.

ONE: Even better. I love her. Anyway, she only took the cocaine when her first husband was dyin'.

TWO: So she says.

ONE: Yeh doubt her? Yeh cunt. If my first wife died—

TWO: Hang on, hang on – fuck. Wha' first wife? Were you married before?

ONE: No.

TWO: Then what the fuck are yeh on abou'?

ONE: Empathy.

TWO: Wha'?!

ONE: I imagined I had a first wife. Dyin' like – just to see if I'd snort cocaine as well.

TWO: And did yeh?

ONE: Yeah.

TWO: Wha' was she like?

ONE: The first wife?

TWO: Yeah.

ONE: Lovely.

340

TWO: A bit like Nigella – was she?

ONE: A bit, yeah. Wha' was it, by the way?

TWO: Wha'?

ONE: Your mother-in-law's allergic reaction.

TWO: What about it?

ONE: What was she allergic to?

TWO: Oh. Horsehair.

ONE: Fuckin' horsehair?

TWO: Traces of it, just. In the sausage meat.

ONE: Hang on. It wasn't part of the fuckin' recipe, was it?

TWO: No – God, no. Why would Nigella want us eatin' horsehair?

ONE: But—.

TWO: It'd make no fuckin' sense, man.

ONE: No. No – yeah. But – it was in the sausage meat?

TWO: Yeah – I told yeh.

ONE: Wha' the fuck was it doin' in the sausage meat?

TWO: Hidin'. I don't know.

ONE: I can understand them fuckin' around with the burgers. The horse DNA in the burgers an' tha'. Horse*meat*, like. But horse*hair*? That's goin' a bit too fuckin' far. An' in sausages. They're made o' pigs, yeah?

TWO: Yeah.

ONE: Well, they've no right to be messin' with them – shovin' the horse DNA into the sausages. It's not natural.

TWO: Sorry – I'm not with yeh.

ONE: I don't mind the burgers. There's always been tha' general agreement. They mightn't be all beef. Just mostly. An' that's grand. I can live with tha'. As long as it's meat.

TWO: But it's not fuckin' beef. Beefburgers should be made o' fuckin' beef.

341

ONE: I couldn't give a shite. Long as it's not slugs or maggots or eyeballs an' tha'. Long as they taste alrigh' – what's the fuckin' fuss?

TWO: Wha' abou' standards?

ONE: Well, that's me point. They can't start fuckin' around with the sausages.

TWO: So. If I'm followin' you right – when it comes to the burgers—.

ONE: Wha' d'yeh mean, if you're followin' me right—?

TWO: Fuck off now, an' listen. Say it was human DNA? In the burgers.

ONE: Grand. It's meat.

TWO: Yeh wouldn't mind eatin' human?

ONE: No. But it depends.

TWO: On wha'?

ONE: Wha' sort of a human it was.

TWO: Wha' d'yeh mean?

ONE: Well, I could never eat a Man United supporter.

TWO: Ah, fuck off.

ONE: It'd make me fuckin' sick.

TWO: Fuck off. A child, say. Yeh wouldn't eat a child.

ONE: Not one o' me own, no.

TWO: Serious now. Say yeh found out, like – they were puttin' orphans in the burgers—.

ONE: No one's puttin' orphans in the burgers. Madonna has tha' covered. But, like – horses. It actually makes more sense to be eatin' horses. Look at them – they're magnificent. Yeh never backed a fuckin' cow in the Grand National, did yeh? Fuckin' cows – wha' do they even do?

TWO: They make beef. An' they do it very well.

ONE: Well – fair enough.

TWO: Yeh like beef, don't yeh? Yeh like a bit of steak, yeah?

ONE: Yeah.

TWO: Then lay off the cows. The cows are grand.

ONE: Okay—.

TWO: We've been underestimatin' cows for years. That's as much as I'll say. For now.

ONE: For fuck sake.

TWO: Did yeh ever look into a cow's eyes, did yeh?

ONE: I've been too busy fuckin' eatin' them.

TWO: Beautiful creatures. In their own way.

ONE: Okay.

TWO: I won't even mention milk.

ONE: Grand – good.

TWO: We'll move on.

ONE: Good idea – yeah. But one thing, just. Are yeh sure now Nigella isn't implicated in any o' this?

TWO: No, no.

ONE: Grand.

TWO: There was no mention o' horsehair in the recipe.

ONE: Okay – good. Cos I was thinkin'. Abou' hospital car parks an' tha'. Someone like Nigella would be ideal – to be in charge. At the barrier, like. Just to give yeh a little smile on your way home. Dressed in black, yeh know.

TWO: An' high heels.

ONE: An' a bit sad-lookin'.

TWO: Wouldn't work with a man.

ONE: No.

TWO: Too like an undertaker.

ONE: An' as well – a sad-lookin' woman is gorgeous. But a sad-lookin' man is just an irritatin' prick you'd want to avoid at all costs.

TWO: Wouldn't be much of a telly programme, but.

ONE: Wha'?

TWO: One o' them reality shows. A celebrity in a car park.

ONE: I don't know. I'm not so sure. Depends on the celebrity.

TWO: *Celebrity Car Park Attendant*. It would need to be a really fuckin' good one.

ONE: Well – Nigella, like. You'd watch Nigella in a car park, wouldn't yeh?

TWO: Ah, yeah.

ONE: For half an hour a week? 'Course yeh would.

TWO: Would she be cookin'?

ONE: I don't see why not. If it was a quiet day. A couple o' muffins from Nigella? It'd brighten your day, a bit. It has all sort o' possibilities, this show.

TWO: You could have cars.

ONE: Well, it's a fuckin' car park.

TWO: There's no need for your fuckin' sarcasm. You're not a fifteen-year-old girl. Yeh might've been in a previous life. Cleopatra or someone – I don't know. But you're not now. So yeh can fuck off.

ONE: I was never Cleopatra.

TWO: Grand.

ONE: I don't believe in any o' tha' comin' back shite. Once you're dead, you're fuckin' dead.

TWO: I'm with yeh.

ONE: You're not comin' back as Cleopatra or a polar bear or a fuckin' daffodil or anythin'.

TWO: Grand.

ONE: Go on.

TWO: I'm just sayin'. Cars. It's a thing we tend to forget – when we think abou' car parks. The fuckin' cars.

ONE: You're actually righ'.

TWO: We're too – well – preoccupied. We're only lookin' for our own car.

ONE: That's true. Specially in a hospital car park. Sorry – go on.

344

TWO: Well – just that, like. There could be somethin' about cars.

ONE: D'yeh not think *Top Gear* kind o' covers tha'?

TWO: Abandoned cars, say.

ONE: Abandoned?

TWO: Think about it. Some poor fucker parks the car, goes in to get the tonsils ou'—.

ONE: And he ends up on a slab.

TWO: Nigella investigates.

ONE: Brilliant.

TWO: Come here – she could do a recipe with tonsils in it.

ONE: Not your man's tonsils, but.

TWO: No. No, no. *Celebrity Cannibal*. That's a different programme altogether.

ONE: I'll tell yeh, but. While we're on the subject. Your man, Clarkson, from *Top Gear* – he was lucky he didn't end up in fuckin' hospital, wasn't he – that time? Slappin' an Irish lad.

TWO: Very fuckin' lucky.

ONE: If he ever comes in here—. Peace process, me bollix.

TWO: Come here – yeh know your man we call Jeremy but his name isn't really Jeremy?

ONE: Yeah.

TWO: Why do we call him Jeremy?

ONE: Two reasons. He failed his drivin' test an' he's a bit of a cunt.

TWO: Ah, yeah—. Did yeh ever eat tonsils?

ONE: Don't think so. You'd never know, but, would yeh?

TWO: Are they edible?

ONE: Well – Jaysis. Everythin's edible, really. If yeh drown it in Bisto.

TWO: Women don't have them, sure they don't?

ONE: I'm not sure – but I think you're righ'. It's one o' the signs, isn't it?

TWO: Signs o' wha'?

ONE: That it's a woman an' not just a man pretendin' to be one.

As ONE *speaks, he takes out his phone and starts composing a text.*

TWO: Then I wouldn't be interested.

ONE: Wha'? Interested in wha'?

TWO: Eatin' tonsils. If it's only men – males, like – tha' have them. What're yeh doin'?

ONE: Textin' the missis.

TWO: Why?

ONE: To see if she has tonsils. An' come here – while I'm at it. It's none o' your fuckin' business.

TWO: I was only fuckin' askin'. Annyway, food is female. Cows, sheep, chickens. All girls. Ninety-nine times out of a hundred.

ONE: I know. I know – that's why I'm checkin'. Wha' d'yeh think of cancer, by the way?

TWO: Oh, I'm all for it.

ONE: I'm serious.

TWO: Well, like – what's there to think?

ONE: Which one would yeh prefer? If yeh had to choose, like?

TWO: Well, definitely not the balls.

ONE: We're too old for tha' one.

TWO: Really?

ONE: Yeah.

TWO: That's brilliant. How d'yeh know, but?

ONE: Cousin. He had to have a medical an' they told him, an' he's the same age as us.

TWO: That's great. What's left?

ONE: Bowels.

346

TWO: God, no.

ONE: It's usually not fatal.

TWO: Don't care. I'd prefer the lungs.

ONE: That's one o' the worst.

TWO: I don't care. It has more style.

ONE: Wha'?!

TWO: Well, think about it. Say you're chattin' to a bird. Your missis has died or somethin'. Whatever – and you're chattin' to this woman.

ONE: Nigella.

TWO: No, no. This is real world we're talkin' about.

ONE: Grand – go on.

TWO: So you're chattin' away there an' yeh tell her you have lung cancer. You're home an' dry. She'll think you're Humphrey Bogart. But tell her you've bowel cancer?

ONE: She's gone.

TWO: Exactly.

ONE: What about prostate?

TWO: I'm not even sure what it fuckin' is. What is it?

ONE: I'm not sure, meself. But I think it's like tha' thing they say about rats. You're never more than a couple of inches away from a prostate.

TWO: Yeah, but what's it do?

ONE: Don't know. But me cousin said it's the one we should be worried about. At our age, like.

TWO: What's the test?

ONE: Finger up the hole.

TWO: Doctor's finger?

ONE: Yeah, has to be a doctor. It's fifty quid extra for two fingers. The cousin said.

ONE's phone buzzes. He picks it up, and reads it like a man who has left his reading glasses at home.

TWO: What's she say?

ONE: Hang on, for fuck sake … Yeah.

TWO: She has tonsils?

ONE: Yeah.

TWO: Well, that's that – I suppose. Like – if your missis has tonsils, then probably all women have them. Back to the drawin' board. Is tha' what's wrong with your da?

ONE: Tonsils?

TWO: No – no. Cancer.

ONE: No, no. Like, he's just old. Very old. The body an' tha'. It's like a machine, really, isn't it? It starts to stop workin'.

TWO: Well – that's already started. Hasn't it? For us, like.

ONE: Yeah.

TWO: We're dyin'.

ONE: It's looking tha' way.

TWO taps the counter, to attract RAYMOND'S attention.

TWO: Two more. (*to ONE*) Just in case.

ONE (*almost cheerfully*): We're fucked.

TWO: Grand. As long as we're all fucked – long as it's fair. I don't give much of a shite. How is he, an' anyway – your da? Were yeh in to see him tonight?

ONE: Yeah, yeah – I was tellin' yeh. I'm gettin' in most nights.

TWO: How was he?

ONE: Ah, well – grand. Not too bad. Actually, not great. Fuckin' terrible, to be honest with yeh.

TWO: Sorry to hear tha'.

ONE: Thanks.

TWO: It's hard.

ONE: He's just – old. Nothin' else, yeh know? He said it himself – 'I'm tired, son.' He's very old.

TWO: What age is he?

ONE:	Ah, he's ninety-four. It's incredible, really. I've seven grandkids. I think. I mix them up with the kids sometimes.
TWO:	Yeah, yeah – same here.
ONE:	Ballpark figure. I've seven grandkids. But there's someone still alive who calls me 'son'. It's mad, really, isn't it?
TWO:	It's brilliant.
ONE:	No question. But anyway. He won't be comin' out. I don't think. Alive, I mean.
TWO:	Yeah, yeah.
ONE:	I hate tha' fuckin' place. Anyway … I could've sworn it was fuckin' tonsils.
TWO:	Adam's apple.
ONE:	Wha'?
TWO:	That's the thing we have tha' women don't have.
ONE:	You're right – good man. But come here. Is the Adam's apple not just another name for the tonsils?
TWO:	Jesus—.
ONE:	I could text her again, I suppose. But it might be—
TWO:	A bridge too far.
ONE:	Kind of – yeah.
TWO:	An' what if she did?
ONE:	Wha'?
TWO:	Have an Adam's apple. An' all other women don't.
ONE:	What're yeh fuckin' sayin'?
TWO:	Nothin'. I'm only—
ONE:	First you're sayin' yeh don't give a shite me father's dyin' and now you're sayin' me wife's a man.
TWO:	No, I'm not!
ONE:	Which?
TWO:	Wha'?
ONE:	Which are yeh denyin'?
TWO:	Wha'? Both – everythin'. Fuck off. Listen—.

349

ONE: Go on.

TWO: There's no way your missis is a man.

ONE: Do yeh want to say that a bit fuckin' louder?

TWO: All I'm sayin' – an' I'm not even sayin' it. All I'm suggestin' is—. She could—. It happens all the time. Look it – your woman in the corner, with Shakin' Stephen. Careful now – yeh know the way she is.

They look – carefully.

ONE: What about her?

TWO: She has three big toes.

ONE: She has ten big toes. She's a big girl.

TWO: She has three – like – official big toes.

ONE: What's your fuckin' point?

TWO: It doesn't stop her from bein' a woman.

ONE: An extra fuckin' toe?

TWO: No—.

ONE: It's not even extra.

TWO: No—.

ONE: So, I'll ask yeh again. What's your fuckin' point?

TWO: None – there's no fuckin' point. I'm just sayin'—.

ONE: Wha'?

TWO: Nothin'.

ONE: Grand.

TWO: - - - She's a good-lookin' woman.

ONE: My wife?

TWO: No – yeah. No – I meant your one with the toe.

ONE looks.

ONE: She is, yeah.

TWO: An' the toe. The fact tha' she has the toe, like – it makes her seem even more attractive. Or interestin'. Somehow. Doesn't it?

ONE: So. Like. If my wife had two Adam's apples – instead of the fuckin' none she actually has – then—

350

TWO: I'm only sayin'—

ONE: I'd be married to Naomi Campbell.

TWO: God, now. I haven't heard tha' name in a fair bit.

ONE: She's never far from me thoughts.

TWO: Still gorgeous, I'd say.

ONE: Why wouldn't she be gorgeous? She's got thirteen toes an' an extra hole in her arse.

TWO: Okay – okay. I fuckin' surrender. But come here. Is it my imagination or is Stephen shakin' less than he used to?

ONE: No, you're righ'.

TWO: Good. I thought it might be me eyes. They're slowin' things down. It must be tablets.

ONE: Your eyes?

TWO: No – Stephen.

ONE: No. Therapy.

TWO: Therapy?

ONE: He's havin' therapy. He told me.

TWO: When?

ONE: Out in the jacks.

TWO: You stood beside Stephen in the jacks?

ONE: No – Jaysis. I stayed well back. What's wrong with your eyes?

TWO: Wha' sort o' therapy?

ONE: He didn't get down to specifics. He just kind o' shouted it over his shoulder. He seemed happy enough.

TWO: That's good, isn't it?

ONE: Yeah – yeah. Stephen's sound.

TWO: Our friend with the toe is all over him.

ONE: Well, there. The therapy must be workin'. A couple o' months ago, he'd've been all over her. What's wrong with your eyes?

TWO: Nothin'. Just the usual.

351

ONE: Wha'?

TWO: Just – well. They're goin' slower. Or they seem to be.

ONE: Wha' d'yeh mean?

TWO: Well, like – somethin' happens. Say a bird goes past. By the time me eyes get there, she's gone. The message from me brain to me eyes – it's takin' longer. It's age, I suppose.

ONE: Hang on. You see the bird, yeah?

TWO: Yeah.

ONE: Then it's not the message from the brain to the eyes. The brain sees fuck all. It's the message from your eyes to the brain. You see her, yeah? Just to be clear now.

TWO: Yeah.

ONE: But it takes you a bit longer than it used to, to register the fact. To get your eyes movin'. Am I righ', or—? Correct me if I'm wrong.

TWO: No, no – that's it.

ONE: It's eye to brain, so. That's the problem. The eyes are grand. It's the brain that's fucked.

TWO: D'yeh think?

ONE: Alzheimer's. D'you eat fish at all? Mackerel an' tha'.

TWO: I fuckin' hate fish. Fuckin' Alzheimer's?!

ONE: I wouldn't rule it out. Did you order those pints?

TWO: Yeah I did. Alzheimer's, but.

ONE: There now. That's encouragin'.

TWO: Wha'?

ONE: The message went straight from your ear to your brain an' you ordered the pints.

TWO: Okay – yeah.

ONE: Well, that's good.

TWO: It wasn't hard, but.

352

ONE: That's not the point. Maybe yeh just need to get your eyes tested.

TWO: I was thinkin' tha' meself. Anyway, but – it's not just the eyes. If there was a woman walkin' across the shop here, you'd need your neck as well, wouldn't yeh? Followin' her, like.

ONE: Good point – yeah.

TWO: Well, that's definitely slower. How come it's called Alzheimer's?

ONE: Some sham called Alzheimer is my bet.

TWO: Invented it.

ONE: Discovered it.

TWO: An' named it after himself?

ONE: Yeah.

TWO: Why couldn't he just have minded his own fuckin' business? The nosy cunt.

ONE: Well, he'd have been a scientist – in fairness.

TWO: But – d'yeh see me point? I'm sure there's always been dementia, like. But then this Alzheimer prick comes along an' claims he's discovered somethin' tha' was there already. He wasn't Christopher Columbus, by the way. And anyway, America was already there as well. Ask any Apache – they'll fuckin' confirm it. Christopher Columbus discovered fuck all. Anyway. People get older, they slow down, they lose some o' the marbles, sometimes all o' the marbles. It's sad – but—. Then fuckin' Alzheimer comes along an' calls it Alzheimer's. It has a name like a disease an' it's fuckin' terrifyin'.

ONE: So – what are yeh sayin'? If it wasn't called Alzheimer's, yeh wouldn't give a shite if yeh had it?

TWO: No – no. I wouldn't go tha' far. But I definitely think I'd give less of a shite.

353

ONE: But – look it. Yeh might forget tha' yeh gave a shite at all. Chances are you'd forget what a shite actually is.

TWO: Yeah – okay—.

ONE: So, it doesn't really matter what yeh fuckin' call it.

TWO: Fair enough. I'll have to think tha' one through. The eyes, but. D'yeh have the Netflix, at home?

ONE: We do, yeah. Load o' shite.

TWO: Flickin' through the programmes an' tha'. Fuckin' *SpongeBob*, *SpongeBob*, *SpongeBob*, *Good Wife*, *SpongeBob*, *SpongeBob*, *Good Wife*, *Good Wife*, *SpongeBob*. The eyes are swimmin'. I nearly fuckin' faint.

ONE: Have yeh seen *The Good Wife*, have yeh?

TWO: No, I haven't.

ONE: Your one who does the investigatin' for them is gorgeous, isn't she?

TWO: The one with the boots?

ONE: Yeah.

TWO: She's lovely.

ONE: She is. There's another thing, but. The Germans have discovered there's life after death.

TWO: Wha'?

ONE: Yeah – I seen it in the *Star*, I think it was. A team of scientists. They're after confirmin' there's an afterlife.

TWO: How did they do tha'?

ONE: Don't know – it wasn't all tha' clear. There was a picture of a bunch o' lads in the white coats – yeh know the ones the scientists all wear.

TWO: Where were they?

ONE: Don't know. Germany is my bet.

TWO: Not in heaven, or on a cloud or somethin'?

354

ONE: No. No. Nothin' like tha'.

TWO: Jesus, but. The afterlife? I don't even believe in the fuckin' afterlife.

ONE: Yeah, yeah – same here. But the fuckin' Germans have found it, irregardless o' whether we believe in it or not.

TWO: Does tha' mean they have the copyright on it? Do they own it, like? The afterlife.

ONE: Don't know.

TWO: It might have been better if it hadn't been the Germans.

ONE: Ah, the Germans are grand.

TWO: No, no – I'm with yeh there. No mention o' Hitler, or anny o' tha' shite.

ONE: Look where they took all the Syrians.

TWO: Where did they take them? The pictures?

ONE: Fuck off. They were decent, is what I'm sayin'. They *are* decent, the Germans.

TWO: No one disputes tha'—.

ONE: Nearly everyone fuckin' disputes tha'.

TWO: Yeah, well, I don't. The Germans are sound. But, like – look wha' they've done with the fuckin' EU.

ONE: Completely different things. The EU an' the afterlife – there's no comparison.

TWO: I fuckin' hope not. All I'd ask of the afterlife—. All I ask is that it isn't fuckin' borin'.

ONE: You're sayin' the Germans are borin'?

TWO: I'm not.

ONE: Well, yeh sound like yeh are.

TWO: I fuckin' amn't. I'm just sayin' – only suggestin' now – that it might've been better if it hadn't been the Germans tha' discovered it.

ONE: Cos they're borin'.

TWO: No. No. They're a bit too organised, just.

355

ONE: Well, yeh see, but. That's probably one o' the reasons why they discovered it in the first place. They organised themselves – got their act together. They saw past next week an' discovered eternity.

TWO: Okay—.

ONE: An' it's in good hands.

TWO: D'yeh think there'll be dogs there—?

ONE: There now – German football. There's no way it's borin'.

TWO: No, it's brilliant.

ONE: Bayern an' Dortmund an' tha'.

TWO: Brilliant – yeah. Is that wha' the afterlife will be like, like? Full o' dead German footballers.

ONE: A big dressin' room. Full o' footballers.

TWO: Could be worse, I suppose. And in fairness – they all speak very good English.

ONE: That's true.

TWO: I wouldn't mind meetin' Gerd Müller. D'yeh remember him?

ONE: I do, o' course. Der Bomber. He isn't dead – I don't think.

TWO: He will be – eventually. A chat with him would be good, I'd say.

ONE: Not for all fuckin' eternity, but.

TWO: No, no. Ten minutes'd be grand. An' there now – tha' could be a problem.

ONE: Wha'?

TWO: In German hands. You'll get exactly ten minutes with each footballer.

ONE: You'll be havin' a laugh with Müller an' a bell will go.

TWO: An' you'll have to move on to Franz Beckenbauer.

ONE: The longest ten minutes of your fuckin' life. Mind you, he'd probably have more goin' for him than Cleopatra.

TWO: What's your problem with Cleopatra?

ONE: Ah, nothin'. I just have a feelin' she'd be a desperate pain in the hole.

TWO: You're probably righ'. Come here, but. Yeh know the way they say tha' when yeh die, you'll be reunited with your dog?

ONE: Eh – I'm not sure I ever heard that—.

TWO: I don't want to be reunited with me fuckin' dog. I had a dog when I was a kid, like. I fuckin' hated him.

ONE: Grand.

TWO: He kept ridin' me leg.

ONE: He'd hardly do tha' in the afterlife. Would he?

TWO: Maybe not – I know what yeh mean. I wouldn't trust the cunt, but.

ONE: That's the thing though, isn't it? The afterlife. Heaven. Whatever yeh call it. Even hell. None o' them are up to much – sure they're not? We're better off stayin' where we are.

TWO: Except we can't.

ONE: I know. I know. - - - He told me he loved me.

TWO: Did he – your da?

ONE: Last night – yeah. I always knew he did, like. It was always clear. He was always—. But – anyway. He told me. An' I told him.

TWO: That must've been good, was it?

ONE: Ah, man.

RAYMOND turns lights on, off, on – and off.

357

Act Two

"Just a Little Lovin", by Dusty Springfield. Same pub, twenty-four hours later. RAYMOND, *in a different shirt, patrols the land behind the bar.* ONE *is alone, texting. He wears his reading glasses. (When not wearing them, they never go on top of his head.)* TWO *enters.*

TWO: Wasn't sure you'd be here.

ONE: I'm here.

TWO: Grand.

ONE: Give this prick a pint, Raymond. (*to* TWO) Just give us a minute with this thing. (*continues texting*) Fuckin' hospital.

TWO: I know—.

ONE: Nearly done—. (*fires off text*) There. (*removes reading glasses, looks at* TWO) You look fuckin' terrible.

TWO: Well, I'm blamin' the fruit.

ONE: Wha'?

TWO: They're sayin' it's bad for yeh now. Fruit, like. It's fuckin' bad for yeh.

ONE: I always said it. Who's sayin' it now, but?

TWO: The fuckin' scientists – who else? All tha' one-in-five bolloxology.

ONE: Fuckin' scientists – they're a fuckin' joke.

TWO: She's fuckin' furious – at home. She's thinkin' o' suin'.

ONE: Suin' who?

TWO: Fuckin' everyone – far as I can make ou'. Says she's suffered permanent spinal damage carryin' all them bananas home from SuperValu.

ONE: Okay—.

358

TWO: I think what's really got her goat is the fact tha' she can't claim the blackcurrant in her rum an' black is one of her daily five. She'll have to replace it with celery or broccoli or somethin'.

ONE: Vegetables are officially still healthy, are they?

TWO: For the time bein'.

ONE: I hate them.

TWO: Same here. Little green cunts. It's gas but, isn't it? How we get suckered in.

ONE: An' there's another thing – while we're on the subject. Three pints.

TWO: One'll do me.

ONE: Three pints is a binge.

TWO: Says who?

ONE: The fuckin' scientists again – an' doctors. I heard it on the radio. Some fuckin' survey.

TWO: That's fuckin' mad. I'd need three pints before I decide whether to go on a fuckin' binge or not.

ONE: I worked it out earlier. I've been on a fuckin' binge since 1975. Three pints, two or three times a month, constitutes harmful drinkin'.

TWO: So – wha'? You've been drinkin' yourself to death for more than forty years?

ONE: Apparently.

TWO: Well, you're not very fuckin' good at it. You look grand.

ONE: Thanks. I'll tell yeh wha' the problem is. An' it's not the drinkin'.

TWO: Wha'?

ONE: The drinkin's grand. The problem is the fuckers tha' do the surveys. They haven't a clue what a good binge is. They've no right to use the word.

TWO: It's ours.

ONE: Exactly. They can fuck off. Three pints in a row isn't a national crisis. It's a fuckin' necessity. Wha' happened your chin?

TWO: Ah, nothing – cut meself shavin', just.

ONE: Cos o' the fruit?

TWO: No, no. Fuck the fruit. I just did – yeh know, yourself. Some o' them aren't too bad.

ONE: The fruit?

TWO: No – the vegetables. Some o' them are okay. Beans, for example.

ONE: Beans aren't strictly vegetables, but.

TWO: Are they not? They're not fuckin' fruit, an' anyway. Are they?

ONE: I think they're just – beans. They're their own thing. But I'm with yeh. Beans are sound.

TWO: An' they're not green either. Which is good. Were yeh in with your father?

ONE: I was, yeah.

TWO: How was he?

ONE: Ah, well—. Not exactly full o' beans. He's run out o' beans – God love him.

TWO: Ah, I'm sorry.

ONE: Thanks. Yeah – so. (*picks up phone*) I'm expectin' the call – any time.

TWO: It's shite.

ONE: It is – there's no escapin' tha'. He kind of—. He slipped out o' consciousness. Last night. He didn't know where he was. Didn't know where the light was comin' from, yeh know. Then he just kind o' stopped talkin' – mumbling, yeh know. Stopped movin' altogether. You'd hardly know he was breathin'.

TWO: I'm sorry.

ONE: So that's it. But – sure, anyway.

TWO: It's shite.

ONE: Yep.

TWO: Peas aren't the worst. When yeh think about it.

ONE: As long as they come out of a tin.

TWO: Definitely.

ONE: It's the healthy stuff that I object to.

TWO: Rips the hole off yeh.

ONE: An' there's nothing' fuckin' healthy abou' tha'. It's not wha' God fuckin' intended at all.

TWO: Some o' them vegetables have – like – corners on them. An' branches, nearly.

ONE: My missis was washin' a bit o' broccoli there, a while back. An' she said a fuckin' nest fell out of it.

TWO: Serious?

ONE: So she said. Although she didn't show us it. I think, meself, she was just tryin' to scare one o' the grandkids back into eatin' meat.

TWO: A vegetarian?

ONE: Yeah – yeah. A lovely kid now – lovely. Annyway, I think the missis thought that if she thought – the vegetarian, like – if *she* thought tha' vegetables were full o' baby chicks an' wha' have yeh, then she'd go back on the meat.

TWO: It makes sense really. Did it work?

ONE: No. Me father but—.

TWO: I understand.

ONE: You do – I know. You've been here, yourself.

TWO: I have.

ONE: An' it's shite.

TWO: It's fuckin' terrible.

ONE: It fuckin' is. But the strange thing is—. It's mad. I feel lucky.

TWO: Good man.

361

ONE: Like, he was grand – in his head, like. Up until – it'd be the night before last, I think. Still havin' the crack, yeh know.

TWO: That's good.

ONE: It's great, really. Fuckin' hell, though. He looks so small in the bed.

TWO: Yeah.

ONE: Cos he wasn't a small man. Isn't a small man. He'd be slaggin' me now, if he heard me. 'Can yeh not wait till I'm fuckin' dead?'

TWO: He'd be jokin' about it.

ONE: He fuckin' would – no better man. Jesus – it was only two – three – nights ago. I'm losin' track – it's all a fuckin' mush. Annyway. He was talkin' about what he wanted put on the coffin – in the church, like. Jokin' about it, he was. To surprise everyone, yeh know. Give them a laugh. So, I suggest one o' Nigella's cookery books. Cos he never even put bread in the toaster, my da. But he says he'd be worried they won't be able to keep the lid on the coffin, if he knows Nigella's up there on top of him.

TWO: An' he's probably right.

ONE: Fuckin' sure. But then – his own idea, like. For the coffin. The Muslim bible – what's it called – the Kerrang.

TWO: The Koran.

ONE: That's the one. The Koran.

TWO: Brilliant. Tha' would get a few people talkin', alrigh'.

ONE: It fuckin' would. Is it anny good I wonder?

TWO: Don't know. I haven't really read it – only bits of it.

ONE: You've read bits of the Koran?

362

TWO: Yeah.

ONE: Why?

TWO: Out of interest, really – the way the world's goin'—.

ONE: Fuck off now – why?

TWO: Well – d'you remember Benazir Bhutto?

ONE: Ah, for fuck sake. I might've fuckin' known. Benazir?

TWO: Well – she was lovely.

ONE: No question.

TWO: An' tragic.

ONE: An' dead.

TWO: But she wasn't when I read it. She was a Muslim.

ONE: So you read the Koran?

TWO: Only a bit of it – a few pages.

ONE: Why? On the off chance she might come in here—?

TWO: No—.

ONE: And yis'd have somethin' to chat about?

TWO: No – fuck off.

ONE: For fuck sake. Where did yeh get it?

TWO: Oh – the wife's Kindle.

ONE: Yeh bought it on your wife's Kindle?

TWO: I didn't buy it – who says I fuckin' bought it?

ONE: Well, who bought it?

TWO: The wife. It was her Kindle. Are yeh fuckin' thick?

ONE: Wha' did she want with it?

TWO: She was thinkin' of convertin'.

ONE: Convertin'?

TWO: Yeah.

ONE: Why?

TWO: So she could tell everyone to fuck off at Christmas. She took the hump, a few years back. Never again, she said – yeh know yourself.

ONE: Tha' makes a certain amount o' sense. You, but—.

TWO: Who says I was thinkin' o' convertin'?

363

ONE: Well, you were readin' their book.

TWO: I read about Arsenal. It doesn't mean I'm goin' to start followin' the cunts.

ONE: Okay – fair enough. What's it like?

TWO: The Koran?

ONE: Yeah.

TWO: Borin' – same as our shite. I'll tell yeh, but.

ONE: Wha'?

TWO: It is a bit excitin'. Yeh half expect the Homeland Security fuckers to come in through the bedroom window. When you're readin' it. There's a bit of a buzz, like. But then yeh calm down an' it's just borin'.

ONE: Tell us, but – what is it about you an' women in authority?

TWO: Wha'? I don't know wha' you're talkin' about.

ONE: Yeh fuckin' do. Every woman yeh fancy—. Every woman yeh ever mention—. The French bird with the scarf.

TWO: Wha' French bird with the scarf?

ONE: The head of the IMF.

TWO: Madame Lagarde.

ONE: That's the one.

TWO: Yeh can't be callin' the head of the IMF a French bird.

ONE: There – listen to yeh. A woman in any sort of authority an' you're fuckin' smitten.

TWO: Fuck off—.

ONE: Thank Christ they're aren't tha' many of them. You'd be a righ' fuckin' basket case.

TWO: You're talkin' shite.

ONE (*sarcastic*): Yeah, yeah – maybe I am.

TWO: Christine Lagarde is very impressive – she knows her stuff.

ONE: An' Benazir?

TWO: She was gorgeous – I told yeh.

ONE: Okay. But Condoleezza Rice?

TWO: She was lonely.

ONE: For fuck sake. An' Hillary Clinton?

TWO: She could've done better than Bill.

ONE: Wha' – you?

TWO: No – fuck off. Not necessarily.

ONE: Then there's Merkel.

TWO: Fuck off now – Angela's sound. You said it yourself – if Angela was Irish, we'd be grand.

ONE: Okay. She'll be up in heaven with the footballers.

TWO: Herself an' Gerd Müller. There's a strikin' partnership.

ONE (*sees someone walk in*): Here – fuck. Talkin' about women in authority. Look who's after walkin' in. Don't look! Now.

TWO: Terry the Tango?

ONE: Well, listen—. Now, I haven't had this independently verified—.

TWO: Go on.

ONE: You remember they did the *Strictly Come Dancin'*, up at the Club—? To send the Under-17 girls to Korea.

TWO: I do, yeah. Did they ever come back?

ONE: Some o' them – yeah. Annyway. D'yeh remember Terry? He was brilliant.

TWO: Fuckin' brilliant.

ONE: As good as the telly.

TWO: Better.

ONE: Annyway, it was his missis—

TWO: Mags?

ONE: You're sittin' up now, yeh cunt. She organised the whole thing for the club. Made a fuckin' mint.

TWO: She ran off with it—?

ONE: No – calm down, for fuck sake. She's managin'
Terry.

TWO: But – like – she's married to him.

ONE: Grand – but now she's managin' him as well. She's
his fuckin' agent, like.

TWO: What's he doin'? Dancin'? He wasn't tha' fuckin'
good.

ONE: No – he's strippin'.

TWO: Wha'?!

ONE: So I heard. I haven't actually seen him.

TWO: Strippin', but. He's – what? He must be fifty.

ONE: If he's a fuckin' day.

TWO: So – Jesus. He's strippin' for oul' ones?

ONE: Young ones.

TWO: Wha'? Ah, Jesus—. It's just for a laugh, but, is it?
It has to be. It's not like *The Full Monty*. He has
a fuckin' job.

ONE: He's booked up to New Year's. So I'm told.

TWO: Come here – does he do the extras? Massages an'
tha'—?

ONE: Is Terry a prostitute? Is tha' what you're askin' me?

TWO: No—.

ONE: Go on over an' ask him yourself.

TWO: Keep your voice down, for fuck sake.

ONE: That'd be some change o' career, wouldn't it? City
Council Drainage Department to the Happy
Hooker.

TWO: You're havin' me on – aren't yeh? Yeh cunt, yeh.

ONE: I'm only tellin' yeh what I heard.

TWO: Where?

ONE: Paddy Power's.

TWO: Ah, for fuck sake—.

ONE: An' what I saw.

TWO: Wha'? Yeh saw wha'?

366

ONE: Calm down. I was up in the hospital, okay? Visitin' me da. An' who do I see? Don't look!

TWO: Terry.

ONE: Terry. Now look. Wha' d'yeh see – that's a bit unusual?

TWO: Hang on – he has one o' those yokes around his neck. Like the things they put around dogs' necks, to stop them from bitin' their stitches.

ONE: It's called a neck brace – that's the medical term.

TWO: Is it part of his costume?

ONE: He did his back in liftin' a manhole cover.

TWO: Hate tha'.

ONE: So he says, an' anyway. I had a chat with him there. In the hospital. Outside the main entrance, yeh know. He was ou' havin' a smoke.

TWO: Was Mags with him?

ONE: She's still in Korea. Anyway, I wouldn't have spotted him, only he called me over. Yeh know what it's like up there – at the main door, like.

TWO: The night o' the livin' dead.

ONE: Spot on. It's hard to tell the difference between the patients an' the ones that are just visitin'. An' I don't think the pyjamas are necessarily the decidin' factor. There's women in pyjamas with handbags an' fuckin' car keys.

TWO: Dressin' gowns.

ONE: Wha'?

TWO: That's how yeh can tell which is which.

ONE: Yeah – okay. But wouldn't yeh think you could tell by how healthy they look – or sick?

TWO: Ah well – in an ideal world, maybe.

ONE: Ideal world, me bollix.

TWO: But, like – in fairness. Yeh can't expect a hospital to be full o' healthy, fresh-faced people, now can yeh?

ONE: But can yeh not expect the visitors to look a bit better than the fuckin' patients?

TWO: But we're all fuckin' patients. Potentially.

ONE: What's tha' fuckin' mean?

TWO: I'm not sure – I don't know. But there's not much difference between the people inside in the hospital an' the people outside of it. Just luck.

ONE: An' age.

TWO: An' all the other shite – yeah.

ONE: Anyway, there was this chap in a wheelchair. Outside, like – at the revolvin' door. He's no legs – they'd been amputated or somethin'. He's got oxygen as well. He takes a blast when he's finished his smoke. Then it turns ou' he's not a patient. He was just in visitin' his wife.

TWO: Well, that's good, isn't it?

ONE: That's me point – I don't know. Is it?

TWO: 'Course it is. What's wrong with his wife?

ONE: Well, she's married to tha' poor cunt, for a start. Tha' can't be fuckin' easy. She's run off her feet – cos he's got none of his own. Nice enough fella, mind you. But it's a bit like the fella in the car park – in his tracksuit bottoms.

TWO: Wha'?

ONE: There should be a dress code or somethin' – if you're visitin' a hospital. You should make the fuckin' effort.

TWO: So – wha'? Your man in the wheelchair should put on a pair o' fuckin' legs for when he's visitin' the missis?

ONE: No – fuck off. She's tryin' to get into North Korea, by the way.

TWO: Sorry – wha'?

ONE: Mags. While she's over there. She's seein' if she can get into North Korea. They're the communists, yeah?

TWO: Yeah – yeah. The last of the Mohicans.

ONE: She'll be sellin' them raffle tickets in no time.

TWO: No better woman. My missis was drivin' me van there.

ONE: Let me guess – done for speedin'.

TWO: She was chargin' home for the start o' *The Good Wife*. She's doin' a law thing with the Open University.

ONE: It was her fuckin' homework?

TWO: So she said. Annyway – she was done. Caught on camera. An' she asked me to take the penalty points – cos the van is in my name.

ONE: She learnt tha' in the Open University, did she?

TWO: Education, man – I'm fuckin' tellin' yeh. Anyway. My question is – would you take penalty points for your missis?

ONE: Not 'would'. Did.

TWO: Did yeh?

ONE: Ah, years back – you were away on your holidays, I think. When we went from miles to the other yokes.

TWO: Kilometres.

ONE: Yeah.

TWO: Wha' happened?

ONE: She took the car down to the chipper.

TWO: Why didn't she just walk?

ONE: Big order, an' her back was at her. So anyway, a couple o' Guards seen her burnin' the rubber on the way back. An' they order her to stop. But she panics. The priority was to get the chips home.

TWO:	The maternal instinct.
ONE:	Yeah, yeah. So the fuckin' Guards ring the bell—.
TWO:	Oh, fuck.
ONE:	An' she told them I'd been the one drivin'.
TWO:	Did they believe her?
ONE:	No.
TWO:	Where were you?
ONE:	Out the back. An' I stayed ou' there till they were gone. So, annyway. The day before she's up in the district court, she drags me down to the fuckin' hairdresser. Gay Larry – d'yeh know him?
TWO:	I do, yeah – 'course.
ONE:	A fuckin' genius. By the time he's finished with us we're fuckin' twins. An' we stand side by side in the dock – in the court, like. Same hair an' in our leisure gear, yeh know. An' the judge – he just gives up. Fuckin' surrenders.
TWO:	Brilliant.
ONE:	It was.
TWO:	Come here, but. Did your missis not mind bein' mistaken for you?
ONE:	Why would she? I'm a good-lookin' man. Fuckin' courts, but. Were yeh ever in court, yourself – were yeh?
TWO:	No – not really.
ONE:	They'd drag yeh up for annythin' these days. Bastards. And now the mobile phones – on top of everythin' else.
TWO:	Wha'?
ONE:	Usin' your phone while drivin' – it's been made illegal.
TWO:	It's been illegal for years.
ONE:	Yeah, but it's really illegal now. A thousand-quid fine if you're caught.

TWO: Yeah, but it's only for a few days. It'll be back to normal after the weekend.

ONE: Shockin' though, isn't it? Last week – listen. I hit a woman pushing a pram – outside Artaine Castle – Tesco's, like.

TWO: With your car?

ONE: Yes, with me car. I was havin' a quick gawk at the Paddy Power's website. But – and this is my point – this is why it's bad law. If I hadn't been backin' a horse, I'd have been goin' way quicker an' I'd have kilt the poor woman. And, in fairness, she saw my point of view – once I got her down off the roof.

TWO: What about the baby?

ONE: Wha' baby?

TWO: In the fuckin' pram.

ONE: There wasn't a baby. It was her husband – her fuckin' life partner. She was bringin' him home from the Goblet.

TWO: Was he hurt?

ONE: Fuck'm. He was textin'. So he wasn't in control of his vehicle. A good-lookin' woman, by the way.

TWO: Was she?

ONE: Oh yeah. Just a bit – yeh know. Life hasn't been kind to her. An' there's a thing—.

TWO: Wha'?

ONE: I was up there – sittin' with me father.

TWO: Chattin'—.

ONE: No – no. There'll be no more chattin'. (*pauses; tries to resume*) But, annyway – fuck, sorry. (*resumes*) Anyway – I'm sittin' there. An' a gang o' little doctors come into the ward.

TWO: Little doctors?

ONE: Yeah.

TWO: Fuckin' dwarfs?

ONE: No—

TWO: Midgets?

ONE: No – hang on. Just young, I mean. Kids, like – trainees. Mostly girls. You could hear their heels on the floor before they came around the corner, yeh know. Like a herd o' fuckin' deers. An' they're goin' from bed to bed – clicky, clicky, clicky. The heels, yeh know. They're with an older woman – a doctor, like. A specialist, I suppose. An' they're listenin' to every word. An' you can tell, they're terrified. Afraid o' being asked a question. An' afraid of the patients – some of them. An' I hated them.

TWO: The little doctors?

ONE: Yeah.

TWO: Why?

ONE: Well—. I know – it's not fair. I mean – they were lovely and they're only learnin' how to do their job an' tha'. But they just look so fuckin' healthy, and you can tell – they'll always look healthy. They'll always be the doctors an' we'll always be the patients. D'yeh know what I mean?

TWO: Class.

ONE: Exactly.

TWO: Us an' them.

ONE: Yeah. An' come here. I'm not sayin' they shouldn't be there or anythin'. They've been brilliant – the doctors. But there's them. An' they all come from the same – wha'? – gene pool. Same accent, same schools. An' then there's everyone else. And normally, I hardly ever think about it. But today – it's not fuckin' fair. It's not righ'. Any doctors in your family?

TWO: No.

372

ONE: Or lawyers – no?

TWO: No.

ONE: Is it cos we're thick?

TWO: No.

ONE: No, it fuckin' isn't. You know what I mean.

TWO: I do. It's the same as the Tuam thing.

ONE: Wha'?

TWO: Like – the mother and baby homes. In Tuam an' tha'.

ONE: Shockin'.

TWO: That's the thing, but.

ONE: Wha'?

TWO: Yeh kind o' get used to it, don't yeh? The stories – all the fuckin' misery. It's been goin' on for years. Am I makin' sense?

ONE: I think so, yeah. Consigned to history, like.

TWO: Exactly – spot on. But then, they're on about eight hundred babies dumped in a tank—.

ONE: An' the nuns—.

TWO: I mean, I haven't seen a nun in fuckin' years. They're like the fuckin' dinosaurs. But then—. Yesterday, I'm readin' abou' the kids in the mother an' baby homes tha' were used for vaccine tests. In 1973. An' I think, 'Oh – my – Jaysis.'

ONE: I was workin' in 1973.

TWO: Me too. Or, I wanted to be. But those kids, like.

ONE: They're younger than us.

TWO: Much younger than us.

ONE: So, it's not history.

TWO: No, it fuckin' isn't. It's current affairs. An' the point is—. One o' the points. Is. Those babies, those women – girls. They didn't go to the right schools either – sure they didn't?

ONE: No.

373

TWO: No – they didn't.

ONE: - - - He looks so small in the bed.

TWO: I know—.

ONE: I just want it to be over.

TWO: I know what yeh mean.

ONE: I know – it's terrible thinkin' like tha'.

TWO: It's not. You just want what's best for him.

ONE: I want him to die.

TWO: You want him to die peacefully.

ONE: Yeah.

TWO: An' he is.

ONE: - - - Yeah.

TWO: Yeah. - - - I thought o' somethin' else for the celebrity car park, by the way.

ONE: Did yeh?

TWO: D'you remember *One Flew Over the Cuckoo's Nest*?

ONE: 'Course, yeah – brilliant.

TWO: A fuckin' classic.

ONE: Jack Nicholson—. (*'does' McMurphy*) 'You're not a goddamn looney now, boy. You're a fisherman.'

TWO: No – shite. *All the President's Men.* D'you remember *All the President's Men*?

ONE: Are you just after mixin' up *One Flew Over the Cuckoo's Nest* with *All the President's Men*?

TWO: I think so – yeah.

ONE: How the fuck did yeh manage tha'?

TWO: Do you never do it?

ONE: No.

TWO: Never?

ONE: Fuckin' never.

TWO: Yeh have to. Grandkids' names an' tha'.

ONE: Ah well, yeah. Names an' tha' – that's different, that's grand. I sometimes call the wife Declan.

374

TWO: Do yeh?

ONE: No, I don't. Just the once. But we all do it – mix up names. Even forget a few. That's under-standable.

TWO: Declan?

ONE: It was dark – fuck off. You're just avoidin' the issue.

TWO: What issue?

ONE: Well, the fact that you can't remember the names of classic fillums.

TWO: I can—.

ONE: But yeh get them mixed up. Alzheimer's.

TWO: Fuck off—.

ONE: I'm tellin' yeh. *One Flew Over the Cuckoo's Nest* is about a bunch o' lads in a mental home an' *All the President's Men* is about two irritatin' cunts goin' after an even bigger cunt.

TWO: Hang on now – *All the President's Men* is a great fillum.

ONE: No question. It's number three in my list o' great fillums abou' cunts.

TWO: Wha'?!

ONE: An' it's a long fuckin' list.

TWO: What's number one?

ONE: *Gandhi*.

TWO: There's no way Gandhi was a cunt—!

ONE: Okay – fair enough. It's more the way he's depicted in the fillum. It isn't the Gandhi I knew.

TWO: Ah, for fuck sake—.

ONE: That's all I'm sayin'.

TWO: You didn't know Gandhi.

ONE: I'll leave it at tha'.

TWO: You're some fuckin' spoofer.

ONE: He lived in Dublin for a while.

TWO: Fuck off – I'm not listenin'. Did he?

ONE: Yeah – yeah. Bought his sandals in Clarks. On the corner of Abbey Street an' O'Connell Street.

TWO: Ah, fuck off.

ONE: What's your idea, annyway?

TWO: What idea?

ONE: I'll tell yeh, hangin' around with you is goin' to be a right pain in the arse – the speed your mind is goin'.

TWO: Deep Throat.

ONE: Wha'?

TWO: From *One Flew Over*— fuckin' *All the President's Men*. Remember?

ONE: Your man in the car park.

TWO: Who told all the secrets to Robert Redford – yeah.

ONE: Brilliant.

TWO: It has possibilities.

ONE: It fuckin' does. So, instead of Redford or the other fella—

TWO: Do you not remember his name?

ONE: I do, yeah – fuck off. What is it?

TWO: Dustin—

ONE: Hoffman. Instead of Redford or Hoffman, we get—

TWO: Nigella.

ONE: Sound.

TWO: And a government insider.

ONE: Revealin' state secrets.

TWO: One a week – yeah.

ONE: Could be brilliant. Some civil servant from – where? – the back of Offaly, tellin' state secrets to a posh woman from England.

TWO: He'll be putty in her hands.

ONE (*thick rural accent*): 'They gave the contract to the Minister's cousin, Missis Lawson, and he never built a hospital before in his fuckin' life.'

TWO (*joins in*): 'Or even a clinic.'

ONE: It could run out o' steam, but – after a couple o' weeks.

TWO: The same gobshite every week – I know wha' you mean.

ONE: Doesn't have to be the same sham.

TWO: Whistleblower – there's the word. A different whistleblower every week.

ONE: *Celebrity Whistleblower.*

TWO: Brilliant.

ONE: I'm not sure abou' the celebrity stuff, but. I couldn't give a shite abou' celebrities, really. Could you?

TWO: No.

ONE: They're all fuckin' eejits, really.

TWO: We're not includin' Nigella in tha'—.

ONE: God, no – fuck, no. No – Jesus. She's essential to the whole thing, like. But we don't want all tha' celebrity shite.

TWO: It's our show.

ONE: Exactly.

TWO: For people like us.

ONE: There yeh go. On before *Match of the Day*.

TWO: Or after.

ONE: Everyone else can fuck off to bed.

TWO: So – wha'? We can do without Deep Throat?

ONE: No – we have him. But only with real scandal.

TWO: Football—.

ONE: As long as it's abou' the football an' not the fuckin' WAGs an' tha'. But corruption an' FIFA –

377

annythin' that influences the game. An' the same with politics.

TWO: Someone takin' shortcuts with the financial regulations in exchange for a few quid an' a wank.

ONE: That's politics.

TWO: Irish politics.

ONE: Same everywhere.

TWO: Probably.

ONE: I'm tellin' yeh – wherever there's a man with a wallet an' a flute, you're goin' to get corruption.

TWO: Yeah – yeah. Did yeh ever do annythin' corrupt, yourself?

ONE: Never got the fuckin' chance. Yourself?

TWO: No.

ONE: That's another door slammed in our faces – the opportunity to be corrupt.

TWO: A few quid an' a wank. It's not askin' for too much, is it?

ONE: I don't think so – personally. But – look it. Here we are. (*looks around*) I don't see anny property developers or fuckin' international financial fellas in tonight, do you? Or high-class hoors.

TWO: There's Terry over there.

ONE: Terry's out of action – for the foreseeable future.

TWO: We'll have to make do with the few pints, so.

ONE: Yep—. (*indicates 'two more' to* RAYMOND) An' pay for them ourselves.

TWO: We're in our natural habitat.

ONE: We fuckin' are.

TWO: Well, like—. I kind o' like it.

ONE: Me too. - - - A few quid an' a wank, but.

TWO: It's a cause worth fightin' for.

ONE: I'm with yeh. Come here but – you watch the nature programmes. How do the animals organise their deaths?

TWO: Wha'?

ONE: Animals. I was thinkin' about it. We've got all this fuckin' – I don't know – industry. Hospitals an' funeral homes – even car parks. Thousands o' people employed. For death. It doesn't make sense, really, does it? Like – how do the animals die?

TWO: They get hit by cars. Some of them, annyway.

ONE: Not deliberately, but. They don't throw themselves under a car when the time comes to die. Like, how do cows die?

TWO: Sledgehammer between the eyes. Then the knife.

ONE: Naturally – if they died naturally. Of old age, like. How would they do it?

TWO: I'd say they go into a quiet corner—.

ONE: Of the field.

TWO: Yeah.

ONE: An' lie down.

TWO: Yeah.

ONE: An' just die.

TWO: Yeah.

ONE: An' with bears and stuff, they go asleep for the winter.

TWO: Hibernate.

ONE: Good man. An' when they're old, they just don't wake up.

TWO: Makes sense. Anyway, that's exactly what's happenin' with your father—.

ONE: He's not fuckin' hibernatin'.

TWO: He's gone to sleep—.

379

ONE: An' he's not wakin' up.

TWO: In a bed instead of a field or a clearin' in the jungle. An' he's bein' well looked after by African nurses.

ONE: Yeah – an' a chap from the Philippines. Nice fella. I think he's gay.

TWO: Grand.

ONE: It's hard.

TWO: It is. But even your little midget doctors – they're lookin' after him too.

ONE's mobile phone buzzes: a text.

ONE: Shite—. This'll be it. (*puts on reading glasses; reads text*) Yeah – it's me sister.

TWO: I thought she was dead.

ONE: No – no. I was mixin' her up with someone else.

He stands.

TWO: You're off—.

ONE: I've to go – up to the hospital. (*grabs his jacket, takes a few steps – stops*) I don't want to—. I—.

TWO stands.

TWO: Come on—. Has to be done.

He puts his hand on ONE'S shoulder. They both walk to the exit.

TWO: We'll get you into a taxi. Paddy the Leper's probably outside on the rank.

ONE: Yeah—.

TWO: At least you won't be needing money for the fuckin' car park.

ONE: That's fuckin' true.

As they exit, RAYMOND turns lights on, off, on – and off.

Act Three

"Just a Little Lovin", *by Dusty Springfield. Same pub, three days later; late afternoon – business is quiet. It slowly gets darker outside as the Act progresses.* RAYMOND, *in the same shirt he wore in Act One, leans on the bar, doing a newspaper crossword, keeping an eye on* ONE *and* TWO, *who sit side by side.* ONE *is in a dark blue suit, white shirt, black tie.* TWO *wears grey trousers, black jumper and jacket.*

TWO: An' the kid tha' sang 'Ave Maria'?

ONE: Me sister's granddaughter.

TWO: She did a good job.

ONE: She did, yeah – fair play. A couple o' notes went astray—.

TWO: D'yeh think?

ONE: Ah, yeah. But the pressure – singin' at your great-granddad's funeral—.

TWO: Not easy.

ONE: No – no, she was grand. Between meself an' yourself, but. I'm only sayin' this. But a grandson o' mine could've done it a bit better.

TWO: Really?

ONE: I think so, yeah.

TWO: Good voice?

ONE: Unbelievable – fuckin' amazin' now. He'd leave the Bublé fucker in the ha'penny place.

TWO: What age is he?

ONE: Six.

TWO: He'd hardly be up to 'Ave Maria', would he? Six?

ONE: No bother to him. Serious little face on him – the gravitas, yeh know. You should hear his rendition of 'Old Man River'.

TWO: Good, is it?

ONE: Fuckin' superb.

TWO: Is his voice not a bit high for tha' one? Like, it wouldn't be broken yet, would it?

ONE: This is what I'm sayin' – it's his face. When he's singin' it. It's unconventional – I'll give yeh that. Yeh wouldn't expect to hear a six-year-old Dublin kid goin' on about workin' all day on the Mississippi. But when you're lookin' at him singin' it—. You'd believe every word.

TWO: Sounds brilliant.

ONE: It is. An' he should've been singin' 'Ave Maria'. In my opinion. But we'll leave it at tha'. The young one did a good job.

TWO: What abou' the big lad tha' sang 'The Red, Red Robin'?

ONE: We had to pay for him – he wasn't family.

TWO: He was very good.

ONE: I thought so.

TWO: Unusual choice, but – wasn't it? For a funeral, like. Or was it?

ONE: Parish policy. They allow yeh one song that isn't religious. A secular song – the priest said. A pop song, or whatever.

TWO: A cousin o' mine died – a few years back now. An' the song was 'The Wind Beneath Me Wings'.

ONE: Load o' shite.

TWO: I'm with yeh. An' Elton John sang tha' one, 'Candle in the Wind'.

ONE: Shite as well.

TWO: Not as bad as the other shite – but yeah.

ONE: Fuckin' 'wind' songs. Some fuckin' dope decided tha' singin' abou' the weather at funerals was a good idea. It makes no fuckin' sense.

382

TWO: I agree with yeh. But then, this mornin', like. Your man gets up an' he sings 'When the Red, Red Robin Goes Bob, Bob, Bobbin' Along'.

ONE: Yeah.

TWO: It was a bit different – was it?

ONE: Me da liked the Andrews Sisters.

TWO: Ah, well, tha' makes sense. That's nice.

ONE: He was in the RAF, yeh see – durin' the War.

TWO: Was he?

ONE: Yeah.

TWO: An' the Andrews Sisters would've been big durin' the War.

ONE: Huge.

TWO: An' they sang 'The Red, Red Robin'.

ONE: No.

TWO: No?

ONE: Everyone thinks they did but they didn't.

TWO: Wha' did they sing?

ONE: Ah, loads of stuff – he had them all at home. 'Boogie Woogie Bugle Boy'. 'Don't Sit Under the Apple Tree'. 'Winter Wonderland'. Ah, fuckin' hundreds o' them.

TWO: So – d'yeh mind me askin'? Why did yeh choose a song tha' they didn't actually sing?

ONE: Well, your man said he knew it. When I mentioned the Andrews Sisters to him. He kind o' launched into it. An' I didn't have the heart to stop him.

TWO: He was brilliant.

ONE: I agree – he was first class. Did yeh see the sweat on him after?

TWO: He earned his few bob.

ONE: He fuckin' did.

TWO: But – I don't know if yeh noticed this. But when he started – the first time he got through 'When

383

the red, red robin goes bob-bob-bobbin' along'. I went, 'Shoot the bastard, shoot the bastard, shoot the bastard, shoot the bastard.' An' I wasn't the only one.

ONE: Me too. An' me sister. The fuckin' priest starin' at us.

TWO: It was automatic – I didn't mean to.

ONE: Same here.

TWO: Cos we used to do it when we were kids.

ONE: Me father would've loved it. He'd've been burstin' his shite laughin'.

TWO: Well, I'm glad. I wouldn't've wanted to cause offence.

ONE: No – it was great. The high point of a fuckin' awful day.

TWO: Good.

ONE: The priest wanted to sing as well.

TWO: Did he?

ONE: He fuckin' did. Tha' one, 'Hallelujah'. I told him to back off.

TWO: Did yeh?

ONE: It wasn't a fuckin' weddin' – I told him.

TWO: How was he about tha'?

ONE: Fuck'm. He can take his fuckin' YouTube fantasies elsewhere. An' Leonard Cohen can fuck off as well. Did your missis like Leonard Cohen, did she?

TWO: Well, she didn't really listen to his stuff—.

ONE: He was a fuckin' miserable prick.

TWO: But I think she liked him. She said he was interestin'.

ONE: Same with mine. Fuckin' interestin'. Just cos he wore a fuckin' hat.

TWO: He was a Buddhist as well.

ONE: Sure, you're nearly a Muslim. Does she think you're interestin'? I bet she fuckin' doesn't. My one has been at me to start wearin' a hat.

TWO: Why don't yeh then? If it makes her happy.

ONE: I'll tell yeh why – I'll tell yeh. If Leonard Cohen walked in here – if he wasn't dead, like – they'd all go, 'There's an interestin' man with a hat on him.' If I walked in, it'd be, 'Will yeh look at tha' fuckin' eejit with the hat – does he think he's Leonard Cohen?'

TWO: You're probably righ'.

ONE: I am.

TWO: Come here, but – how come women's voices don't break?

ONE: Wha'?

TWO: I was just thinkin' there – when you were talkin' about the little lad singin' 'Old Man River'. D'yeh remember your own voice breakin'?

ONE: I do, yeah.

TWO: Me as well. The dog's attitude towards me changed completely. Overnight – just like tha'. He stopped – the minute me voice broke.

ONE: Wha'? Ridin' your leg?

TWO: Yeah.

ONE: Jesus – that's kind of impressive, isn't it?

TWO: It kind of is.

ONE: But it's like the Christian Brothers. The minute your voice broke, they lost interest in yeh.

TWO: Good one. But why doesn't it happen to women?

ONE: Well, the Christian Brothers were fuckin' terrified o' women.

TWO: No – the voices, I mean. Why don't their voices break? Is it the Adam's apple thing again? We have one an' they don't?

ONE: Don't know. But it's just as well, isn't it?

TWO: I suppose so, yeah. But a deep voice – in a woman, like – it can be very attractive. I think, an' anyway.

ONE: Wha'? Benazir Bhutto singin' 'Old Man River'?

TWO: No – fuck off. You're missin' me point.

ONE: They sling their dead in tha' river, don't they?

TWO: Who?

ONE: The Muslims. They throw the bodies into the river in India. The Ganges – isn't it?

TWO: That's the Hindus. The Hindus do tha'.

ONE: Into the river.

TWO: Yeah.

ONE: Wouldn't work here – I don't think. Flingin' your dead into the Liffey.

TWO: No.

ONE: Down to O'Connell Bridge. 'Ah one, ah two—.' It'd be hard not to laugh.

TWO: There'd be a fine as well, I'd say. For throwin' a dead body in the Liffey.

ONE: No, I mean – if it was part of our culture. If it was the way we did it. It'd be hard to take it seriously. Yeh'd throw the body over the bridge an' it'd land in a fuckin' shoppin' trolley.

TWO: They don't throw them in, I don't think. It's more, they slide them in.

ONE: Better off throwin' them, I think. I'd kind o' like the grandkids to lob me over the bridge.

TWO: Nice one – good idea.

ONE: I'd float ou' into the bay with a fuckin' seagull parked on me head.

TWO: Well, it's Glasnevin for me. That's what I'll be pickin'.

ONE: Cremation?

TWO: Yeah.

ONE: I'll stick with the river. – – – Fuckin' mad things, funerals.

TWO: The fuckin' afterlife.

ONE: The Germans found it – I told yeh.

TWO: Never mind the fuckin' Germans. We can stand on our own two feet here. We know better.

ONE: There's no afterlife.

TWO: We know tha' – the both of us. An' d'yeh want to know the proof?

ONE: Go on – wha'?

TWO: All the versions we've ever heard of – all our lives. They're all shite. Fuckin' beaches, virgins, angels, sittin' around listenin' to God goin' on about how fuckin' great he is. For ever? For fuck sake.

ONE: Angels – they've got to be the most borin' fuckers ever invented.

TWO: Eternity, me bollix. Sure, even here – when the crack's good – there's always a point when yeh want to go home.

ONE: This isn't fuckin' heaven.

TWO: Well, it's as good a version of it as any o' the others I've heard. Not great, but it's not too bad – grand for a few hours in the evenin's. But – here's me point—

ONE: You're makin' a lot of points today.

TWO: It's tha' kind o' day – isn't it? A day for thinkin'.

ONE: Yeah.

TWO: Even if yeh don't want to.

ONE: Yeah – you're righ'.

TWO: I've been thinkin' a lot today – an' rememberin'.

ONE: Yep.

TWO: My own father. And me mother, God love her.

ONE: 'Course – yeah.

TWO: We lost a baby, yeh know.

ONE: Did yeh?

TWO: We did.

ONE: I didn't know tha'.

TWO: Ah, it was a long time before we got to know one another. Yeah – so. The second one, it was. Little boy. He only lasted a few days.

ONE: I'm sorry.

TWO: It's a long time ago now – a long time. He'd nearly be forty now.

ONE: Jesus—.

TWO: Fuckin' mad, really—. I think about him – 'specially on a day like today. Or when I'm in among the grandkids. I'm thinkin' abou' the kids he might've had, yeh know. Or wha' sort of a kid he'd've been. She used to say she could feel him in her arms – an' maybe she still does. But, like, imaginin' it all seems part of it.

ONE: It's natural.

TWO: That's exactly it – it's natural. But all this stuff abou' heaven or eternity or the afterlife – it just fucks around with it. Doesn't it?

ONE: How d'yeh mean? I mean – you're probably right—.

TWO: Like you said – it's natural. We've both seen people dyin' an' it's fuckin' terrible but it's also—

ONE: The most natural thing in the world.

TWO: Exactly. Exactly. The most natural thing in the world. An' comin' to grips with it – mournin' an' tha' – missin' them, wonderin' what'd be happenin' if they were still alive. Just bein' fuckin' sad and even angry – they're natural as well.

ONE: Part o' the package.

TWO: Part o' the fuckin' package – spot on. Fuckin' life. Beginnin', middle, end. An' my little fella – he hardly had a beginnin' or a middle but his end was fairly fuckin' spectacular. I remember it like

388

a hand grabbin' me heart an' me lungs an' pullin' them out of me. Right out of my fuckin' chest. Fuck me – it was dreadful. Fuckin' dreadful.

ONE: I can imagine.

TWO: I know yeh can. I know yeh can. It's why I'm here. That's why we're buddies. I'm gettin' confused now. I can't remember wha' I was tryin' to say.

ONE: Heaven – I think.

TWO: Yeah. Dyin' – the way I see it – dyin' is part o' livin'. An' dealin' with it – that's part of it as well. We're men, me an' you. We look after our families as well as we can. An' a lot of it is shite but we deal with it – or we try to. An' heaven – this fuckin' fairyland after we die. That isn't fuckin' dealin' with it. I'll tell yeh what it is. It's an alcoholic's way – a fuckin' addict's way of dealin' with it. Puttin' off the decision – a fuckin' cop-out. Time for a fuckin' drink.

ONE: I don't think I've ever heard you talk as much before.

TWO: That's cos you never shut your hole. An' yeh didn't hear me.

ONE: I did – wha'?

TWO: I said it's time for a fuckin' drink.

ONE: Oh – grand. (*to* RAYMOND) Two more, Raymond. (*to* TWO) If he's not too busy doin' his fuckin' crossword.

TWO: It's only when you're in at this time o' day – it's a cushy enough oul' job, isn't it?

ONE: Here – 'Does fuck all all day until the last hour or so before closin' time. Six letters.'

TWO: Barman.

ONE: Good for the Alzheimer's.

TWO: The crosswords?

ONE: So they say.

389

TWO: Who's 'they'?

ONE: The usual cunts. Scientists an' tha'.

TWO: Fuckin' know-alls. It's fillin' up a bit now, though
        – in fairness. There's Special Trevor – all in black.
        He must've been at the funeral, was he?

ONE: He was, yeah. He goes to everythin'.

TWO: His ma does a good job.

ONE: She does – can't be fuckin' easy.

TWO: Yeh can tell but, can't yeh? If Trevor was a bit less
        special, he'd be grand.

ONE: Well, he's grand anyway, isn't he? Nice poor fella.

TWO: Ah yeah – no question. It was a good crowd.

ONE: A great crowd – yeah. Me sister was delighted.
        The people around here – the neighbours an' tha'
        – they're brilliant. An' actually – yeh need some-
        thin' like today to see tha'.

TWO (*indicating* RAYMOND): He was there an' all.

ONE: Was he?

TWO: Down the back, yeah. He got out before the end—.

ONE: Had to get back to his fuckin' crossword.

RAYMOND puts two fresh pints in front of them. ONE *puts a
tenner on the counter.*

ONE: Good man, Raymond. They're good-lookin' pints.
        (*to* TWO) You'd think he'd stand us a round,
        wouldn't yeh – the day that's in it?

TWO: Gay Larry was there as well. Did yeh see him?

ONE: I did, yeah.

*RAYMOND places his fingers on the tenner, then slides it back
across to* ONE. *He moves away.*

ONE: He only did tha' to make me feel bad.

TWO: An' did he?

ONE: Yeah. But no, people have been brilliant. Gay Larry
        – you were sayin'. He came to the house – before
        the funeral, like.

390

TWO:	To do the hairs.
ONE:	All the girls, yeah. Gave us a deep discount an' all.
TWO:	That was nice.
ONE:	Well, it was. Still cost a few quid, but. He's gettin' married.
TWO:	Is he – Larry?
ONE:	Yeah.
TWO:	That's great. Like Barry Manilow.
ONE:	He's not marryin' Barry Manilow.
TWO:	No, I mean – fuck off. It'll be a weddin' like Barry Manilow's. One o' the new ones.
ONE:	A gay weddin'.
TWO:	Exactly. An' good luck to him.
ONE:	Absolutely. But, like – Barry Manilow. Didn't he have a song called 'Mandy' years ago? A love song, like.
TWO:	Well, she must've wrecked his fuckin' head. Cos he married a chap called Garry.
ONE:	Well, good luck to him as well.
TWO:	An' it kind o' makes sense, doesn't it? Marryin' a man at that age – our age?
ONE:	How d'yeh mean?
TWO:	Well, they can sit up in the bed with their Kindles an' chat abou' the football. Instead of havin' to pretend to be listenin' to fuckin' Mandy goin' on about her health or the state we're leavin' the world in for the grandkids, an' all tha' kind o' shite. It'd be relaxin'.
ONE:	Yeah, yeah – I kind o' get yeh.
TWO:	Where's he from, an' anyway?
ONE:	Barry?
TWO:	Is he Canadian, is he?
ONE:	Don't know, to be honest with yeh. He's shite, wherever he's from.

TWO: No question.

ONE: An' come here. Your idea there, about marryin' a man. At our age, like.

TWO: What about it?

ONE: What if the man yeh married turned out to be gay?

TWO: Wha'?

ONE: You'd be chattin' away abou' – I don't know – whether Sam Allardyce is an even bigger fuckin' gobshite than Rafa Benitez. An' he'd come slidin' across the bed at yeh.

TWO: I never thought o' tha', mind you.

ONE: There'd be nothin' relaxin' about tha'.

TWO: An' it wouldn't be fair – on either of yis.

ONE: How many men are gay, an' anyway?

TWO: Is it one in five?

ONE: I think that's the fruit an' veg.

TWO: That's righ'. It's one in ten – I think.

ONE: It's always one in ten. Anyway. One in somethin'. We'll say ten. So – there's a one in ten chance tha' the man you marry would be gay. That's not too bad. I could live with those odds.

TWO: Then – but – come here. There'd be a one in ten chance you're married to a gay woman. A lesbian, like.

ONE: Fuckin' hell.

TWO: You'd be the one slidin' across the bed. An' that's not on.

ONE: Not in the current climate, no.

TWO: There's always divorce, I suppose.

ONE: Jesus, but – life is fuckin' complicated. An' I'm not so sure abou' the afterlife, by the way. Wha' you were sayin'.

TWO: Wha'?

ONE: Well, I wouldn't be so positive there isn't one. Thinkin' about it.

TWO: Is it yeh think there's an afterlife or yeh want there to be one?

ONE: A bit o' both, I suppose.

TWO: Well, that's understandable.

ONE: Thanks very much.

TWO: Serious. Yeh wish there was an afterlife, therefore—

ONE: Fuckin' 'therefore'?

TWO: I've been thinkin' about it as well – fuck off. For years. Listen – it's not even easy sayin' this. But say there was a heaven an' I died—. I died an' went up, say. Would I be reunited with the baby? Or the baby grown up? A man o' thirty-seven – the way he'd be today – that I don't even know?

ONE: Probably the baby – I'd say.

TWO: So I end up changin' nappies – in fuckin' heaven. For fuck sake.

ONE: I'd say the babies don't shite in heaven.

TWO: Oh, brilliant.

ONE: They just kind o' float around an' smile.

TWO: That'd be nice, actually.

ONE: Except they'd keep floatin' in front o' the telly. I'm just findin' it hard to accept tha' my father doesn't exist any more.

TWO: I know. But he does.

ONE: How does he?

TWO: In you. An' in his grandkids – an' their kids. Every time one o' them laughs—.

ONE: Jesus, we get away with murder on the day of a funeral, don't we? The shite we come out with—.

TWO: Ah now. It's not all shite.

ONE: A fair fuckin' percentage.

TWO: Well, yeh could say that about most conversations.

393

ONE: I'm with yeh there.

TWO: Most of wha' we say is fuckin' drivel. All over the world, men talkin' shite.

ONE: An' it's still brilliant.

TWO: There'd have to be a good bit o' football in heaven, wouldn't there?

ONE: Maybe that's what happens. Yeh get to imagine your own version o' heaven. A bit o' football, a bit o' family, a few pints—.

TWO: More or less what we have now, so.

ONE: No.

TWO: Fuckin' yeah.

ONE: No – just—. We wouldn't be just talkin' abou' football. We'd be able to play as well. An' there'd be no consequences. We wouldn't be vomitin' our guts up on the side of the pitch. Yeh know when yeh see Ronaldo, say, runnin' towards goal? We'd feel tha' – in our legs. An' we wouldn't have to work for it. It would just be there—. An' we could head the ball perfectly – the leap, yeh know, an' hold ourselves in the air for it, an' bang – perfect. An' we could still be ourselves. We'd have a pint at half-time. An' a laugh – slaggin' Der Bomber and Der Kaiser.

TWO: We'd be playin' the Germans, would we?

ONE: Well, they'll be up there annyway, so we might as well. But we can play whoever we want. A Nigella eleven—

TWO: Eleven Nigellas?

ONE: Maybe—.

TWO: Odd numbers are tricky.

ONE: Naomi in goal an' ten Nigellas. Four-four-two.

TWO: I'm not mad about the four-four-two.

ONE: Four-three-three. Kylie Minogue in the Makelele role.

TWO: It's growin' on me, this.

ONE: It's fuckin' heaven, I'm tellin yeh. Maybe I'm just gettin' carried away. But I've a feelin' playin' football against women would be even better than ridin' them.

TWO: Now you're thinkin' like an oul' fella.

ONE: I *am* a fuckin' oul' fella. An' it'll be my fuckin' heaven.

TWO: An' your da will be there as well, will he?

ONE: No! No way. Me da can fuck off. Not in with the football an' the women. It wouldn't be natural. No, I could meet him later. With the family. The kids an' grandkids—.

TWO: An' the wife.

ONE: Yeah – yeah.

TWO: She might have her own version o' heaven.

ONE: An' fair enough – fuck it.

TWO: I never knew your da was in the RAF.

ONE: Yeah – yeah. He joined up in – I think it was 1940. Did I never tell yeh?

TWO: No.

ONE: Yeah—.

TWO: That's amazin', but, isn't it? Was he like Biggles or somethin'?

ONE: Well, there now. There was once – I was a kid. An' I asked him what he was in the RAF – what he did, like. An' he looks at me an' he says, 'Well, son, I was a fuckin' air hostess.'

TWO: Brilliant.

ONE: Yeah – yeah. He was great, me da. Everythin' was an event – d'yeh know what I mean? He'd—. When I came in from the football, he'd examine me knees an' guess how many goals I'd got from the muck on them.

TWO: An' would he be righ'?

ONE: Wha'?

TWO: Would he know how many goals yeh'd got?

ONE: Hang on – he wasn't a fuckin' wizard. It was just a bit of fun. He didn't have magical fuckin' powers.

TWO: I was only fuckin' askin'—.

ONE: Ah, sorry. I was only tellin' yeh tha' one – cos. Like I said – everythin' was an event. He was a mechanic, by the way.

TWO: In the RAF?

ONE: Yeah.

TWO: Mended the planes?

ONE: That's righ' – yeah.

TWO: He went over specially, did he?

ONE: For the War?

TWO: I mean – he wasn't livin' over there when it started.

ONE: I get yeh—. No, no, he went over an' joined. He always said if he'd been a little bit older he'd've gone to Spain.

TWO: Did he?

ONE: So he said an' anyway.

TWO: Strange choice, all the same. Isn't it?

ONE: Wha'?

TWO: World War Two or Torremolinos.

ONE: Ah, for fuck sake—. Hang on – you're havin' me on now, are yeh?

TWO: 'Course I am. Wha' side, but?

ONE: Wha' d'yeh mean, wha' side?

TWO: What side was he on in Spain?

ONE: Wha' *side*?

TWO: Well, it was a war. There's always sides in a war. There has to be—.

ONE: Wait now – hold on. Are you suggestin' my da fought for the fascists?

396

TWO: Well, someone did – cos they fuckin' won.

ONE: Well, he didn't! Hang on – he wasn't even there!

TWO: Grand – okay.

ONE: He wasn't a fascist. Why d'yeh think he went over an' joined the RAF?

TWO: I'm with yeh—. He wanted to fight the Nazis.

ONE: That's righ'.

TWO: An' fair play to him. Did he like it – bein' in the RAF?

ONE: He never mentioned it much. In case some fuckin' eejit called him a Brit an' took a swing at him. He kind o' kept it to himself.

TWO: Yeah – yeah. I can imagine.

ONE: I think tha' was hard for him. But I think he was proud enough of it.

TWO: The planes must've been in some state – comin' back.

ONE: Oh, yeah.

TWO: Although I suppose the ones tha' were really badly wrecked wouldn't have made it back.

ONE: No—.

TWO: So tha' was handy enough.

ONE: What're yeh on abou' now?

TWO: It wouldn't've been like maintainin' the buses.

ONE: Are you comparin' workin' for Dublin Bus with bein' in the Battle o' Britain?

TWO: No – no. Calm down—.

ONE: Fuck off with your calm down.

TWO: Look – all I'm sayin'—. A fair amount o' the planes tha' needed serious repair work never made it back to the depot. An' tha' would never be the case with the buses.

ONE: So, servicin' the buses is harder? A bigger responsibility than fightin' the Nazis?

TWO: Not necessarily, no.

ONE: For fuck sake—.

TWO: I've a question.

ONE: Wha'?

TWO: Can Benazir be in the team?

ONE: No, she can't – fuck off. Fuckin' funerals, but.

TWO: Mad.

ONE: Fuckin' mad. There was a menu of coffins.

TWO: Wha'?

ONE: Tha' was what it was like. A menu. They came to me sister's house – the mornin' after me father died.

TWO: Who?

ONE: Who wha'?

TWO: Came to your sister's house.

ONE: The undertakers – who'd d'yeh think? Who else'd have a menu with fuckin' coffins in it? The Chinese?

TWO: I'm with yeh now – yeah. Go on.

ONE: Well—. They were great – thoroughly professional. Man an' a woman.

TWO: Woman?

ONE: Yeah.

TWO: An undertaker?

ONE: Jesus, look at yeh – sittin' up.

TWO: An undertaker, but. A woman.

ONE: Why not?

TWO: No reason. Makes sense, I suppose. She'd be sensitive.

ONE: He was grand too.

TWO: That'd be her influence.

ONE: What're yeh saying? He'd've started slaggin' us if she hadn't been there?

TWO: Coffins – go on.

ONE: So, yeah – they come in. I'd phoned them the night before. When I got home after me father died. Jesus, it's only three days ago.

TWO: Mad tha', isn't it? Wha' time does with yeh.

ONE: Jesus—.

TWO: An' grief.

ONE: Yeh got tha' one right, bud. Anyway, they come in. I went on across to me sister's an' we met them there – the undertakers. Tea an' biscuits, yeh know – me sister had a plate o' goldgrains. D'yeh remember goldgrains?

TWO: I do, yeah.

ONE: Annyway, they go through the whole thing with us. The whole procedure, like. But anyway, then he says – the undertaker, 'Have yis given any thought to the coffin?' An' as he's sayin' this, *she* takes this menu thing out of her bag.

TWO: Brochure.

ONE: I know what a brochure is. It was a fuckin' menu. Pages an' pages – in a plastic folder. Pictures o' coffins – and the prices. An' she starts to hand it to me sister. But me sister is ahead of her, cos she takes a pile o' pictures out of her own bag.

TWO: Coffins?

ONE: Pictures o' coffins. Off the internet.

TWO: Jesus—. Was there a row?

ONE: Wha'? No – no. They were brilliant. They just kind o' swap the pictures – herself an' herself. Like fuckin' diplomats or somethin'.

TWO: Were they married?

ONE: The undertakers?

TWO: Yeah.

ONE: Brother an' sister.

TWO: Oh—.

ONE: Family business.

TWO: Grand. Go on.

ONE: So, annyway, I'm lookin' at the menu with me sister. Why did yeh want to know if they were married?

TWO: No reason – just curious. Go on ahead with the coffins.

ONE: Okay – yeah. So – annyway, I can't see any difference between the fuckin' things – not really. Some o' them had a bit more brass an' stuff on them. A bit like women, yeh know – jewellery an' tha'.

TWO: Hang on – you're not sayin' women are like coffins—?

ONE: No, I'm not – stop bein' fuckin' thick. I'm only comparin' the handles an' tha'.

TWO: On the coffins.

ONE: Yes, on the fuckin' coffins. Women don't have handles.

TWO: They fuckin' do.

ONE: Not officially. I know what yeh mean – but they don't have fuckin' gold-plated handles. An' crucifixes screwed into their fuckin' foreheads. I'm sorry I mentioned women now. All I wanted to get across was—

TWO: Some coffins have more of the bling than others.

ONE: Exactly.

TWO: Grand.

ONE: But, like – I hadn't a clue. It was like choosin' a Cornetto. Any will do me – I'm not tha' pushed.

TWO: The price, but.

ONE: Well, there yeh go. Fuckin' hell. It wasn't a mobile home we were fuckin' buyin'.

TWO: Did yeh say tha'?

400

ONE: No, no – God, no. I wanted to, but—. I knew I had to let me sister at it. Give her the space, yeh know. It meant more to her, I think.

TWO: The coffin.

ONE: Yeah. She had a wedding ring on her, by the way.

TWO: Who?

ONE: The undertaker.

TWO: Ah, fuck off. Did your sister go overboard?

ONE: With the coffin? No – no, she didn't. Plain was what she wanted. Somethin' masculine, was wha' she said. Did yeh notice me da's coffin?

TWO: Well, I saw it.

ONE: Grand. That's the way it should be. Load o' bollix, really. A lot of it. Isn't it?

TWO: Yeah. And – I'll say this, just. Look after yourself.

ONE: Wha'?

TWO: Just – go easy on yourself. It's a rough fuckin' time.

ONE: I'll be grand.

TWO: Yeah, yeah – I know yeh will. But, like, don't underestimate the impact it'll have on yeh. You're after losin' your father, remember.

ONE: I know—.

TWO: My gums bled when me mother died.

ONE: Wha'? The minute she died?

TWO: No, no. It wasn't a miracle or annythin'. After she died. A couple o' weeks after the funeral. Brushin' me teeth – it was really painful. I had to get a special brush.

ONE: How long did it last?

TWO: Months.

ONE: Stress.

TWO: Grief – yeah. I kind of – I wouldn't admit it at first. I brushed them harder – harden them up, yeh know. There was nothin' wrong. But it was fuckin' agony – stupid. The wife saw my face – an' she knew. So—. I cried a lot as well.

ONE: Are they better, by the way? The gums.

TWO: Ah, yeah. They're sound. You'd recommend the undertakers, so, would yeh?

ONE: They were top class.

TWO: Good.

ONE: Jesus, though. Is this it for the rest of our lives?

TWO: Wha'?

ONE: Well – death.

TWO: Well – we all die.

ONE: And?

TWO: Nothin'.

ONE: For fuck sake.

TWO: I'm not a priest. Or a fuckin' philosopher – fuck off. We all fuckin' die – but it's at the end.

ONE: So – we make the most of it. That it?

TWO: The question is – I think – wha' does 'the most of it' mean?

ONE: Don't know.

TWO: Is it tha' bucket list fuckology?

ONE: What's tha'?

TWO: The bucket list – the things yeh'd like to do before yeh kick the bucket.

ONE: I hate tha' shite.

TWO: Me too.

ONE: Climb Mount Everest, see the Taj Mahal, learn to play the fuckin' piano. I don't want any o' tha'. I don't even want to go up the fuckin' road.

TWO: Same here, really.

ONE: I like me life. I hate admittin' it.

TWO:	Same here.
ONE:	There's no fuckin' 'the most of it'. It is what it is. Me da liked his life as well.
TWO:	Good.
ONE:	Yeah.
TWO:	Maybe that's what it's all about, so.
ONE:	Wha'?
TWO:	Likin' your life – or tryin' to. That's wha' we're here for.
ONE:	Maybe – yeah. That's not so bad.
TWO:	Fuck the Taj Mahal.
ONE:	Come here but – that's probably why heaven – our version – is a pub with a bit o' football.
TWO:	Is it not a bit gay, but?
ONE:	Wha'?
TWO:	Well, the two of us – inventin' heaven. Together.
ONE:	Why is it?
TWO:	Our own little heaven, like.
ONE:	Nigella as well, remember.
TWO:	Yeah, but she's not here, is she?
ONE:	So?
TWO:	She's not here, like – with us.
ONE:	Yeah – so?
TWO:	Well, look it – d'yeh think we'd be in her version of the afterlife?
ONE:	Well, we're younger than the last prick she was married to. An' everyone likes the Irish. Don't they? She likes a laugh – I'd say.
TWO:	Okay – grand.
ONE:	An' there's another thing.
TWO:	Wha'?
ONE:	Who says you'll be in my afterlife?
TWO:	Wha'?

403

ONE: D'you want to be stuck with me for all eternity? Yeh don't, do yeh?

TWO: I see what you're gettin' at. I had me doubts there as well.

ONE: Grand.

TWO: We'd have our own versions – a heaven each.

ONE: Right.

TWO: With a gap in the hedge between us.

ONE: That'll work.

TWO: Grand. A few pints, every few days.

ONE: Sounds good.

TWO: A bit o' football.

ONE: An' no break in the summer.

TWO: No.

ONE: Grand. - - - It's all shite, but, isn't it?

TWO: Eternity?

ONE: Yeah.

TWO: Yeah.

ONE: Death, but. Jesus—.

TWO: Yeah.

ONE: - - -Yeah.

TWO: Still—.

ONE: I know. It's part o' the package.

TWO: You said it yourself there. It's the most natural thing in the world.

ONE: Fuckin' dyin'.

TWO: Yep. Happens to us all.

ONE: It does.

TWO: Grand. But – then, like. Why are we shocked when famous people die?

ONE: We don't expect them to – I don't know.

TWO: Davie Bowie.

ONE: Fuck me – tha' was shockin'.

TWO: Why?

ONE: We think they should be – I don't know – immortal.

TWO: Aretha Franklin.

ONE: The same, really.

TWO: Chuck Berry – he was ninety.

ONE: He was still Chuck Berry – yeh know what I mean?

TWO: Maybe it's the music. We love it, like – so we love them. An' then they die. It's like a little bit of us.

ONE: Beethoven – how did he die?

TWO: I don't like Beethoven.

ONE: Doesn't matter – how did he die?

TWO: He was deaf.

ONE: Yeh can't die of deafness.

TWO: Yeh can if yeh step out in front of a lorry.

ONE: There'd've been no lorries in his day.

TWO: Well – people just *died* back then, I'd say.

ONE: How d'yeh mean?

TWO: It's what I was sayin' to yeh there, a few nights ago. Like, when, say, our grandparents – or no, back further. People just died. Like – they came to the end. Alive one minute, dead the next. No reason – no fuckin' diagnosis.

ONE: Just accepted.

TWO: Yeah – exactly. Just happened.

ONE: Hasn't changed much, has it – really?

TWO: No – you're right. We all die. We just have to accept it.

ONE: Yeah—. Easier said than done, but.

TWO puts his arm across ONE's shoulders.

TWO: True.

ONE: I'm for home.

He stands.

TWO: We won't have one more, no?

ONE: No. No, I want to get home. See the kids—.

TWO (*standing*): Grand. I'll walk yeh home.

ONE: Yeh fuckin' won't. The way this conversation's been goin', you'd slidin' your hand down the back of me fuckin' trousers.

TWO: Come on, yeh cranky cunt. (*to* RAYMOND) Good luck, Raymond.

ONE: See yeh now, Raymond.

They start to exit.

TWO (*sings quietly*): 'When the red, red robin goes bob-bob-bobbin' along—'

ONE: Shoot the bastard, shoot the bastard, shoot the bastard, shoot the bastard.

They exit. RAYMOND *takes their glasses from the counter, and wipes the counter.*

RAYMOND: For fuck sake—.

Lights flicker – off, on, off, on – and off.

THE ZOOM PINTS

1

ONE: Shift your phone a bit there. I can see your cooker behind yeh.

TWO: What's wrong with tha'?

ONE: We're pretendin' we're in the boozer. An' there's no cooker in the boozer – as far as I remember.

TWO: Okay – there. Tha' better?

ONE: Yeah, yeah – a bit. Is tha' your fridge?

TWO: Ah, look it – I'm in the kitchen.

ONE: Okay—.

TWO: I'm not gettin' rid of – the wha' – the white goods. Just so you can pretend you're in the local an' life is grand an' normal. I'm not puttin' the fridge ou' in the garden every time we skype for a pint.

ONE: Okay—.

TWO: I'll tell yeh wha', but. Here's a thought.

ONE: Wha'?

TWO: You know your man tha' sits a bit down from us?

ONE: Your man with the head made o' Lego?

TWO: That's him. Just pretend the fridge is your man.

ONE: Now that I'm looking—.

TWO: Wha'?

ONE: The fridge actually does look a bit like him – from here, like. The handle's like one of his ears.

TWO: Grand, so. We're up an' runnin'.

ONE: Yeah—. It's a bit sad this, but, isn't it?

TWO: It's better than nothin'.

ONE: Remains to be seen.

TWO: Ah, it is. How're yeh gettin' on, an' anyway?

ONE: Okay.

TWO: You're not bored yet, no?

ONE: I was born bored.

TWO: Yeh were not—.

ONE: So my mother always said, an' anyway – God rest her.

TWO: That's just daft.

ONE: I looked up at the midwife an' yawned. Apparently.

TWO: Ah, lay off. What abou' the cabin fever? Are yeh gettin' out for a walk most days?

ONE: I don't like walkin'.

TWO: Wha'?

ONE: I was never tha' keen on walkin'.

TWO: Wha'?!

ONE: Puttin' one foot in front o' the other – what's the point?

TWO: I read somethin' somewhere. Or it might've been the radio. But anyway, it said – all walkin' is, is tryin' not to fall over.

ONE: Tha' makes sense.

TWO: Toddlers, like—. When you look at a toddler learnin' to walk, all he's doin' is tryin' not to fall on his face.

ONE: An' that's it for the rest of our lives. Tryin' not to fall on our faces. I don't know abou' you but I expected a bit more from life.

TWO: Yeah, but—.

ONE: Come here – what's tha' your drinkin'? It's not a pint.

TWO: No – I timed it badly. I ordered a slab o' cans – on the internet, like. But they haven't arrived yet.

ONE: That's bloody typical.

TWO: Five o'clock this mornin', I ordered them – in fairness.

ONE: That's loads o' time. Unless you ordered them from the Spar in Afghanistan – did yeh?

TWO: No – Coolock.

410

ONE: There yeh go – it's unprofessional. What is it, annyway?

TWO: Wha'?

ONE: Your drink!

TWO: Oh, yeah. Hand sanitiser – an' tonic.

ONE: Wha'?!

TWO: We've loads of it – way too much. Left over from the Ebola an' the foot an' mouth, d'yeh remember?

ONE: Drinkin' it, but – you're drinkin' it? It's for your hands, man!

TWO: So is water – when you think about it. You wash your hands with water—.

ONE: For twenty endless seconds – I know.

TWO: And yeh drink water as well.

ONE: Ah now – that's no argument—

TWO: 'Course it is—. Hand sanitiser. The buzz and the inner cleanliness – all in the one glass. (*gulps*)

ONE: Don't!

TWO: Aaah – it's goin' down a treat.

ONE: Hang on, hang on – you're havin' me on, aren't yeh?

TWO: I might be – yeah. But look it – cheers.

ONE: I don't do the cheers.

TWO: I know. That's why I'm drinkin' the sanitiser.

411

2

ONE: I'm just shiftin' my phone a bit – here. Now – look it. We're not lookin' straight at each other.

TWO: Ah – that's good. It's like we're side by side.

ONE: Like normal – yeah. In the boozer.

TWO: That's gas.

ONE: On the stools, like.

TWO: Technology, wha'.

ONE: You're drinkin' a pint this week.

TWO: Oh, yeah – God, yeah. Come here, but. Wha' d'yeh think of the social distancin'?

ONE: I'm all for it.

TWO: Really – are yeh?

ONE: Add an extra metre – I say. The further away the better.

TWO: Ah, now.

ONE: All the bloody huggin'.

TWO: What's wrong with the huggin'?

ONE: Men huggin' – men our age, like. It's pathetic.

TWO: Is it?

ONE: Not so long ago – a few years back, just. We barely said Howyeh when we met. Now, but – we're supposed to hug each other an' even ask how we are. I mean, I couldn't care less how you are. How are yeh, by the way?

TWO: Not too bad.

ONE: Good.

TWO: I've a bit of a cough.

ONE: Is it a 'cough' cough? Or are they bringin' your good suit down to the cleaner's?

TWO: No, it's just a cough – ordinary – just now an' again. An' I don't have a suit.

ONE: Your good hoodie then.

TWO: I've a nice grey one.

ONE: That'll work. But come here. If only one good thing comes out o' this crisis yoke – it's men'll stop huggin' each other.

TWO: You might be right.

ONE: I am.

TWO: Just men?

ONE: Wha'?

TWO: Women. Would you object if the women are still huggin' each other?

ONE: No – I could live with tha'.

TWO: Nigella huggin' Naomi Campbell?

ONE: I could definitely live with tha'.

TWO: What abou' your man from the Department o' Health?

ONE: I wouldn't be huggin' him – no.

TWO: I don't mean—

ONE: Not after Nigella.

TWO: Hang on, hang on. We're not talkin' abou' huggin'. We've moved on from the huggin'.

ONE: Wha'?

TWO: Your man – Tony Holohan.

ONE: He's top class.

TWO: The chief medical officer.

ONE: No – he's top class.

TWO: He speaks plain English.

ONE: There yeh go. He's always bang on.

TWO: An' calm – an' reassurin'. An' what I really like about him – he's Tony.

ONE: None o' the Doctor Anthony Holohan.

TWO: Exactly. Or the other one – where the doctor is such an important doctor, he's a mister.

ONE: He's one o' the lads.

TWO:	I'd say, so – yeah. Who does he follow – d'yeh think?
ONE:	Not Spurs.
TWO:	God, no – Jaysis, no.
ONE:	An' not the rugby.
TWO:	No – no. The football an' the GAA, just.
ONE:	I've a theory.
TWO:	Go on.
ONE:	D'yeh know the way men who follow the same team all start to look like one another?
TWO:	No—.
ONE:	Ah, yeh do.
TWO:	Like – Man United supporters all have pointy heads?
ONE:	Exactly. An' Man City supporters—
TWO:	We've never seen one o' them.
ONE:	Well, that's true. But annyway. Me theory.
TWO:	Go on – yeah.
ONE:	I've examined the shape o' Tony's head – an' he's a Bohs fan.
TWO:	Like us.
ONE:	Up to Dalymount every second Friday – cheerin' on the Bohs.
TWO:	Have yeh seen him there?
ONE:	It's just a theory. I've no documentary evidence. I haven't seen him wearin' a Bohs scarf at the press conferences, like.
TWO:	It makes sense, but. Followin' the Bohs has prepared him for gettin' the country through the virus.
ONE:	Who says football isn't essential?
TWO:	Some doctor.
ONE:	Not Tony.
TWO:	Never.

ONE: Come here, but – back there, earlier. You didn't ask me how *I* was.

TWO: Did I not?

ONE: No, yeh didn't.

TWO: Ah – d'yeh need a hug?

3

ONE: Sit up there – I can't see yeh.

TWO: D'you really want to see me?

ONE: Not really, but – there. That's better. You're sweatin' a bit there, are yeh? Are yeh alrigh'?

TWO: Well, I was ou' for me walk there. Nothin' illegal now – I was well inside me 2k. But I seen a couple o' Guards comin' towards us. An' I started runnin'.

ONE: Why?

TWO: It was automatic. I thought I was fourteen again.

ONE: That's brilliant.

TWO: Well, it was – although runnin'—.

ONE: A killer.

TWO: A challenge. The wife was furious.

ONE: Why?

TWO: I left her behind. I legged it on me own, like.

ONE: Did they arrest her?

TWO: Why would they arrest her?

ONE: Well, she's married to you, for a start. Tha' has to be some sort of an offence.

TWO: Ah, lay off.

ONE: I've been ou' walkin' a bit, meself.

TWO: Good man.

ONE: Now tha' we're not supposed to – it kind o' makes sense.

TWO: Funny tha', isn't it? There's people ou' walkin' tha' haven't inhaled fresh air since Michael Collins was shot.

ONE: The bit I don't like – I've started smilin' at people I don't know.

TWO: Same here.

416

ONE: It's desperate – I can't help it. And – like – the wife always said it was the thing she liked about me – the fact that I didn't smile.

TWO: Wha'? Ever?

ONE: I smiled on the day o' me Holy Communion and it got me nowhere. But the wife – she said she was sick of smilin' men.

TWO: An' now you're smilin'.

ONE: Not at the wife, but – so that's okay. Only at people I don't know.

TWO: The marriage is safe.

ONE: That's another thing, but.

TWO: Wha'?

ONE: The reality shows.

TWO: I hate them.

ONE: Yeah, but she loves them. *Celebrity House* an' *Celebrity Dinner* – they're doin' me head in.

TWO: Come here – I've an idea for a good one.

ONE: Wha'?

TWO: *Celebrity Virus*.

ONE: I'm sittin' up – go on.

TWO: The celebrities get to choose their viruses. For charity.

ONE: Hang on – the celebrities aren't goin' to want the coronavirus. None o' them are tha' desperate.

TWO: No – listen. It'd be an old virus – nostalgia. Measles an' chickenpox – the nice viruses.

ONE: Or leprosy.

TWO: Is leprosy a virus?

ONE: I'd say it is. It's serious an' anyway.

TWO: Big time.

ONE: Leprosy's no joke – I'll tell yeh tha'.

TWO: A cousin o' mine—

ONE: Hang on – I'm stoppin' yeh there. You're not goin'
to tell me your cousin had leprosy.

TWO: No.

ONE: What then?

TWO: He read a buke.

ONE: Abou' leprosy?

ONE: Yeah – he got it for Christmas.

ONE: Not his main present?

TWO: Ah, no. No.

ONE: Did he say it was a virus?

TWO: I can't remember. I was tryin' to eat me trifle. But
come here. The *Celebrity Virus* idea – it could have legs.

ONE: Not if it has leprosy.

TWO: Ah, stop it.

ONE: On a serious note – are yeh listenin' there?

TWO: I am, yeah – go on.

ONE: Me sister's son. Her youngest lad. He's a nurse.
An' – well – he came home.

TWO: From the shops?

ONE: From Australia!

TWO: 'Course, yeah. All the shops are shut, an' anyway,
aren't they?

ONE: Hang on – I can't see yeh – stop hidin'. Are you
havin' me on again?

TWO: Ah, I am. But it's brilliant.

ONE: Isn't it? Makes me proud.

TWO: So it should.

ONE: D'yeh know what he is? An' I don't gush – you
know me. He's a hero.

TWO: He is. They're all heroes, aren't they?

ONE: Well, they are. An' another thing I'll say – they
didn't lick it off a stone.

TWO: Come here, you – are you smilin' there?

ONE: No, I'm not!

4

ONE: I can't see yeh – where are yeh?

TWO: Here—. I was just washin' me hands.

ONE: I'm sick o' washin' me hands.

TWO: I'm sick o' bein' told to wash me bloody hands. Every time I turn on the telly.

ONE: I've no hands left, hardly. I was washin' them earlier an' one o' me fingers fell into the sink.

TWO: Red raw, mine are. An' now we're stuck in the house for the bank holiday.

ONE: The wife was ou' the back earlier, diggin' a tunnel to Wexford.

TWO: Was she – yeah?

ONE: But she got a warnin' on WhatsApp. The Guards were out on the road with metal detectors. Searchin' for people with shovels.

TWO: Did they catch many?

ONE: It was like *The Great Escape* out there.

TWO: Brilliant.

ONE: They pulled Steve McQueen out o' the shore beside Paddy Power's.

TWO: Talkin' abou' Steve McQueen. D'you remember *Butch Cassidy an' the Sundance Kid*—?

ONE: Steve McQueen wasn't in *Butch Cassidy an' the Sundance Kid*.

TWO: I know he wasn't.

ONE: Then I won't be able to remember him in it—.

TWO: No, listen – tha' was just me way of introducin' the subject.

ONE: Wha' subject? The films tha' Steve McQueen was never in?

TWO: Just listen, will yeh—?

ONE: Go on – wha'?

TWO: Okay—. I was thinkin' abou' words tha' have changed their meanin's over the last month or so.

ONE: 'Self-isolatin'', 'cocoonin''.

TWO: I was thinkin' more o' 'droplets'.

ONE: Droplets?

TWO: The virus is in the droplets, like, an' if we inhale them—.

ONE: I know.

TWO: I know yeh do. But – like – a few weeks ago, droplets were only droplets – little drops, like – nothin' to be scared of. An' d'you remember tha' bit in *Butch Cassidy* – 'Raindrops Keep Fallin' on me Head'?

ONE: Brilliant – yeah.

TWO: With Paul Newman on his bike, and Ally McCoist on the handlebars.

ONE: Ali McGraw.

TWO: Was it?

ONE: Ally McCoist played for Glasgow Rangers – he was on *A Question o' Sport*.

TWO: Oh, yeah—.

ONE: Why would Ally McCoist be up on Paul Newman's handlebars? It makes no sense, man.

TWO: Ali McGraw then.

ONE: No.

TWO: No?

ONE: You're mixin' her up with Katharine Ross. Katharine Ross was on the handlebars.

TWO: Ah, Jaysis – it might as well be Michael D. Higgins on the handlebars.

ONE: Sorry – go on.

TWO: Well – the song. 'Raindrops Keep Fallin' on me Head'. It's lovely. Isn't it?

ONE: Yeah.

TWO: Now – take out 'raindrops' an' put in 'droplets'. Droplets keep fallin' on me head. It isn't Paul Newman on his bike now, is it?

ONE: No – Jaysis. It's Vincent Price with a meat cleaver.

TWO: The whole isolatin' thing, but—. Is it gettin' yeh down?

ONE: Ah – it's alrigh'.

TWO: Yeah—.

ONE: But, like—. Not bein' able to be with the grandkids an' tha'. It makes me feel a bit useless.

TWO: Yeah. But you were always useless.

ONE: Well, yeah – that's a comfort. But come here – there's a thing.

TWO: Wha'?

ONE: One o' the grandkids. She was watching somethin' on the news. Abou' this woman who was a hundred – it was her birthday, like. An' all her kids an' grandkids were in the front garden lookin' in through the window at her. An' she said – the granddaughter said – tha' she wanted to look at me through the window on *my* hundredth birthday.

TWO: Ahh—.

ONE: So anyway, tomorrow mornin' they'll all be in the front garden an' I've to pretend I'm a hundred.

TWO: That's brilliant. Is it even your birthday?

ONE: No.

5

TWO: Come here – d'you remember what the boozer looks like?

ONE: Not really, no.

TWO: Same here.

ONE: I mean, I can't remember what *I* look like, an' I looked at meself in the mirror earlier.

TWO: D'you know what I *do* remember?

ONE: Wha'?

TWO: Where my elbow should be – exactly the feel of where it should be on the bar.

ONE: I know exactly what yeh mean.

TWO: It's like when yeh get your leg amputated but you can still feel the leg.

ONE: My leg was never fuckin' amputated.

TWO: I'm at the kitchen table – here, like – an' it's grand for holdin' a knife an' fork. It's perfect. But it's all wrong for holdin' a pint. Like – me elbow remembers the boozer better than the rest o' me.

ONE: I can't wait to get back. That'll be the sign, won't it?

TWO: Wha'?

ONE: When the country's barmen are the frontline workers again. We'll be back to normal.

TWO: The doctors an' the nurses, but – they've been brilliant.

ONE: Ah, no question. But I'll tell yeh.

TWO: Wha'?

ONE: I was down in SuperValu there this mornin'. An' they were lettin' all the health workers skip the queue an' go on ahead o' the rest of us.

TWO: Ah now – that's right an' proper.

ONE: I agree – I'm with yeh. But when the pubs reopen an' they want to skip the queue – order their pints before the rest of us—.

TWO: They can fuck off.

ONE: Exactly.

6

TWO: Yeh know the way there's no planes an' hardly any car engines these days. So, like, we can hear all the birds?

ONE: Yeah.

TWO: I fuckin' hate birds.

ONE: Same here.

TWO: I fuckin' hate them.

ONE: Me as well, yeah. Nature, generally – I hate it.

TWO: Not on the telly, but.

ONE: No, no – the telly's grand. Gazelles an' giraffes an' tha'. Brilliant.

TWO: But not ou' the back.

ONE: No – that's me point. I don't want to see a fuckin' gazelle hoppin' over the back wall. An' it's the same with the birds. If there's a programme about them, grand. But they can get the fuck out o' my fuckin' garden.

TWO: I mean – I like a bit o' traffic.

ONE: Same here – yeah.

TWO: If I hear some poor fucker goin' over the ramp outside doin' sixty – I love tha'.

ONE: It's a story, isn't it?

TWO: That's it – a story. You're wonderin' what's his hurry, if he's alone. Is he chargin' away from somethin' or chargin' to it?

ONE: It's the same when you hear a siren—.

TWO: You're thinkin', 'What's the story?'

ONE: What's the fuckin' story – exactly. Every time yeh hear an engine.

TWO: But the fuckin' birds—.

ONE: Fuckin' tweet tweet tweet.
TWO: There's not much of a story in tha', is there?
ONE: They're blockin' out the stories – the cunts.

penguin.co.uk/vintage